Silent Evidence

Clea Koff is a forensic anthropologist and author. Born in London and raised in England, East Africa and the US, she was a member of the first international forensic team brought together by the UN in 1996 to investigate evidence of war crimes and crimes against humanity, commencing in Rwanda after the 1994 genocide. She subsequently worked for the UN International Criminal Tribunal for the former Yugoslavia in Bosnia, Croatia and Kosovo. *The Bone Woman* (2004), her memoir about this work, was published in the UK, US, Australia and Canada and sold in translation to ten languages worldwide.

Silent Evidence

Clea Koff

avon.

Published by AVON
A division of HarperCollins*Publishers* Ltd
1 London Bridge Street
London SE1 9GF

www.harpercollins.co.uk

HarperCollins*Publishers*
Macken House, 39/40 Mayor Street Upper,
Dublin 1 D01 C9W8
Ireland

This paperback edition 2024

First published as *Freezing* in the United States by
Severn House Publishers in 2011
1

A catalogue record for this book is available from the British Library.

ISBN: 978-0-00-868775-5

This novel is entirely a work of fiction.
The names, characters and incidents portrayed in it are
the work of the author's imagination. Any resemblance to
actual persons, living or dead, events or localities is
entirely coincidental.

Set in Sabon LT Std by HarperCollins*Publishers* India

Printed and bound in the UK using 100% Renewable Electricity by
CPI Group (UK) Ltd

MIX
Paper | Supporting
responsible forestry
FSC™ C007454

This book contains FSC™ certified paper and other controlled
sources to ensure responsible forest management.

For more information visit: www.harpercollins.co.uk/green

For Sam (aka Steelie)

A note for the reader

Although Agency 32/1 does not exist, it should.

It is based on the Missing Persons Identification Resource Center, a California non-profit founded by the author in 2004 to link families of missing persons with coroners holding thousands of unidentified bodies across the United States. MPID has since closed.

- The plot and characters of this book are fictional.

- The statistics on unidentified bodies are fact.

- Forensic profiles of missing persons are hope.

2005

DAY ONE

Tuesday

1

The distinctive tang of warming eucalyptus reached Jayne as the breeze intensified. She took her eyes off the California Highway Patrol officer standing next to the Jeep and glanced at the trees. They were half a block away, shimmering where they flanked the 101 Freeway in its elevated sprint across the San Fernando Valley. Jayne looked back at the officer. He was listening to static-bound information from his radio while his eyes traveled over the Jeep's roll bar, dipped into the back and then returned to Steelie's slim frame in the driver's seat. Steelie's hand was resting casually on the gear stick but her expression was hidden by a faded pink baseball cap.

The officer holstered his radio. 'You're the scientists?'

Jayne nodded but he was already beckoning their escort: a CHP motorcycle officer parked nearby. The motorbike rumbled to life and the officer rolled over smoothly, keeping a foot on the ground as he looked back. His demeanor was serious below a helmet and sunglasses.

Steelie gave a loose salute and the bike moved forward, zigzagging around police cars that had made a maze of the parking lot that spread out from under the tiered overhang of the Sunkist Headquarters building. Near the northwest corner, the bike peeled off, leaving Steelie and Jayne to face a wall of Chevrolet Suburbans with government license plates. The massive vehicles were stationary with engines

3

humming and headlights burning, but no one alighted to meet them.

Steelie kept the engine running but pulled off her cap. She ruffled her short hair and the silver streaks above her ears that had instigated the college nickname of 'Steelie' feathered in with the blonde.

Her blue eyes were troubled. 'If this was Buenos Aires circa 1978, we'd be running for our lives right about now. Where is everyone?'

Jayne had been wondering the same thing. She knew that at least one person was here because he'd asked them to come. Problem was, her imaginings of their reunion after all this time had involved a dinner cruise not a crime scene – and she'd only come to this one because he'd been the one asking. *He's probably guessed as much*, she thought. Annoyed, she bent down into the footwell to tie a double knot in her bootlaces.

Steelie abruptly turned off the engine. 'I see your man.'

Jayne managed to stay on task in the footwell. 'He's not my man.'

'Well, he's on his way over and... looks to me like he's still sporting dark blond hair over a furrowed brow over green eyes over a smirk atop five feet eleven inches of I-don't-know-what's-under-that-suit-but-I'll-take-it.'

Jayne straightened up, hoping Steelie was exaggerating. She wasn't. At a distance, FBI Special Agent Scott Houston appeared unchanged from five years earlier when they'd met him by chance at Quantico. She and Steelie had been there for a conference while he'd been there for training. On their very first night, in the campus bar, Scott had made a beeline for Jayne. They'd flirted over drinks every evening

4

for the rest of the week, breaking off from their respective colleagues to talk at a corner table, their intense mutual interest superficially justified by the overlapping nature of their work. Jayne had been so attracted to the thirty-something, athletic, clear-voiced and clear-thinking man that she'd kept in touch with him through long-distance phone calls ever since.

As they'd got to know each other, the flirtation had deepened but Jayne's confidence that Scott wanted to do more than flirt had waxed and waned because he'd never suggested they fly to see each other. Jayne hadn't suggested it either; she'd even become glad of the distance. Bouts of insomnia and hypervigilance over the years had left her feeling ninety-five rather than thirty-five and she figured she had some of the outward changes to go with it. Now Scott was here in LA and she'd only had two days' notice. Not enough time to get five years of sleep or, like, a butt lift.

Pushing her sunglasses into her hair to constrain waves that had been whipped into something unruly on the drive over, she alighted just as Scott reached the Jeep's front bumper. He was close enough for Jayne to catch his quick assessment of her from head to toe and she resisted the urge to suck in her stomach – any more, anyway.

'Not bad,' he said as they shook hands slowly.

Elated, Jayne tried for nonchalance. 'You're not looking so bad yourself.'

His mouth twitched into a grin. 'I meant how fast you made it here. Speeding, were you, Steelie?'

Steelie was coming around the car with her toolbox. 'You want our help or not, Houston?' She returned his grin as she clasped his hand briefly.

Scott looked pleased. 'Follow me. I'll introduce you to the team.'

Jayne reached into the back of the Jeep to retrieve her own toolbox and steadied her breathing. There was still something between her and Scott, even without the dinner cruise low light and mood music. For now, that was all she needed to know in order to switch to work mode and she followed the others.

On the far side of the Suburbans, a huddle of five men broke up, lowering clipboards and clearing throats. Four of them were dressed like commandos and Scott introduced them as Special Agents Steve Weiss, Duane Sparks, Tony Lee and Xavier Tollen. They were collectively known as the 'Critters' from the Federal Bureau of Investigation's Critical Stabilization and Recovery Unit, there to maintain chain of custody for any evidence collected that day. Scott then addressed his team, inclining his head toward the women.

'Jayne Hall and Steelie Lander. They run Agency 32/1, an outfit that does forensic profiles of missing persons, matching them up with unidentified bodies or living Does. I called them in because they're forensic anthropologists and they do dental as well. Steelie here's a triple threat 'cause she's also a lawyer, so watch your P's and Q's. These are the people who're going to tell us if everything we've got is human, so we defer to them at the scene. Okay?'

There were polite nods all round and then Scott said he needed a minute to brief the newcomers. The Critters cleared the area but the one man Scott hadn't yet introduced kept his stance, feet spread, one hand held over the other in front of his body, causing the fabric of his suit to pull slightly over muscular arms. Jayne thought he was in his mid-thirties like she was, with skin about as brown as her own, but his dark hair was straight and his eyes... She averted hers. He had been looking at her looking at him.

Scott was gesturing at him. 'My partner, Special Agent Ramos.'

Jayne started. 'You're Eric?'

He stepped forward to shake her hand. 'Uh-oh, what's he been saying about me?'

'No, nothing – I mean, it's a pleasure to meet you.'

He smiled. 'In that case, Scott, I'll get you your money later.' He turned to greet Steelie.

'Alright, let's get started,' Scott said. 'We're dealing with a single vehicle accident around 5AM on the 101 right here behind us. A guy's car takes out part of the side railing. He tries to get out of a DUI charge by telling Highway Patrol he rear-ended a van, then had to swerve to avoid a body.'

'A body lying on the freeway?' Jayne interrupted.

'No, that's the thing. He says the body came out of the van he hit. Happened to have noticed the van earlier because it had a peach on the license plate and he'd just had a bellyful of peach schnapps.'

'Peach plate,' Steelie said. 'Georgia?'

'Got it in one. So, there was no sign of a body but CHP reports that the side railing scraped off part of the front of this guy's car. Anything could have dropped down under the freeway because it's one of the sections with a berm sloping off it on the north side. Lots of vegetation, creating a basic ravine situation. They secured the area as soon as their flashlights picked up what they thought were body parts.'

Jayne looked toward the ravine. 'How many BPs are we talking about?'

Eric answered her. 'We don't know yet.'

'Okayyy,' Steelie said. 'I don't want to seem uninterested but why were you so insistent on calling us in? Why not Rudin or Sweetzer? This is their beat.'

Scott said, 'Coroner's office can't spare Rudin because of the crematorium investigation and they said Sweetzer's on her honeymoon. But... there's another reason.' He crossed his arms and took a deep breath, only to look up at the sky.

Jayne looked to Eric. He was focused on a tarmac fissure at his feet.

Then Scott exhaled the story like a confession. 'Eric and I have some open cases from Georgia involving body parts. All female, none yet identified. We believe they're related to the disappearance of a number of sex workers in and around Atlanta. We figured it for one serial killer, not a bunch of different Johns.'

Eric took up the story. 'Our boss wasn't convinced by our reading of the facts so he scaled back our investigation even though we still had decent leads. But Scott and I... we couldn't let it drop. Our boss found out, transferred us to LA. But we know that killer's still out there.'

Jayne scanned Scott's face. 'You didn't tell me that's why you were transferred.'

He looked away.

Steelie sounded interested. 'What makes you think the material in the ravine is related to your Georgia cases?'

Eric said, 'If the material is human, then it's the MO of dismemberment in combination with the type of vehicle. Multiple witnesses recalled the missing Atlanta women last being seen getting into a van.'

Scott added, 'When CHP notified us early this morning that there was a van wearing a Georgia plate involved in this mess, we made it federal and put on our thinking caps.' He finally met Jayne's eyes. 'And I called you.'

'So you want us to confirm human, non-human, sex? What else?' Jayne said. 'Because this isn't our area anymore. Our agency deals with families, not bodies.'

'Ever noticed how the wick goes all the way through a candle?'

She wasn't ready for the change in subject.

Scott re-started. 'A candle couldn't burn if the wick didn't go all the way through. That's why you can burn it from either end.'

'And that applies here... how?' She looked over to see if Steelie was following this but she'd only lifted an eyebrow.

Eric put his thumb out toward Scott. 'He's trying to say that we're all doing the same thing, just starting at different ends. You're trying to make IDs by starting with missing persons; we're starting with their bodies. I've heard from Scott that you two did more than your fair share of body work with the United Nations. If anyone's qualified to check out this site, it's you guys.'

'So,' Scott said. 'Can we do this?'

Steelie nodded, so Jayne held out her hands in acquiescence.

Scott called out to one of the Critters, who walked over holding an array of nylon straps with attached clips.

He spoke with a deep voice when he identified himself as Agent Weiss. 'When we get over to the site, you'll see that the best way to climb up there is for me to winch you up. Can I get you two fitted out?' He unfurled the straps to show they were fixed into a harness that resembled underpants.

Steelie stepped forward to get into the rig as the others watched. Leaning on Weiss' shoulder for balance, she called out playfully, 'Y'know, Scott, you didn't have to go to all this trouble just to see me in some underwear.'

Eric choked back a surprised laugh. 'Hang on. How long have you guys known each other?'

'Since Houston here was still in training pants.'

'Not pants,' Scott corrected quickly. 'I was *at* a training session. And it was a uniform.'

Steelie was clearly enjoying herself. 'It was a training gun, though, right?'

Eric looked to his partner. 'Is she talking about the red ones we use at Quantico?'

But Scott was looking at Jayne. 'Can't you rein her in?'

'No,' Jayne said, stepping into her own harness. 'I can't.'

Steelie still had Eric's attention. 'When Jayne and I were at Quantico, we watched a classmate of Scott's run a semi-covert op to steal his gun.'

Eric looked at Scott in disbelief. 'From the back of your pants?'

'She didn't succeed,' Scott downplayed. 'And then I stole hers.'

'Yeah!' Steelie said. 'And she yelled at him from the other side of the bar like he was NASA Control: "Houston? We got a problem." So then he—'

'Eric doesn't need the rest of that story,' Scott said firmly. 'You ready, Jayne?'

They followed a CHP officer to the edge of the parking lot and clambered over a low concrete wall to descend into the ravine where they hiked along the bottom for a short distance. Past the Sunkist property line, the ravine narrowed and became more overgrown: eucalyptus, vinca, shreds of plastic bags, all sprouting with equal vigor. It was darker and cooler because the sun hadn't filtered down yet. The group fell silent.

The officer slowed and called back to them, pointing to the left where the berm led up to the freeway. 'The material's up there. We marked a wide perimeter with flags. The slope is steep and it is slippery.' He stepped to the side, using the trunk of a small tree as a handhold.

Jayne and Steelie hung back while the Critters moved in to do their work. Then Scott turned to the anthropologists and said, 'Alright, Thirty-Two One, tell us what we got.'

The two women moved to the front of the group, the clicks of the power buttons on their flashlights echoed by clicks on others as people followed their lead. Ten seconds passed as they looked up the berm from below. Brown leaves, wet leaves, wet tissue exhibiting pale red blotches.

'Well, it's human. I can tell you that from here,' declared Jayne.

'In that case,' Scott said, 'I authorize you to take a closer look.'

Weiss clipped their harnesses to a rappelling rope and checked all the connections. Once they were lined up with Jayne in front, he started winching and she and Steelie climbed the slope. As soon as they were parallel to the body parts, they leaned toward them at various angles.

Steelie called down to the others. 'We're not going to touch anything because you guys will have to detail-photo this first, okay?'

11

'Ten-four, ma'am,' came the reply.

Jayne murmured, 'I'm seeing two arms, present from the shoulder down, all fingers present. A chunk of thigh and knee... left. You seeing the same thing?'

'Yeah, and I've got another chunk of torso down here. Everything's wet.'

'Is it just wet around the BPs? Or is that condensation?'

They both looked around. Everything else was dry and dusty, like Southern California should be in the summer.

'What's the deal?' Jayne asked. 'The parts aren't fresh but they don't look like they're decomping either.'

'They're not,' Steelie replied. 'Listen. Hear that?' She held her hand up and Jayne stopped moving, cocking her head to the side.

In between the rushes of sound that accompanied the passing traffic on the freeway above them, there was a distinct sound. *Sip, sip... sip... sip, sip*. Then, before their eyes, out of the tissue visible in the cross-section of the exposed left knee came a droplet. It was a watery red shimmer, hanging, then dropping from the tissue onto the bed of leaves below.

'Not decomping...' Steelie said. 'Defrosting.'

They straightened up.

Jayne called out, 'Houston.'

'Yo,' came his voice from below.

'We got a problem.'

12

2

Jayne swore as she unlocked the door of the low-slung brick building while balancing the two Styrofoam cups of coffee, plus the bag of donuts. She'd just registered how bright the sign above the door was: *Agency 32/1*, illuminated by both daylight and spotlight.

The agency wasn't much to look at but it had a good view: the back-end of Dodger Stadium and surrounds – low hills of eucalyptus and oleander sectioned by midsummer's nut-brown scrubland. If you left the stadium and went to the agency as the crow flies, you'd cross the 5 Freeway, the Los Angeles River, the rail yards and San Fernando Road before landing in the front parking lot. Just five spaces, two marked *Reserved* and three marked *Visitor*. One reserved space was for Steelie's Jeep Wrangler, which was so compact it made Jayne's adjacent old, cream-colored Ford truck look like a 1950s fridge.

'Guess what? I forgot to turn off the lights earlier,' Jayne called out to Steelie, who was approaching with their toolboxes.

'The real question is,' Steelie peered inside the donut bag with a practiced eye, 'did you remember to get me a lemon-filled?'

'Is today Tuesday?'

Steelie filched the bag off of Jayne. 'It's so nice to be predictable.'

They went into the building, Jayne crossing in front of the counter where their volunteer receptionist would sit when she arrived at nine. Carol was a retired grief counselor who claimed she would rather sit all day at the agency than at home. She dealt with phone calls, incoming and outgoing mail, file creation, petty cash, tea and watering the one plant: an aloe tree named Fitzgerald.

Jayne passed through the double doors just beyond reception to go into her office. She caught a glimpse of Steelie trotting past her other door, which opened into the hallway and led to the kitchen, restroom and laboratory. Sitting down at her desk, Jayne swiveled her chair to switch on the computer to the left and the lamp in the center. From the right, she selected a fresh legal pad and pen. Then, from the cabinets that flanked the wall behind her, she pulled one file out at random.

Each agency file described someone who had gone missing, but it wasn't a missing person report. It was a family history, a story told by those who knew the missing person and remembered falls from first bike rides or someone's favorite candy. Jayne and Steelie translated those falls and candy into a database of healed fractures on bone and cavities in teeth, all in the hopes of identifying some of the 40,000 dead bodies that languished in coroners' offices throughout the country.

But Jayne didn't start with data in the morning. Mornings were about the stories, in case a fresh look made something jump out.

The file she pulled today included a transparent sleeve with a photograph of a smiling twenty-two-year-old. Jayne automatically zeroed in on the teeth. The left central incisor

– tooth number nine – was slightly twisted. It gave the woman an earnest look and would help identify her body if it was lying in the morgue. Although she was unable to say her name, her bones and teeth would speak for her. Jayne flipped to the dental chart at the back of the file to check that number nine's mesial torsion had been noted. It had been. It was time to look through the transcript of the interview she'd conducted with the missing woman's parents. She opened the stack of pages to the right place and smoothed the file down.

Several pages in, she heard the jangle of the bells hanging from a string on the front door. The sound was followed by Carol's crisp, 'Morning all,' which seemed to encompass not just Steelie and Jayne but the missing person files too.

Jayne walked to her doorway to see the plump, white-haired woman placing her canvas bag on the front counter. 'Thanks for coming in, Carol.'

Carol waved her hand in dismissal. 'It's been nine months. You can stop thanking me.'

Steelie arrived to greet Carol and Jayne turned back to her office, thinking about the grant applications for the agency's third year of funding, which included a modest salary for their receptionist. It was too late to adjust the requests for the second year and she hoped Carol would keep accepting lunch as compensation. She picked up the transcript again.

Steelie came to stand in front of her desk. 'Which one have you got today?'

'The girl from Tarzana.' Jayne waited expectantly.

Steelie put a finger to her lips and then pointed at the file. 'Bulbous frontal, twisted front tooth, missing from her job at… Victoria's Secret?'

'Jesus. I don't know how you do it. We've got a hundred case files and you can always remember details like that.'

Steelie bowed as she walked backwards toward the hallway.

Jayne called after her, 'Was it X-rays in the package yesterday?'

Steelie nodded. 'Just getting to them now.'

*

Scott wrapped up the call on his BlackBerry and summoned his team from where they'd been talking to Highway Patrol on the edge of the Sunkist parking lot.

'We've got the green light from Quantico to process this scene.' He held up his hand as two of the Critters began to move toward the open rear doors of the Suburbans. 'Hang on. After we get the material, it's going to the LA County coroner, not Virginia, so bag it for local transport, not shipment.'

Eric looked like he wanted to ask a question but Agent Sparks got in first. 'Do you want us to stick to the perimeter CHP established?'

Scott turned to Agent Weiss. 'Steve, what'd you see when you put up the rappelling line?'

'The body parts look like they were thrown down from above. Sparky thinks they've rolled a bit but neither of us saw signs that this was the dismemberment site. Tony?' Weiss gestured an invitation to the Critter to his left, who was holding a stack of plastic photo markers with surgical-gloved hands.

Agent Lee shook his head. 'I haven't seen anything

beyond the immediate area where they're dripping. And the Chips kept their perimeter well wide of that. I wouldn't go wider.'

'In that case, let's use their perimeter line and note that,' Scott said. 'But Tony, can you photo-doc outside the perimeter? Get the whole ravine?'

'I can, once Xavier brings over the *whole* lighting rig.' Lee threw a meaningful glance at Agent Tollen.

Tollen grinned. 'Oh, you wanted *all* the lights? Not just the two I brought over already?'

Scott left the Critters talking among themselves and headed back to the ravine. Eric walked briskly to catch up and fall into step beside him.

'You told Quantico this might be related to the Georgia cases?'

'Yes,' Scott replied.

'So...?'

'So, they're not biting.'

'Did you explain about the cuts?'

Scott nodded.

Eric continued. 'I went up while you were on the call. There's something too neat about the body parts. Too clean, maybe? I think you should climb up and take a look yourself.'

Scott climbed over the wall in a swift movement and carried on. 'I was about to do just that.'

*

Steelie's voice called out from the intercom on the desk telephone. Jayne activated the microphone. 'Steelie, you can only be in one of two other rooms in this tiny building.

17

Why are you using the intercom?'

'Why did we buy phones with intercoms if not to use them?'

As usual, she had a point. 'Okay, what is it?'

'Can you come down to the lab? There's something here you should see.'

Jayne walked down the hallway and turned into the last doorway on the right. Steelie was at the base of a U formed by the countertop on three sides. She was perched on a stool, looking at an X-ray clipped to the large wall-mounted light box. Papers were spread out across the countertop below. Jayne came up to look at the film.

It was a radiograph of a man's head, taken from the left side. The bony parts were milky-white, as were the teeth, although the metallic fillings were bright white where the metal had blocked the light from passing through the X-ray film. Something else was stark white but in an unexpected place. Jayne leaned in, her eyes traveling above the eye sockets, perhaps between them, an inch or so back from the forehead.

She turned to look at Steelie. 'These *are* antemortem films, right?'

'Yep.'

'So he was walking around...' Jayne blinked back at the X-ray. 'With a bullet in his head?'

'That's what I came up with.'

'What case is this?'

'Thomas Cullen.'

'From Twentynine Palms?'

'The same.'

'I remember interviewing his folks. They didn't mention

18

that he had a bullet in his head. Are you thinking war wound or something?'

'Too young for Vietnam, AWOL for Afghanistan and Iraq.'

'What about Desert Storm?'

Steelie swung back to the X-ray, pulling herself closer to the counter and pointing at the film with the eraser end of a pencil. 'Actually, here's what I'm thinking: from the angle of the bullet I'd say he shot himself through the roof of the mouth but he didn't count on the ol' sphenoid bone being there, let alone being so convoluted, and the bullet lodges. Pain associated with shot is numbed by shock at still being alive. Never even tells his family he tried it.'

'Are there any shots of the maxillary bones?'

'Not in this batch. I reckon the doc took these to see where the bullet was and determine if they were going to dig it out.'

Jayne rocked back slightly. 'They *had* to leave it.'

'Probably.'

'And it would make him identifiable as hell.'

'Yep.' Steelie was warming to the subject. 'According to the file, the missing persons detectives only asked Cullen's parents for his dental records. It wasn't until the parents came to see us that they started to look for medical X-rays. Didn't even think they'd find any. So... since the dental hasn't made the match yet, I think we should put out an ACB.'

Thirty-Two One had developed the All Coroners Bulletin, or ACB, to notify coroners with unidentified bodies when there was new information about highly identifiable characteristics on missing persons – details that

19

couldn't have been included in the original police report and therefore wouldn't be in the FBI's national database. The ACB was in its pilot phase, with strict usage guidelines the agency had established in concert with coroners nationwide.

'This'll be the first one. We'll have to follow protocol to the letter, Steelie.'

'I know the rules: unknown or suspicious circumstances only.' She indicated a manila folder on the counter. 'I've got the Cullen file right here. I'll check it out.'

The lights suddenly dimmed and the lab computer behind them turned off, only to restart itself.

'Shit. Brownout,' they said simultaneously.

'They're getting to be weekly,' Steelie said. 'We've got to get that generator, Jayne.'

'I know. They say it's going to be a long, hot summer.'

'It's LA. It's always a long, hot summer.'

Jayne gave her a humorless smile.

Steelie grinned. 'I'm here all week. But seriously, is our budget still strapped?'

'Since you asked me this morning?' Jayne pushed off the counter.

When Carol announced Scott Houston on line one later, Jayne answered the phone at her desk before she took her eyes off the sentence she was reading, which made her sound distracted.

'Scott. How are you?'

'Good, but you sound tired. We get you up too early this morning?'

'Very funny. What's up?'

'When was the last time you ate?'

20

'You sound like my mother,' she said as she swept the last donut crumbs on the desk into the trash.

'Actually, I was trying to ask you to lunch.'

Jayne looked at her watch but suddenly couldn't take anything in, pleased out of all proportion. 'Is it lunchtime already?'

'Is that a ladylike way of saying, "No, thanks"?'

'Only a more gentlemanly invitation would get you a ladylike response.' Jayne was focusing now.

'Oh, really? I'll send round an embossed card with gold edging next time.'

'I'd be interested to see "In-N-Out Burger" written in calligraphy.'

He chuckled and then said, 'How about Cal Plaza?'

'Downtown?'

'Why not? It's only ten minutes from your shop.'

'I know. I mean, Cal Plaza's great but you just moved here! I'm surprised you've even heard of it.'

'Hey, I get out,' he protested.

Jayne's bubble burst. *He's been out with someone? Already?*

He spoke into her silence. 'Is that a yes?'

'Yes.'

'Okay, I'll pick you up in fifteen.'

'With Eric?'

'Nope, Eric will be eating with the Critters at the site.'

'They're still there, then?'

'You fishing, Jayne?'

'No! I was just wondering—'

'Relax! I'll tell you all about it at lunch.'

Jayne returned to the lab where Steelie was just hitting

21

the *Print* key on the computer.

Watching the document emerge, Jayne said, 'Scott's going to bring me up to speed on their body parts case.'

'Cool. When?'

'Noon.'

'A lunch date,' Steelie chirped.

'No one used that word.'

Steelie pretended to look puzzled. 'Wait, "lunch" or "date"?'

Jayne gave her a quelling look.

Smiling, Steelie relented. 'I've got something more interesting than Agent Houston and his body parts right here.' She whipped the paper out of the printer tray and handed it to Jayne.

It was the ACB. It looked serious and official:

* * ALL CORONERS BULLETIN * *


```
Dear Coroner/Medical Examiner,
    In the matter of CULLEN, Thomas
    DOB 03-01-1959, NCIC# M-004517592
Please be informed that the
aforementioned individual sustained GSW
to palate and sphenoid with projectile
remaining lodged in sphenoid and visible
on attached LEFT radiograph dated 04-15-
1992. For further information, contact:

Steelie Lander
Agency 32/1
```

'That looks good,' Jayne said. 'What did the police have for Cullen's circumstances?'

'Missing Persons logged it in as unknown. Cullen had asked for a few days off work, didn't return, car was found at John Wayne Airport. I think he went to take his life just as he'd tried to before but this time he wanted something more reliable for him than a handgun. Pills, maybe.'

'Go on.'

'He flies up to Alaska, to see the ex.'

'What ex?'

'It's in your interview transcript: the girlfriend who left him in '91. I think their break-up was the reason he tried this number.' Steelie tapped the X-ray image of the bullet.

'Okay.'

'He tootles up there, says goodbye or what-have-you, takes his pills and suddenly he's Alaska's problem.'

'Could be.'

'Well, whatever happened to him, if he's been found and they've done a craniotomy – or even if an anthro pulled the maxillae to X-ray the teeth – they would've been clued into the old bullet. Even if he's alive and has amnesia, this X-ray is key. The fact that the police didn't know he had a bullet in his head when they did his missing person report warrants the ACB.'

'I'm already on board, remember? Where's the checklist for the protocol?'

'Right here.'

'Let's sign it so you can get this sent out.'

As they finished up, they could hear lively chat between Carol and someone in reception.

'That'll be your lunch,' Steelie said.

23

'If it is, he's early.' Jayne felt a frisson of excitement at the thought of Scott rushing over to see her, even if it was only a working lunch.

She followed Steelie to the front of the building where they found Scott leaning on Carol's counter, listening with rapt attention as she concluded, '—afford it on my salary.'

Jayne found herself just enjoying the sight of Scott standing in their little reception area but Steelie was quick off the draw. 'Houston, don't try to tempt Carol away with your government wages.'

He stepped back from the counter with a smile, hands raised, palms out. 'I would never do that to the agency. You should know that about me.'

Carol began to clarify. 'Agent Houston and I—'

'Please call me Scott.' He all but twinkled at her.

She inclined her head and continued. 'Scott and I were just comparing the V6 and the V8 when used in the four-wheel-drive Chevrolet Suburban.'

He gestured at Jayne and Steelie. 'You knew Carol rode shotgun with her mom when she drove the Alaska Highway in the Forties?'

'In a wood-panel Suburban,' Carol added with pride.

'Of course we knew,' Steelie huffed.

Scott leaned on Carol's counter again. 'I look forward to continuing our discussion another time.'

Jayne and Steelie had never seen their receptionist blush before and exchanged an amused look. Then Jayne propelled Scott out the front door and into the heat of the day.

3

The mist of California Plaza's fountains kept its amphitheater of granite steps cool even when the Santa Ana winds were blowing hot over Los Angeles. Every riser supported a person's back and every flat surface was a perch for buttocks and take-out sushi. Scott and Jayne had opted for hot dogs and they sat at the top step with their backs to Angel's Flight, the funicular that used to carry people up and down Bunker Hill for twenty-five cents. All talking had been deferred in favor of eating, so there was just the hum of others' conversation, the occasional outburst of distant laughter, and the unpredictable *fwap* of the fountains' geyser-like water jets falling back to the granite floor.

Jayne popped the last bit of ketchup-drenched bun into her mouth and mumbled, 'Now, *that* was a good idea.'

Scott murmured agreement as he wiped his mouth and held a hand out for her paper hot dog boat. Stacking it with his, he walked toward a trashcan as Jayne watched. She was trying to understand why she was so uncharacteristically comfortable in the open plaza. It had to be the position on the steps that Scott had subtly chosen. It was at the top of the amphitheater without any businesses behind it, which translated to a bird's eye view with limited foot traffic at one's back. Then she noticed that they weren't covered by close CCTV here either. Most of the cameras were

25

mounted on the buildings across the way, tilted down to cover entryways of boutiques and eateries.

Scott was striding back now, his eyes scanning the perimeter. This was the other reason she was comfortable: he was as vigilant as she was.

Once he was seated next to her again, she said, 'Now, give me the skinny on the body parts and tell me why we had to come to the best spot in Downtown to not get overheard.'

'Worked that out, eh?'

'Spill.'

Scott leaned forward, elbows on his knees. 'Okay, the Bureau's directed us to move the freeway body parts over to the LA County Coroner's Office, where you know they're going to the bottom of their list—'

'Wait. How come they'll go to the coroner? I thought that once the FBI has a case, that's it.'

'Well, the boys in Virginia don't want another bunch of body parts to deal with, especially when those parts don't include a head. Not without the locals at least trying to ID them first. We get to keep the investigation into the vehicle because that could go interstate but we've been directed to move the body parts to Mission Road ASAP.'

Jayne immediately thought of the Automated Fingerprint Identification System. 'Could you run the fingerprints through AFIS? Fingers were present on both hands.'

'You know that fingerprint matching only works when the vic's prints are already on the system for another reason, like a criminal record, right?'

'Of course, but it's worth a try, isn't it?'

'Maybe, but the Bureau would be on me like a fly on shit

if I started accessing AFIS for a case I've been told isn't the Bureau's. So AFIS has to be initiated by the coroner when *he* gets the case.'

'Which will be when the bottom of their list makes its way to the top.'

'Exactly. But I think your agency can help.'

She looked at him and waited. They were sitting so close that she could see the hazel flecks in the green of his irises.

Scott lowered his voice. 'I climbed up to the body parts and had a look at the cuts. They were precise, right? At anatomical locations to make dismemberment easier?'

'I'd agree with that. So?'

'So, whoever's carrying them around in a freezer is a pro. And we only know he was driving around because a drunk rear-ended his van.' Scott glanced over his shoulder. 'Can we go over there?'

Jayne followed him across to the metal railing that overlooked Bunker Hill. If Scott was looking for total privacy, he had it here. It was like being on the edge of a cliff, complete with a breeze whistling in her ears. Scott was speaking with a quiet urgency so she leaned over to hear him better, bumping into him for only an instant but his shoulder left a warm memory on hers.

'Those body parts seemed freezer-burned to me, Jayne, not just frozen. I think someone's been holding onto them a long time – maybe even years. That translates to zero active police investigations into those victims as missing persons. They'll have been overtaken by newer cases like always happens. But those vics will still have *family* looking for them. If they haven't been to your agency yet, someone'll send them there.'

Jayne didn't see how this request merited cloak-and-dagger treatment. 'You want us to check our database? That's no problem. Just give us the autopsy or anthro report when it's ready.'

'I was thinking that maybe you could do an anthropology exam yourself and then check it against your files.'

Now she *was* surprised. 'But the coroner's going to want to do an autopsy. You can't precede that with anthro. And Steelie and I don't work for LA County.'

He looked at her intently. 'What if you did an external, non-invasive sort of... preliminary exam?'

'Wait a minute, Scott. What is this?' When he looked down without answering, she continued. 'You know, ever since Eric said that this case was the reason you got transferred to LA, I've been trying to work out why you never mentioned it. We must've been on the phone tons of times while—'

'I couldn't.'

She made a noise of exasperation. 'I *do* know the meaning of sub judice, you know. You could've told me the outline without compromising the case.'

He made a gesture like he wanted her to lower her voice. 'No, Jayne, I meant I literally could not tell you. After certain... things happened with the case, Eric and I decided our phones weren't safe. We communicated in person or by private messaging between our BlackBerrys. Plus, we had to fly under the radar so our boss couldn't see the number of hours we were putting in on leads he considered dead ends. There were only two other agents in the office we could trust with what we were doing and I didn't talk to anyone by phone on this. Not anyone, okay?'

28

She took in his expression: earnest, concerned. She wanted to ask him what those 'things' were that 'happened' but that could wait. She kept her voice low. 'Alright. So tell me about the situation here. Do you have the same constraints you had in Georgia?'

'Theoretically? No. New office: new supervisor. But if the body parts from this morning are related to the case in Georgia, then Eric and I need to know ASAP. Has a Georgia serial killer gone mobile? Does California need to be on alert? Are there any clues on the 101 Freeway that will help us solve the Georgia cases? The best way to answer those questions is to ID the body parts. You know that as well as I do.'

'I do, but it sounds like you want us to do this external exam just because you don't want to wait for the coroner's office. Or is there something more?'

'Listen, superficially, those body parts have characteristics that look like one of my cases, so I think of them as part of my case; doesn't matter that they turned up in LA instead of Atlanta. I'm ready to ID them but then the Bureau takes it out of my hands and gives it to people who've got so many bodies to ID, they've become statistics.' He tilted his head back and forth as though getting a kink out of his neck. 'Maybe I don't like that so much.'

She almost laughed. 'That doesn't sound like "maybe".'

'Yeah, well, Eric pointed out that it's no coincidence that "bureaucracy" and "Bureau" share the same Latin root.' He paused. 'Look, we've been told to make the transfer as soon as possible. In my experience, that means we've got two days with the body parts in our cold storage. Could you do an exam and a report for me in that time?'

29

'Could you provide X-ray facilities?'

'Sure.'

She thought about it. Then she asked, 'How will this be cleared?'

'Don't have to clear it; material's in our custody.'

She cocked an eyebrow. 'So Steelie and I come into the FBI building on a visitor tour but happen to examine some human remains before leaving with the other tourists?'

'No...' Scott looked amused. 'I'll put you onto our site log but we're talking about a non-invasive look-see. *I'm* clearing you. I'll take responsibility.'

Jayne looked into the distance at the ivory bulk of County-USC Hospital and the summer-drawn smog blanket above East LA. She felt small against the spread of the city and the knowledge that it took millions of people living their lives to make that haze. Then she thought about the paupers' graves where the county buried bodies that had never been identified or claimed. She knew Steelie's opinion of these group interments: it was excellent that LA County cared enough to do them but they were still mass graves. Jayne could easily picture the body parts from the freeway ending up there in a few months, with only some taxpayer-funded strangers to intone a few words over them. Scott's request offered a chance to change that picture. It made her hopeful.

Looking back at him, she could tell he already knew what she'd decided. She returned his smile. 'Alright, count us in.'

4

When Scott dropped Jayne off at the agency, she knew she was the first one back because Carol's 'Out to Lunch' sign was still hanging on the front door. The phone started to ring as she walked in. She picked it up at Carol's desk.

The caller's voice was loud. 'This is Ron from A-1 Electrics?'

Jayne wondered if he was asking her or telling her. She sat down in Carol's chair. 'How can I help you?'

'Yeah, I'm calling about the generator?'

'The generator?'

'Yeah!' Chewing gum snapped and clicked. 'I've got a... uh, two-stroke Give-All generator with shut-off switch to deliver and I just need to confirm your address.'

'I don't know what you're talking about.'

'If you're worried about the installation, that's all included.'

'That's nice but I didn't order a generator and neither has anyone else at this address, to my knowledge.'

'Well, ma'am, I've got the receipt right here.'

'Who ordered it?'

'Let's see.' *Snap-snap-pop*. 'I don't have a name on the requisition sheet but there's a note about angles.'

'ANGLES? Is it an acronym?'

'Or... angels? Angel's Flight maybe?'

'What?' Jayne stood up so abruptly she almost yanked the phone off the desk by its cord as she tried to see if Scott was still in the parking lot.

'You still there, ma'am? It *is* all paid for.'

She straightened the phone. 'Ron, I'm going to put you on hold for a minute.'

She punched the hold button and dialed out on another line.

'Houston.' He was on speakerphone and she could hear ambient noise in the background.

'Scott, I've got a guy on the other line asking me where I want my new generator. You know anything about this?'

'No-o-o.'

'No?' Jayne was incredulous and her words came out like bullets. 'I find that very hard to believe because he just told me that it's for Angel's Flight. Now that's too much of a coincidence in my book.'

'Let's say I do know something about it. Why are you so angry?'

'You can't just turn up here and start giving me gifts!'

'Let me reassure you right now that I don't think the way to a woman's heart is through gas-powered machinery. It's for the agency.'

Jayne was too hot under the collar to feel mortified. 'I know *that*! What I meant was, you can't just give me gifts for the agency. We're governed by 501(c)(3) regulations. Any gift has to be a legit donation and – dammit, Scott, I can take care of this place myself!'

'Well, that's not what Steelie said to Eric in relation to this.'

Jayne faltered. 'Steelie?'

'Yeah. She got to talking with Eric about the brownouts this morning, mentioned your office needs a generator but doesn't have the funds, and Eric decided to organize a donation to the agency. All by the book.'

Before Jayne could muster a response, Scott continued. 'Plus, we don't want your computers going down while you're working on anything related to our discussion at Angel's Flight.'

'I see. Well, in that case, thank you. We'll send you a donation receipt. Or send it to Eric…' She petered out.

'Take your time, Hall.' He sounded amused. 'Ten-four.'

Jayne pressed the button to retrieve Ron on line one and politely organized the delivery of the generator for Thursday.

She'd only been back at her desk for a few minutes when she heard Carol and Steelie enter the building.

Steelie immediately asked, 'Good lunch?'

'Thank you for your interest,' Jayne said drily as she followed them to the small kitchen where they were putting leftovers in the fridge. 'It was very nice and I agreed that we'd go to the FBI's Wilshire office tomorrow at eleven.'

She explained Scott's theory about the freeway body parts and his desire for a preliminary report.

Steelie sounded doubtful. 'And the coroner's office isn't going to have a problem with this?'

'Apparently not.'

Carol looked at the two anthropologists. 'If Scott's cleared it on his end and you wouldn't be compromising a future autopsy, then you wouldn't be interfering with the wheels of justice turning down at the coroner's office. Maybe you'd even grease them a little.'

Steelie jerked a thumb toward Carol. 'Ever noticed how everything she says sounds sensible?'

Carol gave Steelie an indulgent smile. 'All I'm saying is that this request fits into the agency's mission, in my view.' The bells on the front door rang out. 'I'll go,' she said.

Steelie watched her pad away. 'I have to say that I did like the big team feeling this morning: being on that hillside with the Critters, having Scott and Eric waiting for our input, plugging it into their investigation.'

'I liked it too,' Jayne said. 'Oh, and your loose lips have won us a generator.'

'No way!'

'Yeah. Eric and Scott are going to donate one to the agency.'

'Wow.' Steelie's broad smile collapsed when she caught Jayne's expression. 'Don't tell me you did one of your don't-think-me-ungrateful-but-we-can-do-it-ourselves numbers on them? Oh, you didn't!' Steelie threw up her hands. 'Y'know, not everyone is paternalistic or even chauvinistic—'

She broke off when the sound of a sob traveled back from the front of the building. She motioned with her head that she'd be in the lab.

Jayne slipped quietly into her office from the hallway but the double doors to reception were already closed, which was no doubt Carol's doing. Jayne didn't want to interrupt what the doors' mottled glass panels allowed her to make out: Carol, in full grief-counselor mode, had sat down next to the visitor. The crying, which had started as though a dam had burst, was subsiding but Jayne sensed that the force of the tears had only been dammed up again, not spent. And was it ever?

It was possible that the visitor wouldn't stay for an interview on the first visit. Sometimes it was enough for family members to walk through the agency's front door and deal with what that represented: they'd reached the stage where they were considering the possibility that their missing relative had been found dead. They would return when they felt stronger.

A darkening across the room made Jayne look up. The visitor was leaving. A knock on the door a moment later was Carol.

'That was Solana,' she said, sitting in the chair facing Jayne's desk. 'Here about her son Roberto, missing for six months. She was referred by the Alstons in Pasadena.'

'Some referral. We haven't been able to find their daughter.'

'Well, you'll be interested in what Solana said, then. She started working for the Alstons as a housekeeper a few months ago. At some point, they asked her if she would live-in. She said she couldn't and then broke down. They thought she was afraid she was going to lose the job if she didn't live-in but then she explained to them how she didn't want to be away from home for any twenty-four-hour period in case Roberto came back and she wasn't there.'

Jayne shook her head sadly. 'How many times have we heard that before?'

'Exactly. So that's when the Alstons shared that their own child had gone missing almost six years ago but discovering the agency recently had helped them focus their energies... given them hope of some sort of answer. Solana agreed to pay us a visit but, as I'm sure you heard through the door, it took a lot out of her.'

'Do you think she'll come back?'

Carol considered this as she stood up. 'I don't know. It's taken her weeks just to come inside, having driven past a few times. But I gave her one of our brochures to take home.'

'Thank you.' Jayne could hear Carol humming quietly as she returned to reception.

*

Scott walked into the office he and Eric shared on the fourth floor of the FBI building in Westwood and saw his partner on the phone. He wondered if information was coming in from a law enforcement officer who'd seen their Be On the Look Out notice for the van hit by the drunk on the 101 Freeway. Even busy cops still paid attention to BOLOs. He set one of the cups he was carrying down onto Eric's desk.

Eric hung up the phone and turned to face him. 'That was Detective Schrader over in LAPD Robbery Homicide.'

'He call you?' Scott winced as he scalded the roof of his mouth on the coffee.

'She, and I called 'cause I got to thinking: we've got the BOLO notice out for the van but the perp will have had to stop to repair it, maybe even disguise it. So, we don't just have to wait for a hit on the BOLO. We can go out and track him down.'

'Body shops?'

'The *right* body shops.'

'Did the detective give you their watch list?'

'Yeah. She gave me eighteen shops that have come to their attention for handling stolen vehicles.'

'What radius from the body parts?'

'I asked for a five-mile radius from the nearest freeway exit to the north, which was… uh, Van Nuys Boulevard. We can expand it if we have to.'

'Chances are the perp didn't drive too far once he realized he lost his load out the back door.' Scott was already getting up and he grinned at Eric, who was trying to get some coffee down and fast. 'You ready?'

Eric swallowed. 'Just remember whose brilliant idea this was.'

Scott resurrected the competitive trade-off they'd started in Atlanta. 'You want a gold star? I'll give you one if we get a lead on the van.'

'Yeah, I've heard that before,' Eric grumbled but he was getting up with alacrity and the two agents left the office.

*

Steelie didn't move from the lab all afternoon. Carol did crossword puzzles at her desk until 4PM, when she watered Fitzgerald and then made tea for everyone else. Jayne pulled together the material they'd take to the FBI office: biometric forms, sliding calipers, rulers. Then she checked the agency email account.

There were seven new messages in the inbox since she'd last checked: three were spam, two were lurid spam, one was from the server warning account-holders that old messages would be deleted, and one was from a family looking for a missing relative they believed was alive. The last email was of a type that the agency regularly received: relatives of missing persons didn't want coroners' freezers scoured for their relatives but still got in contact for any scrap of information that might lead them down a fresh path to find that relative.

Carol came to the doorway. 'It's just going on five, so I'll take your cup and then I'll be going.'

'Thanks, Carol. See you tomorrow.'

The email inbox refreshed with a new message and Jayne smiled as she read it. She went to the lab where she found Steelie hunched over her keyboard.

Jayne went to stand next to her. 'You won't believe who just got in contact.'

Steelie's eyes didn't leave the screen. 'Who?'

'Gene.'

'As in, India Tango One?'

'His call sign was India Tango Five, as you well know.'

'But he was number one in his own mind. Probably still is.'

'Well, you'll have a chance to see for yourself because he's flying into LA and suggested we all get together for dinner.'

'I'll be busy.'

'You don't even know what day it's going to be!'

'If it involves Gene and dinner...'

'He's not with the FBI Lab anymore,' Jayne dangled.

Steelie looked at her. 'Oh? What's he doing now?'

'Didn't say.'

'Well, whatever it is, I'm sure he's still number one.' Steelie turned back to the computer.

Jayne looked over her shoulder at the screen. 'How's it going?'

'I posted the ACB onto the network and it's reading fine. Now we just need a reply from someone.'

All the electrical equipment hummed and buzzed as another brownout swept over the neighborhood.

'Hope you weren't working on anything important,' Jayne said with irony.

'Just bring me that generator. In fact…' Steelie stretched her arms above her head. 'Let's take that as a sign and get out of here.'

'Yeah. Let's lock up.'

Jayne replied to Gene's email and then the two women moved through the building, turning off lights and locking the safe that held X-rays and original photographs that would later be returned to clients.

'Keep watch, Fitz,' Steelie said to the office plant as she stepped out the door and locked it behind her.

It was still warm outside but the light was mellowing, the sun beginning to consider a descent somewhere behind Griffith Park's tallest peaks. Steelie and Jayne were both heading in that direction, Jayne to her apartment facing the Silverlake Reservoir and Steelie to her cottage in Atwater Village.

They pulled out of the agency's parking lot to join commuters for whom San Fernando Road was just a way to avoid a particularly congested part of the 5 Freeway. Halted next to each other at the first traffic light, Jayne could hear Steelie's radio: 'It's slow-and-go on the Golden State Freeway this evening, folks…' She smiled at her friend before the light turned green.

5

Scott drove east on Beverly Boulevard with the sun at his back, frustrated that none of the body shops on Eric's list had so far generated a lead on the van. One shop owner merited a second visit; that was on for tomorrow.

He turned on the radio and then glanced at the station ID as he registered a female voice that evoked Hollywood movies from the 1940s in its clipped yet throaty intercontinental tones. He could hear two other voices, both American, whose contributions suggested one was a chef and the other was a landscaper. Then the intercontinental voice returned, requesting that a caller put her question, and Scott upped the volume, hoping to catch the name that went with the voice.

Caller: 'Hi, Marie? Or any of your guests today, I know we're all supposed to be doing xeriscapic gardens these days but do you ever find that your yucca tree, well... disappoints?'

Marie: 'Oh, chop it down, darling. And eat its roots for dinner.'

Scott heard the caller's astonished gasp and smiled to himself. The host, Marie, had to be Jayne's mother. Over the years, Jayne had told him about Marie's voice – and her radio show – but he'd never have guessed that

40

British schooling in Venezuela followed by thirty years in California could produce a voice like the one he was hearing now. He looked in his rearview mirror before changing lanes. The small white car behind him indicated at the same time and Scott accelerated to get in front. The studio guests were chiming in.

Andrew: 'I'd recommend dry white wine to go with yucca, however you cook it.'

Jess: 'The main thing to remember with xeriscapic gardens is that, once they're established, *don't* water them. I take it you've been watering your yucca?'

Caller: 'Well... yes. You see, it's right next to the azalea, which just *loves* water, so it's hard to integrate the, um, Mexican yucca.'

Marie: 'Listeners, we must all remember that it's *xeriscapic*, not xenophobic, that we're aiming for in these troubled times. And that goes for the Rose Garden as well.'

Theme music and a voice advising that this episode of *Weekends with Prentis* had been a repeat drowned out any other comments Marie might have made, leaving Scott trying to picture a woman who used a food show to sling veiled political arrows at Dubya's post-9/11 White House. Jayne had told him that her mother's ability to cast a spell over people had so far kept her out of trouble. Apparently, the spell wasn't due only to her voice but also to her looks, which Jayne had described as 'like Catherine Deneuve, but browner'.

Realizing he'd missed his turn, Scott hung a quick right onto Spring and continued down to the light at 2nd Street. He noticed that the white car was still behind him and making the same right turn. Now it was pulling over to the curb and two Skid Row residents were approaching it. Scott's traffic light clicked to green, so he pulled right, tracked back to his building and turned into the underground parking lot, the gate lifting and then closing behind him.

As he went up the elevator to the fifth floor, he finally allowed himself to think about how good it had been this morning to see Jayne in person, not just hear her voice coming down a phone line. The physical attraction mattered and everything about her – her dark, wavy hair that he wanted to touch echoed in dark eyes that seemed shy and defiant at once; her golden skin with that one beauty mark at the base of her throat; her curves that made him hope she liked to eat real food; and her serious, sometimes sad, insanely beautiful mouth that he could make smile if he said the right things – *all* of it had produced the same pull he'd experienced the first time he'd seen her from across the bar at Quantico. He'd almost forgotten this morning that he was at a crime scene with Eric and a convoy of Critters. Eric. Scott smirked as he got out of the elevator. His partner had picked up on something right away, though he'd held off raising it until Scott had been on the verge of leaving to meet Jayne for lunch.

Scott unlocked the door to his apartment and went in, activating down-lights as he walked into the kitchen. He stepped around the packing boxes on the floor so he could turn on the oven and pull lasagna out of the freezer. Then he leaned against the counter, remembering how Eric had tried to arrange his face into a neutral mask after he'd overheard Scott ask Jayne to lunch.

Eric had opened with, 'So. How long's this been going on?'

Scott had tried to sound blank. 'Nothing's going on.'

'Then it's been a whole lotta nothing.' Eric had paused. 'Was it going on while you were with Mindy?'

'Mad Mindy?'

'Don't change the subject. What about Callista or whoever you brought to Angie's fortieth. Was it going on then?'

When Scott had been too embarrassed to admit the truth, Eric had burst out laughing. 'I don't believe it! Jayne's been the one this whole time? Y'know, I always wondered why you dated such lightweights. It was weird, man. Angie and I used to talk about it – oh shit, *Angie*. I can't wait to tell her!'

Scott had pointed at Eric's chest. 'Don't tell Angie anything. Plus, Mindy and Callista – and Helen for that matter, who was a rebound thing and you know it – were not lightweights when it came to my wallet.'

'That's because you kept giving them consolation prizes every time you skipped out on barbecues or bowling or whatever those kinds of chicks plan.'

'Tapas. For couples.'

'Spare me. Anyway, it's not your wallet that's in danger with Jayne.'

'What's that supposed to mean?'

'I've never seen you look at someone the way you looked at her this morning. And I've seen you look at a *lot* of people.'

Scott had frowned. 'How did I look at her?'

'It was a little... wolfish.'

'That can't be good.'

'Yeah, you might want to work on that.'

Just then, a CHP officer had walked in their direction and Scott had levered himself into the driver's seat of the Suburban.

Eric had leaned on the door so Scott couldn't close it and lowered his voice to a confidential tone. 'So why haven't you been seeing her this whole time – even long distance? And why didn't you tell me about her?'

'Precisely so we wouldn't have this conversation.'

'Man, you need this conversation if you haven't made a move on her yet. Five years? Really? You're lucky she's still around – and available.'

Scott's face must have betrayed him because Eric had asked, with incredulity, 'You don't even know if she's single?'

Scott had covered breaking eye contact by putting the keys in the ignition. The car had sounded a warning.

Eric had been adamant. 'You *really* need this conversation.'

'I'm handling it.' Scott had made to close the door.

Eric had stepped away and said, 'Just try not to screw up lunch. We've got a case riding on this.'

*

Jayne pulled her truck close to the top of the driveway fronting the redwood two-story that housed her apartment. She climbed the concrete staircase on the left side of the building, rising above a neat lawn that held its own under an ancient fir tree. The only neighbor was downstairs, but his front door was on the opposite side of the duplex so Jayne enjoyed the sense of privacy and ownership she felt every time she ascended to her landing, which was why she'd finally bought some terracotta pots and filled them with plants.

She had lived there for several years after moving out of her graduate student apartment in Westwood and refusing the tempting offer of a cottage at the end of her mother's sprawling garden. She loved the apartment's location because it was directly across the street from the Silverlake Reservoir. The large, sparkling body of water was a clear space in a busy neighborhood so drew a faithful crowd of joggers and dog-walkers to its perimeter every day. Some of the faces were familiar to Jayne but she'd never actually talked to anyone.

Expecting her mother to drop by, she left the front door open to the security screen while she put together a light supper in the kitchen. When Marie arrived fifteen minutes later, Jayne marveled once again at her mother's timing. The sunset sky made Marie's silk shirt shimmer in concert with the bronzer that glinted from her impressive cleavage all the way up her neck. Highlights in her dark hair emphasized a style usually achieved on magazine photo shoots by using large fans.

As Marie swept through the doorway, her every move produced a melody as bangles met and dangling earrings swayed, but she immediately turned Jayne by the shoulders and gestured back at the landing with a manicured hand.

'Darling, has it ever occurred to you that you'd get more dates if you kept something other than cacti by your front door?'

Jayne wriggled out of the pseudo-embrace. 'Is that advice about gardening or relationships, Mom?'

'You should have something like gaura pinks. Or maybe gaura lindheimeri – you know, the white ones. Just a few pots, uneven in number.'

'What, so I can find the man who has just one similar pot and say, "You... complete me"?' She faked a swoon as she crossed to the kitchen to finish preparing their roast chicken and avocado sandwiches.

'You're so irreverent, darling. That also keeps people away.'

Jayne cut the sandwiches into triangles. 'This gaura. Is it the wispy one you planted all over your garden?'

'You've noticed!'

'Then, no thanks. Too feminine.'

'What's wrong with a little femininity?' Marie cast an apparently critical eye around the open-plan apartment.

'Nothing. For you. It's just not my style.' Jayne walked over with the tray of sandwiches and a wooden salad bowl. 'Can you grab the iced tea?'

Once Marie joined her, Jayne ushered her onto the deck facing the reservoir. She had covered the patio table with a white tablecloth and decorated that with tea lights and rose petals whose pink tones were deepening as they dried.

Marie fluttered her fingers over the petals. 'I thought you said feminine wasn't your style?'

Jayne smiled, pushing bits of avocado back into her sandwich. 'I just like winding you up.'

They ate for a bit. Then Marie folded some butter lettuce and speared it neatly with her fork. 'Steelie said you're seeing Scott.' In went the lettuce.

Jayne had known this was the real reason for Marie's last-minute visit so she was prepared. 'Not "seeing", Mom. I've seen him. We've all seen him.'

'Now just a minute, darling. The last time I set you up with someone – that perfectly nice teacher *and* a Venezuelan – you stated that you'd rather spend an hour on the phone with Scott Houston than five more minutes with *el profesor*. I remember that quite distinctly.'

Jayne left her sandwich unfinished on the plate. 'Let me get the strawberries.'

Marie called after her. 'And now this Scott Houston is here.'

Jayne was very much aware of this reality. In fact, she'd been wondering what he'd been doing every night since he'd moved to LA. She emerged with the tray holding bowls of berries and a jug of cream. 'So?'

'So, I didn't raise you to be a five o'clock fish.' She fixed Jayne with her 'severe' look, which consisted of one arched eyebrow while she tilted her chin up. 'You remember the five o'clock—'

'Yes, yes.' Jayne waved a hand. 'The fish that's been sitting out all day at market and no one wants to buy old fish or whatever. I told you I don't like the commodification of women inherent in that metaphor. It's ridiculous. I'm not a piece of seafood. Nor am I on a shelf.'

'You're up on this deck! Most evenings! All weekend! You're hiding up here with I don't know what memories from some mass grave or other haunting you, and you've given yourself nothing for comfort other than...' Marie gestured wildly. 'Than spiky *cactaceae*!'

47

Jayne couldn't argue with that. She looked to the reservoir. Its surface was rippled in its best imitation of a lake as night fell. She could see through the fir trees to the hills on the other side where the lights of distant houses glittered.

Marie began to fold and re-fold her napkin. She spoke more softly. 'I worry about you.'

'I know.'

'You don't talk to me about everything you saw when you were overseas and I know that's because you talk to Steelie—'

'Steelie's single too but you never harangue her about it!'

'Because, as I learned when she and I were doing her garden, she's often busy with her lawyer friends and with her hobbies.'

'Her bowling? I see she finally convinced you that it's an acceptable hobby.'

'I am not speaking specifically of bowling. I am saying that Steelie has a support system in the form of actual people. Multiple people. I do not often worry about Steelie. In fact, *she* thinks you need someone in your life, a partner, so it all falls into perspective.'

That surprised Jayne. 'Really?'

Marie managed to frown without actually involving her forehead. 'Don't you talk with her about this?'

'Talk about dating with Steelie? I can almost hear her saying *yech* and spitting a loogie out onto the sidewalk.'

Marie smiled but wasn't distracted. '*Cariña*, be serious. You both spent years helping to uncover war crimes – *war* crimes for heaven's sake – and now you've gone on to do other work that drains you. Maybe in a different way but it drains.'

'It is draining sometimes. But it feeds me, too. I like what I do.'

Jayne watched the candles on the table flicker in the breeze, threatening to go out but then flaring back up triumphantly.

'Even if it breaks your heart almost every day?' Marie sounded curious, not judgmental.

'Mom, it's the people who come to us whose hearts are broken. I just have an empathetic sort of... heart-stretching.'

Marie nodded and then poured cream over the berries. 'Listen, from what you've told me over the years, Scott is the perfect person for you to spend time with now that he lives here. You have interests and sensibilities in common. He might not have been on the same forensic missions as you but he understands what went on over there.'

'Maybe.' Jayne stacked slices of strawberry on her fork, thinking that her mother was only half-right. Scott would understand what went on over there but would Scott understand what was going on over *here*, with her? And if she did tell him – about Benni in particular – would he then see her as she saw herself: sad, broken, guilty? It would mean the end of the flirting, the teasing, the promise, the hope. Jayne dropped her forehead onto the back of her hand at the thought of it.

Marie spoke softly. 'Have the nightmares started again?'

Jayne looked up, startled; she had almost forgotten her mother was there. She took the excuse on offer. 'Not really, they're just infrequent. Can I finish your berries?'

Marie slid over her bowl. 'Why don't you come up to the house when things get bad?'

'I've thought about it.'

'But?'

Jayne sighed. 'I'm afraid I'd never leave again. Like some kid who got older but didn't grow up.'

'I thought you'd say that, which is why I brought you this.' Marie pulled a small plastic bag from her lap and handed it over.

Jayne saw the name of the local pharmacy and pulled out the contents: night-lights, pack of two. She smiled. 'Thanks.'

'Perfect for my daughter, who has definitely grown up. Maybe a little too much.' Marie put her hand to Jayne's chin and caressed it before squeezing her cheek like she was still a baby.

Jayne put her hand over Marie's. Her mother cajoled but she also understood and for that Jayne was grateful. They sat in companionable silence until the breeze picked up enough to blow out the candles.

She roused herself. 'You want coffee, Mom?'

'No, darling, I've got to go. I'm judging the student exhibits at the Garden Expo in Pasadena tomorrow, so it's an early night for me.'

Jayne saw her mother down to the driveway where Marie's sleek, sky-blue Mercedes 450SL was parked behind her truck. As she walked back up the stairs to her door, Jayne looked at the much-maligned cacti and laughed to herself. They did look like sentries: totally unapproachable and silent.

After Jayne cleared up, she locked the sliding door

and went to bed, banishing all thoughts of real people as she pressed 'Play' on the cassette deck resting on her bedside table.

She didn't hear the man on her front doorstep when he smashed one of the cactus pots. The measured reading of *Gaudy Night* had taken her into a rare dreamless sleep.

DAY TWO

Wednesday

6

Eric's voice was quiet. 'Here he comes.' He pushed off of the Surburban's door to allow Scott to get out. They had been waiting for Al Corso, the owner of the body shop on Magnolia Boulevard, to emerge from his office. When Corso saw them advancing, he came to a standstill and threw out his hands, causing his nylon briefcase to wave around.

'What? You not done with me yet?' His tone was aggressive and resigned all at once. 'I answered all your questions, didn't I?'

'Yeah,' Scott said casually. 'We just didn't like your answers so much, Corso. Thought we'd give you another chance.' He flicked his fingers toward his palm to show that Corso should come with them.

Corso looked at each of them, then his shoulders slumped and he walked to the Suburban with an agent on either side. Eric hopped into the back next to Corso while Scott got in the driver's seat. The door locks thunked closed.

Eric used a friendly tone. 'Mr. Corso, are you familiar with the term "obstruction"?'

The body shop owner held up his hands. 'Look, I told you what I know.'

'No. You told us you had a van in here for bodywork but that you didn't get its license plate number.'

55

'That was true!'

'But you remembered that it was a California plate?'

'Yeah?' Corso sounded tentative.

Eric punched him lightly on the shoulder. 'Don't get nervous! I'm just reminding everyone of what you said last time.'

The man tried to smile.

'So it was a California plate, but you didn't get the number,' Eric rejoined.

'Uh-huh.'

'And you said that you couldn't remember if it was a vanity plate or a regular one.'

'So?'

'I wondered if you knowing that we're looking for this van because it's at the center of a federal murder investigation might help jog your memory?' Eric smiled at him.

Corso's voice came out at a higher octave. 'Murder?'

Scott leaned around from the front. 'And not just murder. We have evidence to suggest that the guy driving the van cut people up into pieces.'

'I-I-I didn't know about any murder! The guy didn't look like a murderer.'

Eric was calm and took over the questioning again. 'The guy who brought the van in.'

'Yeah. I told you, he was just a nobody, maybe forty years old, nothing weird about him.'

'And he paid cash.'

'Everyone pays cash!'

Eric fixed him with a look. 'Let's talk about the other cash.'

'What other cash?!'

'Come on, Corso. We know he paid you hush money. And don't pretend you haven't been in this business long enough to note the plates even before you start working on the vehicles. Come on. How else do you think we found you? LAPD gave us your name 'cause you've handled stolen cars.'

'But this one *wasn't* stolen.'

Eric raised his eyebrows. 'How do you know?'

Corso drew breath and then froze. He had walked straight into the trap Eric had laid. 'Okay, fine, look – look. I've got a contact at the DMV now. He checks plates for me because of all the problems I had with the cops. I've been trying to go straight, okay? I only just got this place out of Chapter Eleven.' He gave Eric a look of appeal.

Scott spoke without turning around. 'We don't want to hear your bankruptcy bullshit. Tell us about the plate on the van or we'll be telling LAPD that you're hacking into Department of Motor Vehicles files.'

'Okay, okay! The plate was like I said: California. It was clean.' Corso unzipped his briefcase and pulled out a sheet of paper. He ran a finger down the page and then read out a license plate number.

Eric confirmed that Scott was writing it down and then looked back at Corso. 'So if it was clean, why the hush money?'

'I don't know! The guy just pulled out the cash – three hundred dollars – and I knew exactly what it was for. I didn't want to take it but he said, "Remember, I know where you live." That shook me up.' He looked indignant. 'I didn't want to play with a guy like that so I took the money, okay? I've got kids to feed, a mortgage.'

Scott said, 'Get out, Corso.' His words were punctuated by the sound of the door locks lifting.

'Wait! What about the LAPD? What's going to happen?'

'Just get out,' Eric repeated.

The body shop owner got out of the car, clutching the unzipped briefcase to his chest.

Scott spoke as he dialed his cell phone. 'I'm calling the plate in.'

Eric moved up to the passenger seat and read the notes Scott was making during his call. As soon as Scott hung up, Eric pointed at the notepad. 'The van's registered to a woman?'

'The *plate* is registered to this woman, who's clean. NCIC shows no arrests, no convictions, living at an address in Woodland Hills since 1990. Now, Corso didn't check to see if the plate went with the van that came into his shop.'

'You thinking the perp comes out here from Georgia and borrows the license plate to cover his tracks after he gets hit on the freeway?'

Scott looked grim as he turned the ignition key. 'All I know is, this is the only van we've found that matches the drunk's vague description *and* needed rear door repair since Monday.'

*

The FBI office on Wilshire was in a ten-story building constructed in the 1970s when concrete slabs and deeply inset, tinted windows were in vogue. Only the barricades at the front curb hinted that a warren of government offices lay behind the unremarkable exterior. Inside, elevator number two was moving silently upwards, carrying Steelie, Jayne and Special Agent Steve Weiss.

Weiss had cleared the anthropologists through security after they arrived from the visitor parking lot but as the elevator reached and passed the fourth floor, where Scott and Eric's office was located, Jayne and Steelie exchanged a look.

Steelie cleared her throat, watching the floor numbers. 'Uh, where are we going, Steve?'

'I'm afraid that's classified, ma'am.' He smiled at her as the elevator doors opened on the tenth floor. They walked into a foyer with keypad-controlled doors marked 'Restricted Access'. Weiss punched a code into the one directly ahead and a buzzer sounded.

He opened the door wide. 'Welcome to Critter Central.'

Jayne went in first and immediately felt she was in a clinical space the likes of which she hadn't encountered since being in the UN morgue in Kosovo. There were no windows so the large room was lit by rows of fluorescent tube lights. Nearest to them, metal tables held microscopes and camera equipment, while the walls were lined with filing cabinets and bookshelves with recognizable forensic science reference texts. The far side of the room looked like a wet lab with fume hoods in the middle of the worktop, plus cabinets marked for hazardous materials.

Steelie was clearly impressed as she looked around. 'So *this* is where you guys hang out?'

Weiss nodded. 'And Tony Lee, who did the photography out by the freeway, is just through that door, in the cool room.'

Jayne digested that. *The cool room. Of course. A mini-*

morgue. She shouldn't have been surprised that the Bureau had all this kit hidden inside an office building but it still felt like a leap in time to a place she'd tried to leave behind.

Special Agent Lee emerged from the door at the end of the room. He was wearing blue scrubs and had two reddish stripes across his cheeks where the elastic straps on a filter mask must have pulled tight. There was another stripe across his forehead and his dark hair looked flattened. He raised a hand in greeting.

'Mornin', Thirty-Two One. Been expecting you.'

Weiss said, 'I'll leave you to it, then.'

Steelie and Jayne followed Tony into an anteroom that was divided by a bench and had lockers on one side.

Tony explained, 'We'll do the examination in the cool room itself because we're trying to keep the material as cold as possible on account of the coroner needing it next. Here's the protective gear. Shoe covers and safety glasses are over here.' He gestured to a container. 'I'm here to run the fluoroscope for you, capture whatever images you want, take photos and move the material if necessary.'

'Basically cater to our every need,' joked Steelie.

Tony smiled. 'Exactly.'

Jayne was glad Steelie had made the joke. She was beginning to feel tense about seeing the body parts out of the natural environment by the freeway where leaves and detritus had masked the brutality of the cuts. The clinical setting would make the parts look more like a dismembered body – one body in particular, one person in particular. *No,* she told herself. *Don't think of Benni.* Jayne felt Steelie nudge her. She took the mask Steelie had been offering her but shook her head in response to the question in her

60

friend's eyes.

Jayne pulled up her hood and followed the others into the cool room, another windowless space whose chill was a shock. Most of the overhead lights were switched off but a panel illuminated the center of the room above the fluoroscope where the portable X-ray machine was cantilevered parallel to the floor. Its posture made it resemble an out-of-commission oil derrick. Black body bags were each on their own gurney in a queue next to the fluoroscope.

'Sorry for the "CSI" effect with the lighting,' Tony said, only slightly muffled through his mask. 'Just trying to keep radiant heat to a minimum but let me know if you need more light.'

He pulled the nearest gurney toward the fluoroscope and unzipped the body bag. It held the severed leg. The pale flesh was damp and had defrosted; blood pooled darkly in the recesses of the body bag. Jayne was relieved that her first instinct was to move closer to get a better look. She and Steelie positioned themselves on either side of the gurney, while Tony stayed by the fluoroscope.

'The cut goes through the femoral shaft,' commented Steelie. 'Looks like midway up the thigh.'

'And the other cut's just under the patella,' Jayne said.

'Trying to avoid sawing through bone again?'

'Maybe. Can't tell which cut he tried first.'

'How much of the patella have we got?'

'I don't think he even nicked it. Take a look.' Jayne moved to the right to examine the proximal cut, while Steelie bent down to look at the patella, its tip just visible among the ligaments and fat of the knee.

'We don't have much to go on for sex,' Steelie said.

'Not when we can't expose the femur to do a mid-shaft circumference.'

'Even that's just an indication.'

There was silence as the anthropologists looked at the leg, tilting their heads this way and that.

Tony cleared his throat. 'The thigh's not shaved. Would that indicate male?'

'Possible but not reliable,' Jayne replied, her eyes still on the leg. 'Not all women shave their thighs and plenty of men do, like swimmers and cyclists. If you can take photos of each cut and from above, we can move on to the fluoro.'

'No problem.' He went into action, the recharge of the camera's flash whining as he took two shots from each vantage point, the latter requiring a stepladder that he wheeled over from the corner. Before turning on the fluoroscope, Tony brought over three lead vests and they slipped the heavy material over their heads, adjusting them by the shoulder sections until the vests could rest there without too much discomfort.

Tony turned switches on the fluoroscope and began pushing and pulling its lens over the severed leg. An X-ray image of everything in the lens' path beamed out of a screen on an adjoining trolley.

Jayne asked, 'Can you bring it in a slow sweep from one end to the other?'

The anthropologists' eyes flicked between the partial leg and the screen, trying to orient the gradations of gray that represented bone and tissue.

They all noticed that the cut at the top of the femur didn't reveal any shards of metal or metallic fragments, as might have been expected from forceful cutting action. Steelie asked Tony about the apparent absence of trace evidence.

'Yeah,' he replied. 'Sparky – Agent Sparks – said there are indications that the perp washed the body parts after he'd done the cutting.'

As the fluoroscope traveled down the thigh, they saw faint, lighter marks at the distal end of the femur.

'Hold it there, just above the knee,' said Steelie. 'Lines of fusion?' She looked questioningly at Jayne, who was staring at the screen.

'Looks like it. Move it down a fraction, Tony... and back up?'

He pushed the lens to where it had been a moment before.

Steelie said, 'Lines of fusion.'

'I'll be damned,' breathed Jayne.

'Talk to me, Thirty-Two One,' said Tony, glancing back and forth at each woman.

Steelie pointed at the TV screen. 'See those lines at the top of the knee? That's where the epiphysis, or growth plate, is in the process of fusing to the shaft of the femur. Fusion happens at standard ages across populations and sexes. So, because we can see that line, we know you've got a teenager or someone in their early twenties, regardless of sex.'

He gave a low whistle.

'Make a print of what you've got on the screen now,' Jayne said. 'Then can you flip the leg over so we can see the same region from the posterior?'

'What label do you want?'

'Distal left femoral epiphysis.'

'Can you spell that?'

'Left femur will be fine,' Steelie clarified.

Jayne looked at the fluoroscope screen and felt a frisson of excitement to see that pale jagged line: an identifying marker to narrow the search. A start.

Tony tapped buttons at a keyboard beneath the screen and then raised the fluoroscope's neck to make space to turn over the leg.

He handled the leg carefully, supporting it at each end, barely raising it off the gurney before laying it back down on a section of body bag that wasn't bloody. Removing one of his two layers of gloves, he returned to maneuver the fluoroscope toward the back of the knee.

Similar pale lines were again visible on the fluoroscope screen, even easier to discern without having to look through the kneecap.

Steelie said, 'I think it's either close to fully fused or it finished fusing not long before death, and that's why we can still see the line. Another shot, Tony.'

He worked with the machine, then asked, 'Want to take it from the top again?'

'Yep,' said Steelie, 'then let's move on to the next bag.'

Nothing remarkable came up on this second pass. Tony re-bagged the leg and Steelie and Jayne watched him discard his dirty gloves and double-glove again with clean ones. When Tony brought over the next gurney, Jayne realized she was no longer apprehensive about how the contents of the body bag would affect her. She had moved on to thinking about the person who made the cuts and did the killing.

She was thinking about bringing them to justice.

*

Scott and Eric drove in silence until they were at the base of Jeffdale Avenue in Woodland Hills. The street didn't extend far up the slope before making a sharp turn but the split-level houses in matching pastel tones produced suburban uniformity. Number 3180 was on the left side of the street. The double garage door was closed but there was an oil mark on the driveway concrete as though a vehicle that leaked fluids usually sat there.

Scott's eyes were on the oil stain. 'It's either in the garage or it's on the road right now. Let's get a look in the garage first.'

'Then you're on door-knock duty?'

Scott nodded and jutted his chin at the glove box. Eric unlocked it and removed two pieces of small electronic equipment. They strapped the gear next to the handguns at their waists before donning FBI-marked windbreakers.

They approached the side of the garage and looked in the window. The glass was dusty and had cobwebs in the corners but the van inside was clearly visible. It was white with a blue stripe down the side and sported a roof rack.

Eric nodded to Scott and they put in the earpieces that would allow them to communicate with each other once they were separated. Eric started moving quietly down the side of the house. Scott waited until Eric transmitted that he was in position and then stepped out from the side of the house to ring the doorbell.

The woman who eventually answered the door looked like she'd been sleeping even though it was already late morning. Her strawberry-blonde hair was pushed up at the crown and the cut-off denim shorts she wore were creased. Scott waited for her to stop yawning in his face before he held up his badge.

'Ma'am, Special Agent Houston, FBI. Are you Tracey Ellen Redding?'

'Yeah.'

'Does anyone besides you reside at this address, ma'am?'

'I've got a friend here visiting.'

'Is he or she at home with you right now?'

'No. Why?'

'Ma'am, could I speak with you inside?'

She shrugged, apparently uninterested. 'Sure.' She left the door open behind her as she walked off, her flip-flops slapping against the floor tiles.

Scott followed her, noting that the house had a glass sliding door from a rear patio. The door was also visible from the kitchen counter where the woman was pouring herself a glass of flat Coca-Cola out of a two-liter bottle.

Lighting a cigarette, she asked, 'What's this about?'

'Is the van parked in the garage yours, Ms. Redding?'

'Yeah. I own it. It's paid off.'

'And have you been fully cognizant of its whereabouts for the past several days?'

She squinted at him through a haze of smoke. 'You asking if I know where it was?'

Scott nodded.

'Sure I know. I mean, I let Sky use it the other day, but I know where he was.'

'Who is Sky?'

'My friend who's staying with me.'

66

'Were you aware that the van was recently involved in an accident that required repair work, Ms. Redding?'

The woman looked alert for the first time and exhaled smoke. 'No...' Then she turned around and looked at the kitchen cabinets as though she could see through them into the garage. 'I think you're wrong about that. Sky would have told me.'

'Where is your friend at the moment?'

She took a deep drag on her cigarette. 'Actually, I don't know where he is. I was taking a nap before you rang the doorbell and woke me up.' She stubbed the cigarette out in a small plate that held some toast crumbs. 'He could be anywhere. He takes walks in the hills.' She gestured with her hand as though waving away flies.

Just then Scott's earpiece reverberated and he heard Eric say, 'FBI – identify yourself, sir,' then a grunt followed by, 'Code four!'

Scott launched into a run even though his partner had transmitted that he was okay. Scott hadn't liked what he'd heard and had pulled his Glock from its holster by the time he had the sliding door open. Eric was holding a man down in the dirt between a rangy evergreen bush and the stucco wall of the house. The man was struggling and cursing but Eric was already handcuffing him so Scott turned to find the woman.

She was just arriving at the door and began shouting at the man Eric was now pulling to his feet. 'Why didn't you tell me you were in an accident in my van, huh?'

'Shut up!' the man shouted back, spitting dirt out of his mouth, his face red with anger and exertion. His hair was pale next to the red of his forehead while the veins of his neck were twitching above the collar of his NASCAR logo T-shirt. 'For once, woman, shut your trap.'

She turned on her heel, screaming that he would find his things on the front lawn.

'Enough!' Scott's voice was authoritative and the man stopped struggling in Eric's hold but still looked angry. 'What's your name?' Scott demanded as he holstered his gun.

The man focused bloodshot eyes on him. 'Sky Horton.'

'You got any aliases, Mr. Horton?'

The man shook his head.

'What about time inside? We're going to check, so you may as well speak up or you'll look like you're trying to hide something.'

This set the man off but now his tone was aggrieved. 'Listen, I know I should have reported it but I don't have the money to pay the damages and it isn't even my van. It's not like I hurt anyone, for Chrissakes!'

Eric spoke. 'Should have reported what?'

'The accident.' The man tried to twist to make eye contact with Eric. 'That's why you're here, right? Did the City call you?'

'Tell us what happened.'

'I backed into the traffic light, alright?' He looked back at Scott. 'It was a tight turn and I was in a hurry. I didn't even realize the thing was there until I hit it and the light came down with a godawful crash. I almost swore it moved while I was turning!' He tried to twist again.

The agents looked at each other. Then Scott said, 'Mr. Horton, you're going to accompany us to our office for questioning.'

68

'I'm owning up to it, man! I'll pay the City! Can't we work something out?'

'Right now,' replied Eric, 'you're looking at a charge of assaulting an identified federal agent and that's just for starters. We'll cover the rest of this at our office once we've examined the van. Move forward.'

7

Tony Lee had brought out the dismembered torso and Jayne was finding it more frustrating than the leg. Whoever had made the cuts had aimed just below the ribcage but just above the pelvis, avoiding cutting through bone even on the spine, where the cuts had been squeezed in between vertebrae. The flesh didn't yield any clues either: no scars, no tattoos, no perimortem bruising. When Tony turned it over, there were some moles and beauty marks on the back, along with some hair toward the base, but not enough secondary sex characteristics to even start a sex determination. Tony photographed everything before turning on the fluoroscope.

On X-ray, the epiphyses of the vertebrae were clearly fused.

'Okay, fusion puts this one easily over seventeen and more likely over twenty-five,' Steelie said. 'So we're still at an MNI of one.'

'MNI,' Tony repeated. 'Minimum number of individuals?'

'Yeah,' Jayne answered. 'So far, we can't confirm that this is the remains of more than one person but I suspect that the leg's a youngster while the torso's over twenty-five. Let's move on to the next bag before we make grand pronouncements.'

Jayne caught Steelie's look and knew what it meant:

70

there wasn't enough information yet for them to reliably compare these body parts with any profiles at the agency as Scott had hoped.

Tony was switching over the gurneys and unzipping the third body bag. It was the left arm and hand. Here, the cut was above the humeral head, allowing a careful disarticulation of the shoulder joint.

'If the person who cut this nicked anything, it would have been the scapula. The humerus itself looks unscathed,' Steelie said.

Jayne was leaning in toward the gurney. 'You notice how much cleaner these cuts are than the other parts we've seen so far?'

'Want a photo of that?' asked Tony.

'You read my mind.' Jayne stepped back to give him room at the gurney's edge.

Next was the fluoroscopy. The humeral head looked small on the screen, which suggested female, but Steelie and Jayne wanted a better estimate. Tony took a shot of it so they could measure it with calipers.

In pulling the fluoroscope down the length of the arm, they had to stop twice to take shots of old, healed fractures: one mid-shaft on the humerus and the other on the ulna close to the wrist.

'Defense wounds?' Tony asked as he typed in a label for the second shot.

'Looks like it,' replied Jayne.

'The ulna's got a classic parry fracture.' Steelie demonstrated the defensive pose by holding one arm out diagonally in front of her chest and then her face, trying to imitate the position the ulna would have been in when hit. 'Nasty.'

'Badly healed, too,' Jayne said.

Tony looked at the hand with its chipped burgundy nail polish. 'Are you thinking this is a different person to the leg and torso?'

'Well, all the epiphyses of the arm bones are fully united, so we're looking at someone older than their mid-twenties,' began Steelie. 'Plus, those sunspots on the forearm suggest an older person. We might be able to narrow it down by looking at the structure of the bone on the X-ray prints you give us.'

'Which isn't something we do all that often,' Jayne said. 'Usually, we deal with X-rays taken at a known age and don't need to examine internal structures.'

'But since we don't have much to go on with this material, we'll try everything we can,' Steelie rounded out.

'Want to move on to the other arm?' He looked at her expectantly, one hand on the gurney.

'Sure.'

As Tony switched the gurneys for the last time, Jayne felt deflated. They weren't getting very far. All the parts had pale skin, all were post-pubescent and therefore it was more difficult to discriminate between them given the parameters of their non-invasive examination. Body parts that might give a clear indication of age, like the pelvis or the teeth, were not in this batch. Jayne felt her hopes for identifying the victims fading.

She suddenly felt weighed down by her lead vest. She shifted it and stretched her back uncomfortably.

Tony moved as though he wasn't wearing a lead vest, exposing the right arm in the body bag with efficient movements. The arm lay slightly sideways in the bag so he moved it parallel to the edges of the gurney. His gloved hand momentarily supported the fingers with their polished nails and Jayne had a sudden, violent image of a dead woman being led in a waltz. She looked at the ceiling to banish the image from her mind, causing her mask to pull on the skin under her cheeks. The sensation brought her back to reality.

She was mildly tired from this kind of concentration and the standing, and the cold was getting to her. Gruesome images fed on her fatigue, she knew that already. *Just one more body part*, she told herself.

She looked down when she thought Tony had photographed the arm from every angle. It was a right arm and appeared, superficially, to be the match for the left arm they had just examined. Tony drew the fluoroscope down along the severed limb, pausing briefly to take a shot of the small humeral head. Then the fluoroscope's lens resumed its journey, Tony carefully keeping it in line with the arm, and Jayne's mind began to drift to where they'd get the reference material to improve the age estimate for both humeri.

'Jesus *Christ*!'

Steelie's exclamation made Tony freeze and Jayne jump. She looked at Steelie, who was staring at the fluoroscope screen. Jayne immediately followed suit. And there it was, a thing the killer couldn't have known about – unless he'd had an X-ray machine.

The surgical plate was screwed into the humerus at about midshaft. It would have been applied by a surgeon, could have an identifying number and might just lead an investigator to that surgeon's patient records. *Surgical plate as homing pigeon*, Jayne thought, and then realized they wouldn't identify this person from the agency's files. They didn't have a single client who had reported a woman missing with a plate in an arm, nor had they received any X-rays that showed plates on examination. But it was the first real lead on the identity of this woman and therefore the first real lead on her killer.

Tony was looking at the screen. 'I guess this is a good thing?'

Steelie pointed at the image. 'You just got yourself a lead, Tony.'

*

Scott looked up as Eric walked into their office and sat down heavily at his desk. Scott raised his eyebrows interrogatively.

Eric shook his head.

'Everything checked out?' Scott said.

'Yeah. The City confirms that well after our van got hit on the freeway yesterday morning, someone put a traffic light out of commission at Winnetka and Hatteras.' Eric consulted his notepad. 'They lifted traces of white paint on the light post and had just started searching for the vehicle that did the damage. The Critters have examined the Redding woman's van. No suspect biological traces, no work on the van besides the body work on the back doors.'

He looked up at Scott. 'What did you get from Redding on interview?'

'She alibied Horton, under caution, for the time the van we're looking for was hit on the freeway. And given how mad she is at him, I think it's a safe bet she wouldn't cover for him.'

'So we're back to square one.'

'Not exactly.'

'How so?' Eric said.

'Let's expand your body shop theory,' Scott said. 'We started with the ones that have handled hot cars, but if it's our perp from Georgia, he doesn't know which shop to go to out here in California, does he? He picks whatever is convenient from the freeway and figures that, with enough incentive, he can keep the shop quiet.' Scott pulled a printout closer. 'I've got twelve more body shops we can check in that radius you set up around the accident site.'

Eric groaned. 'Twelve?' He came to scan the list over Scott's shoulder.

'And here I was, thinking you'd be pleased 'cause there's still hope for your gold star.'

Someone knocked on the open door. Weiss was waiting for their attention.

'Heard you guys were in the building. Thought you should get this from Thirty-Two One direct.'

At his summons, Jayne and Steelie appeared. Both their faces bore the hallmarks of working with biohazard – marks from protective gear around their noses, cheeks and foreheads – but they also looked excited.

'You found something?' Scott said.

Jayne made the announcement. 'There's a surgical plate in one of the arms.'

Neither agent reacted at first. Then Eric said, 'What does that mean for the case? Do you know who she is?'

Steelie smiled. '*We* don't know but you're probably

gonna know. Tony's working on it now, up in your lab. Said he'd stay through lunch.'

Jayne said, 'If the plate is batch-stamped or coded in any way, and you add in that it's screwed into the right humerus of a woman between the ages of twenty-five and sixty, then you guys are about as close as you're going to get to a shortlist of people who had this procedure done from that batch of plates.'

'There are a couple of *ifs*, though,' Steelie cautioned.

'But there's another way we could search, right?' Eric said. 'Using the National Crime Information Center database, we could generate a shortlist of all missing women in that age range with a plate in the right arm.'

'That too,' Jayne agreed.

'It'll only work *if* she's been reported missing,' Steelie said. 'And *if* the person who did the reporting knew about her surgery or alerted the cops about the medical records, and *if* the cops actually uploaded those records into NCIC. And we know that doesn't always fly.'

But Scott had been thinking. 'Was there a scar? Like, from the surgery?'

Steelie smacked her forehead lightly and turned to stare at Jayne. 'Of course! We were so focused on the plate, we forgot about tissue.'

'So,' Eric said. 'We should be able to do a simple search on "scar, upper right arm" and it doesn't matter if whoever put in the misper report knew what kind of surgery or accident led to that scar.'

The room went silent.

Jayne gave Steelie a wry smile. 'And you always had a low opinion of these law enforcement types.'

Scott said, 'He just wants the gold star I promised him.'

Jayne raised an eyebrow. 'Is that what they teach you at Quantico? Carrot and stick?'

He paused, locking eyes with her. 'Well, you've been there—'

Steelie cut in. 'No, we were only there for a few days giving our two cents on NCIC 2000. At the time, your main object of study appeared to be a beer bottle.'

Scott dragged his eyes away from Jayne to respond to Steelie. 'Then you wouldn't know that the Bureau stalwarts who train us think the only place for a carrot is in a side salad – shredded.'

'And even then, it's suspicious,' Eric quipped.

Scott grinned. 'Plenty of stick around, though.' He got to his feet. 'And we should escort you out before our boss comes in here wielding his.'

8

Steelie and Jayne stopped for a late lunch on their way back to the agency. While she ate, Jayne gave some thought to where she would eat dinner with Gene later. She didn't canvass Steelie's opinion lest it turn into another recounting of Gene's shortcomings from the old days. Jayne remembered them well but she'd already agreed to meet up. It would be impolite to back out now.

Carol stood up when they walked into the agency. 'Steelie, your lab computer made a loud beep a few minutes ago.'

'Ooo!' Steelie sped off down the hallway.

Jayne called out after her, 'I'll just bring all this biometric equipment in by myself, then?'

Carol laughed. 'I'll help you.'

They went to the laboratory together.

Steelie was at the computer. 'Check it out! Our first message via the All Coroners Bulletin. From a coroner in Anchorage about Thomas Cullen.'

Jayne pulled up a stool and read the text, whose font was all capitals. 'They're calling this a courtesy message and... they do have a John Doe with a projectile in the sphenoid but it can't be Cullen because this person died from the gunshot wound.'

Steelie nodded. 'Looks like they ascribed the bullet to a perimortem GSW.'

Carol made a noise of surprise. 'Could they confuse the two?'

'Maybe they didn't. Maybe it's not Thomas Cullen but someone who *actually* died from shooting himself the same way.'

Jayne had been putting away equipment but now looked back at the coroner's message. 'It's a decent match on the identifiers though: Caucasoid male, forty years old plus or minus five, five-foot-nine plus or minus two inches, dark brown head hair, eyes brown, body found in 1998.'

Steelie shrugged. 'So he's a forty-year-old white guy with brown hair and eyes, no known scars, marks or tattoos. No wonder they've never had any hits in NCIC. There's almost nothing there to discriminate between him and thousands of other missing men.'

'That's really sad,' Carol said.

Jayne tilted her head to the side. 'Send them another message, Steelie.'

'I was planning on it. I was going to encourage them, in polite language, to compare any X-rays they've got with the one we digitized. They haven't done that yet.'

'Alright, I'm going to write up the report on the body parts for Scott and Eric. Let me know if you hear anything. You want tea, Carol?'

'I'll make it for everyone.' Carol followed her out.

By the time Steelie came to Jayne's office later, she was tidying the papers on her desk, preparing to leave.

Steelie said, 'Did you get an acknowledgment from anyone on our report?'

'I did. Tony said he'd make sure that Scott and Eric saw it when they got back.'

79

'Which was when?'

'God knows.'

Steelie perched on the edge of the desk. 'So, where are you meeting Gene tonight?'

'They put him up at the Omni—'

'Who's "they"?'

'His company, I guess. So I'm picking him up—'

'He doesn't have a rental?'

'No…' She waited for Steelie to interrupt again but she didn't. 'And I'll take him to Little Tokyo.'

'Which restaurant?'

Jayne stopped pulling the papers together. 'I don't know. We'll walk around, see what takes our fancy. If you're so curious, why don't you come too?'

Steelie gave a little shudder. 'I hear your cry for help and yet I am not moved.' She went out the door but then stuck her head back around it. 'But call me when you get home afterwards.'

Jayne nodded. She finished at her desk and left the others to close up the office.

At home, she changed clothes and put on mascara and lip gloss, realizing that it had been almost a decade since she'd seen Gene. They'd been at Kigali Airport in Rwanda. She'd still had a pair of well-used leather gloves sticking out of the back pocket of her cargo pants even though she and Steelie were leaving the mission in a matter of hours. He'd been wearing dusty boots, on his way to UN HQ, staying in the mission for another six months as he'd joined the team late, on loan from the FBI Lab. Jayne belatedly wondered if she'd recognize him now and was glad he'd suggested the rear entrance of the hotel. It was less busy there and would make him easier to spot.

Glancing at her watch, she picked up her bag and went out to her truck, making a mental note to stop by the Home Depot at some point to purchase new plants for her porch. She would have to do more than just sweep up the mess of broken pottery left the night before by raccoons or possums.

The traffic on Sunset Boulevard was still heavy but the evening's milder temperatures were layering in and Jayne drove with the windows down, listening to an Oscar Peterson compilation but not minding hearing music from nearby cars when at stoplights along the boulevard.

Twenty minutes later, she pulled into the Omni Hotel's curved driveway, its facade looming skyward, dwarfing the people gathered at the curb. A young valet made eye contact with her, raising his hand, but she shook her head as she drove past him slowly, scanning faces. When she had made the full circuit of the driveway, she pulled to the curb in front of a taxi and twisted in her seat to look for Gene out the back window. Just then, her passenger door swung open and a man dressed entirely in beige leapt in as she pulled her bag to safety.

'Christ, Gene, you gave me a fright!'

'Sorry, I was afraid you were going to drive off without me.'

He leaned over the bench seat and gave her an awkward sideways hug, the zipper of his windbreaker scraping against her cheek slightly. When they released each other, she looked at him and was glad he'd spotted her because she might not have recognized him after all. His blond hair was turning white and his cheeks seemed to droop,

81

which changed the shape of his face altogether. His long body was still lanky, which made him appear youthful, and his pale eyes were as penetrating as ever, their dot-like pupils making it seem as though he were focused on and displeased with whatever he was looking at. But his smile transformed everything, as it always had.

'So, how the hell are ya, Jayne Hall?'

His exuberance was infectious and she laughed. 'Not bad, thanks. How was your flight?'

'Hey, when it's business class, it's always good.'

She gave him an admiring glance. 'Nice.' She pulled away from the hotel and headed back the way she came, then turned onto Tom Bradley Boulevard. 'So, what classy business brings you out to LA?'

'Oh, I've been working for an electronics company that's looking to open a West Coast office. Sent me out here to take a couple meetings, get the lay of the land. I won't bore you with the details.'

'But when did you leave the FBI Lab?'

'Years ago!'

'I didn't know.' Embarrassed to be so out of touch, Jayne was formulating an apology when he spoke again.

'Hey, how much of your life do you want to spend dealing with crime and criminals?'

She glanced at him. 'You miss anything from those days?'

'Nope! The job I have now is dull and that's the way I like it. I can get my excitement elsewhere. Seeing you and Steelie is the highlight of this trip. Speaking of which, is she meeting us at the restaurant?'

Having parked at a meter, Jayne got out of the truck,

raising her voice over passing traffic. 'She couldn't come tonight. Pretty busy this week.'

Gene waited until she'd joined him on the sidewalk. 'She still mad at me, then?'

'Ummm…' Jayne smiled and started walking.

'Argh!' He threw his hands up in the air and caught up with her. 'How long can someone hold a grudge, for God's sake! It's been almost ten years.'

'She's like an elephant; she never forgets.'

'And now you two are running this charity. How's that going?'

'It's good. Early days yet.'

'How long since your doors opened?'

They'd crossed into the center of Little Tokyo and were walking past tea houses and gift shops. 'It's been about a year now.'

'I only glanced at your website but it looked like you're trying to work on the backlog of bodies around the country?'

'Yeah.'

'Pretty ambitious.'

She shot him a look. 'What, just because it's a big job, we shouldn't bother?'

'You know it's not just a big job, Jayne. It's damn near insurmountable.'

She didn't like the way he made air quotes with his fingers around 'big job', like she and Steelie hadn't accurately assessed the nature of the problem. She wanted to say, *Well, with attitudes like that!* Instead, she said, 'Depends on how you look at it.'

'You're saying the glass is half full, not half empty.'

83

'Yeah.'

'Bullshit.'

She stopped walking and turned to look up into his face, remembering that he always managed to make his height feel like essential superiority. She was suddenly glad Steelie wasn't there; it would save her having to post bail after Steelie was arrested for punching Gene in the mouth.

'It's not bullshit, Gene. Perspective makes a difference and if that means people like me and Steelie keep trying to put names to bodies – especially those difficult to identify – then that's a good thing.'

Jayne felt like his eyes were boring right through her but then he broke into a grin.

'That must be the face your sponsors see when you're asking for grants.'

She couldn't tell if that was a compliment and didn't get a chance to ask because the host of the restaurant they'd stopped in front of asked if they'd like to see the menu. He was holding out a large, vinyl-covered book that Jayne accepted.

They stepped closer to the doorway to get light to read by and walked into the scent of food. She and Gene nodded to each other and followed the host past potted trees to a table near the front window.

They shared several dishes, telling old stories and arguing good-naturedly over details.

As they finished up, he asked, 'Remember when you fell down the ravine in Rulindo?'

'Oh, we can laugh about it now but you guys left me down there way too long.'

'We knew you weren't hurt too badly.'

'I could have broken my ankle!'

'But you didn't.'

'I think I did sprain it or something. It's never been the same.'

'Really? You should get it checked out.'

'A bit late for that, don't you think?'

He gave her a speculative look. 'You, ah, ever get checked out by a psych?'

'Why? Did you?'

'When I got back to DC. But you didn't answer my question.'

'No, I never saw anyone.'

'Still could.'

'I suppose.' She paused. 'Did it help you? I mean, not that you needed help, per se.'

Gene thought for a moment. 'It helped me get some clarity about what I wanted to spend my life doing. Working in Rwanda kinda opened things up for me.'

'How do you mean?'

'I guess I felt some freedom there. When I got back home, I decided to pursue it; give myself permission to enjoy life, not stay beholden to my government job and the road to a pension.' He tapped his cup thoughtfully and then smiled up at her. 'You charge by the hour or what?'

Jayne smiled back.

He said, 'And you? What happened for you after the Kigali mission?'

'More missions, in other countries.'

'That's right. I think I got news of you and Steelie every now and then from the so-called Balkan hot spots. All mass graves?'

She nodded. 'Barring a few multiples and a few places where we expected bodies but didn't find any. Carcasses of animals maybe, but no human remains.' She looked out the window. 'Those were the worst. Thinking you were going to find them and then you didn't and you know they're still waiting for you. Even now, while we're sitting at this table in this window, they're still waiting for us.' She wasn't looking at anything now; her perspective had internalized. 'Or people like us.'

'But that's why you started the agency, right?'

She looked at him gratefully. 'Yeah. That's a nice way of looking at it.'

'Hey,' Gene laughed. 'I actually *do* charge. By the minute.' He looked at his watch. 'That'll be seventy-five cents, lady. Next!' He called out as though to a waiting patient but the host thought he was summoning the bill and came over.

Jayne tried to smother her laughter.

Gene took the bill. 'I got it.'

*

Eric pulled out of the driveway of yet another body shop and nodded at the manager, who was waiting to close the gate after the Suburban. Eric watched him in the rearview mirror and said, 'Someone's not too happy we held him back after class.'

Scott was flipping through pages in his notebook. 'He was uneasy, wasn't he?'

'For a guy whose business is supposed to be on the up-and-up.' Eric was driving with some haste along the broad boulevards in Van Nuys.

Now Scott was almost talking to himself. 'How could he flatly deny they've ever had a vehicle in there from Georgia?'

Eric pulled in to park next to a Tommy's Burger stand where the short queue suggested the first dinner rush was over. He looked at Scott meaningfully.

But Scott was still musing. 'Wouldn't you expect someone to say, "I don't remember; let me check my files"?'

Eric kept his eyes on his partner while lowering the windows to let the car fill with the scent of grilling food, enjoying watching how fast Scott got the message. It didn't take long with grilled food; only barbecue got Scott's attention faster. And there it was: Scott threw his notebook on the dash, still preoccupied but finally getting out of the car. Within a few minutes, they were standing at the counter with food in front of them.

Before eating, Scott pulled out his BlackBerry but didn't do anything with it.

Eric chewed some of his chilli burger. 'Why don't you just call her?'

'What? Who?'

'You don't look innocent, Scott. You can't *do* innocent.'

Scott took a deep breath, stretched his arms over his head, arched his back, twisted his torso and exhaled.

Eric protested, 'I'm trying to eat here and you're acting like it's the warm-up for the long jump.'

Scott re-holstered his phone and took a deliberately large bite of his meal.

But Eric wasn't finished. Compared to other times his partner had wanted to ask a woman out, Scott had displayed an unusually high level of interest in Jayne Hall. It

87

had been followed by an equally unusual level of *in*action. 'What are you worried about – with Jayne, I mean?'

Scott chewed for a while. 'I'm not worried. I just don't want to start something while we're working together.'

'That didn't stop you with Mindy.'

'Yeah, and look how that turned out.'

'And Jayne isn't an agent like Mindy, so I don't buy that excuse on any level. Nor does it explain what you've been doing for the past five years.' Eric was beginning to think that Scott's interest in Jayne went beyond dating. Curious, he prodded some more. 'You want me to find out if she's involved with someone? I'll ask her. I'll ask Steelie.'

Scott was fierce: 'Don't.'

'Jesus. Fine, I won't, but Jayne's not...'

'Not what? My type? I know that already.'

'No, that's not what I'm getting at.' Eric thought back to the two times he'd seen Jayne Hall. He could see why Scott was attracted to her looks; she was a nice-looking woman. But she was thoughtful and reserved, maybe even sensitive, with a smile that came late to the party. Eric knew that his perception had likely been influenced by the fact that Jayne had always been next to Steelie Lander. Steelie was clearly a bantamweight fighter who wore her heart on her sleeve and joked her way, at high speed, through anything that came at her. As for Scott, one thing Eric knew about him was that he dated women who were all over him already, women who would give him a toothbrush and expect a ring in return. But Jayne... she'd apparently been satisfied with just talking to Scott on the phone for five years, so maybe something else was going on – with her.

Eric chose his words carefully. 'I'm saying I don't think she's necessarily easy to read.'

'I know.' Scott took a bite of food and then talked through the mouthful. 'I can't believe I'm taking advice from a guy who was married and divorced before he was thirty.'

'That's why I'm giving you my advice. So you can avoid my mistakes.'

'You can't do the dad role, Ramos. I'm older than you.'

'Really? It's so hard to tell sometimes.' Eric's tone was light but he felt an undercurrent of concern. In Atlanta, he'd seen Scott get distracted when his romances went haywire and it had never done their casework any good. Now, with the chance to find this serial killer on the boil again, the chance to vindicate themselves with their old boss and maybe even get promotions, Eric needed Scott focused on the job or happy with his woman. Preferably both.

*

Jayne turned her phone's ringer back on as she and Gene strolled slowly back through Little Tokyo to her truck. The phone hadn't chirped to signify new voicemail so she wasn't sure why she imagined she would have missed a call from Scott. He was on her mind as she thought about how soon they might have an evening like this.

They'd had dinner together on the phone often enough. Scott had usually been eating at his desk in Atlanta, having stayed late on a case, while Jayne was at home, feeling giddy whenever his calls came after she'd showered so she'd just be wearing a nightshirt. He'd only ever asked her once what she was wearing but it wasn't one of those nights; she

89

was too honest for her own good, and thereby felt she had missed the chance to go down that path with him.

But she'd never forgotten that he'd asked.

Gene broke into her reverie as they got into the truck. 'If you're not too tired, I wouldn't mind seeing this place of yours.'

Her mind hadn't shifted gears yet. 'My apartment?'

'Sure, that too.'

'Oh!'

He laughed and Jayne pulled away from the curb, telling herself to pay attention. 'Sorry, I—'

'Don't apologize. Seriously, I wouldn't mind seeing your office *and* your apartment. I'd like to see these places that are giving you so much therapy.'

Jayne suddenly turned right on Main Street. 'Alright,' she said brightly. 'We'll swing by the office, then have coffee on my deck.'

Gene nodded and settled back on the seat, his elbow resting on the open windowsill, the warm night air lifting his hair off his forehead.

When she turned into the agency parking lot, the light above the front door was on and the security lights were illuminating the corners of the building.

Gene got out of the truck and stretched his long legs. 'This is it, huh?'

Jayne unlocked the front door and entered to disable the alarm. She turned on the lights as she let him in.

He looked around appreciatively. 'Nice.' He walked over to Carol's desk and picked up one of the agency brochures. 'Can I have one of these?'

'Sure. Wanna see the rest of it?' She went into the next

room. 'This is my office. I do the interviews with families and friends of the mispers in here.'

'Hence the sofas and tissues.'

'Are you being flippant?'

'That came out wrong. You do the interviews and then, what, you do the profile off of them?'

'In part, and in part off any documentation we can get our hands on.'

Jayne started down the hallway but then realized Gene hadn't followed her. She turned back to find him. He was looking at the filing cabinets behind her desk.

'Are these all your cases?'

'Yes.'

'How many do you have?'

'About a hundred.'

'And how many have you matched up to bodies?'

'Seven so far.'

'Not very many.'

'Yeah, but if one of those seven was, say, your father, would that matter? Those seven count for a lot.'

'True. Sorry, I'm used to dealing with evidence, not identifications. So, where do you keep the files you've closed?'

She pointed at the top drawer of one of the cabinets and then watched in disbelief as Gene walked over as though to open it. 'We keep them locked for obvious reasons.' She was beginning to wish she hadn't agreed to this detour.

'I was just interested. Must look kinda empty. You got any plans to fill it up faster?'

'Well, if you'd follow me, Mr. Enthusiasm.'

This time he did follow her, past the kitchen to turn into the lab across from the restroom.

'This is where Steelie does the odontograms and the biometrics and we digitize relevant photos. It's basically an anthro report done from antemortem instead of the body.'

Gene was turning round, looking at different items on the counters and walls.

'And this,' Jayne said, pointing at the computer terminal, 'is where Steelie runs the All Coroners Bulletin, which – once it's out of its pilot phase – will be one of our best tools to speed up the rate with which we close cases and fill that file drawer.'

He looked curious. 'How does that work?'

'If we come across particularly identifiable characteristics that weren't included on the original missing person report, we get to instantly alert coroners through this dedicated network. It bypasses NCIC.'

He whistled. 'That's pretty good.' He looked preoccupied for a moment then asked quickly, 'You made any IDs through it yet?'

'No, but before you spread any more of your good cheer, I'm calling the glass half full on this one.'

'Yeah, you might be right about that.' He looked at the computer and lapsed into silence.

Jayne said, 'I'll just go to the restroom and then we'll head over to my place.'

When she came out, she looked in the lab but there was no sign of Gene. She shut off the lights there and moved forward to her office. She found him sitting at her desk, revolving slowly in her chair.

He pointed at her good-naturedly. 'I can see why

you keep going. You've broken the big problem down into smaller pieces, haven't you? I bet you do a lot of compartmentalizing.'

'I don't know about that. But I do like it if I can tell when something's over, when a job's done.'

'What about in the rest of your life?'

'What about it?'

'Do you compartmentalize there, too?'

'I don't know! Come on, let's go.'

Fifteen minutes later, she and Gene were walking through the front door of her apartment. While he used the bathroom, she put on the kettle and wiped down the table on the deck. When Gene emerged, she indicated the coffee fixings.

'How do you take it?'

He called back to her as he walked over to the bookshelves. 'Black, thanks.'

As she put the grounds into the press, she watched him, noticing how his height was even more obvious now that he was in her home. He was reaching for a book on a high shelf that she needed a footstool to reach.

He flicked through the book and then returned it to the shelf. 'No books on forensics?'

'They're all at the agency.'

He turned and looked at her with a surprised smile. 'You have boundaries when it comes to forensics? I'm shocked,' he joked.

Jayne poured hot water over the coffee. 'I don't know about you but Spitz and Fisher was never my first choice for bedtime reading.'

'So, you *do* compartmentalize.'

93

'What is it with your fascination as to whether or not I compartmentalize, as you put it?' She carried the tray of coffee and cups out to the deck.

Gene followed her out. 'I'm just curious about how you keep working in forensics and still have a normal life. I wasn't very successful at it.'

They settled down at the table and Jayne sugared her coffee. 'Well, I never worked for the Bureau for one thing, and I never said I have a normal life.'

'But you're expecting a hot date soon, right?'

'Gene!' Jayne almost spat coffee in her surprise.

He grinned at her. 'Hey, people who've done the type of work we've done sometimes have trouble finding someone who "gets" them. And I take it from your reaction that you don't get a lot of hot dates.'

'I didn't say that.' Jayne wiped her chin.

'You missed a spot.' Gene leaned over and presumptuously wiped his thumb beneath her lower lip. 'I was really just trying to find out if you had a boyfriend right now. The way you checked your phone earlier...?'

'No. I mean – no.'

'Riiight.' He sounded unconvinced.

'Okay,' Jayne countered. 'Since you're so smug, why haven't you mentioned your fabulous wife and kids back at your massive condo with attached two-car garage?'

Gene inclined his head. 'Because it's a house – my mom's house, incidentally – not a condo, with a one-car garage that's filled with other stuff so there's no room for the car. No wife, but there've been some... dalliances.'

'Well, I'm sure your garage has everything labeled and organized because you like to compartmentalize, just as you

94

allege I do. Am I right?'

He looked thoughtful and then admitted, 'Pretty much.'

'Yeah, I bet your mom loves having you around.'

'Actually, she passed away.'

'Oh, I'm sorry.' Jayne felt like she was on the back foot yet again. She could have sworn he'd implied that he lived with his mother.

Gene was shaking his head. 'Don't be. It was for the best. Alzheimer's.'

'Oh.'

'Trust me, you don't want to live with someone who has that kind of dementia. She didn't know who she was most of the time and she sure as hell didn't know who I was by the end. It's pretty weird to have your own mother not recognize you. Makes you wonder who *you* are.'

'I don't know what to say,' Jayne faltered.

He shook his head. 'She's been gone a few years now. And I worked out who I am.'

A car passed below them on the street, its occupants singing loudly along with their stereo. Their voices died away with the air and were replaced with the sound of cricket calls.

Gene drained his cup and stood. 'I should probably get going.'

'I'll drive you back.'

'No need. You look tired.'

'It's no trouble.'

'Seriously, no need. But you said you had a copy of that photo we took at Kigali Airport?'

'Right, I do. Give me a second to find it.'

They went indoors and she left Gene there while she

went outside and down the stairs to her storage room off the driveway. It took a few minutes to find the right box and she carried the whole thing back upstairs.

They went through the box together on the dining table, looking at her snapshots from Bosnia. Streets of shelled houses in Brcko, carts of ripe peppers for sale on the shoulder of the road to Tuzla, a bright new gas station on the highway to the Croatian coast. When they came to the photos from Rwanda, the Kigali Airport shot was near the top. Jayne put the duplicate in an envelope and gave it to Gene. They walked to the front door.

'I'll keep in touch,' he said.

'It was good to see you.'

'Tell Steelie I said hi.'

Jayne smiled a bit sheepishly. 'Will do.'

She thought he was bending down to kiss her cheek, so she leaned toward him, but he reached her first and pressed his lips to hers. It wasn't a bull's eye, landing partly on her mouth and partly on her cheek, and she panicked for a split-second, afraid he would try again – afraid she'd misread everything. But he turned to leave, raising a hand in farewell.

Jayne locked the door behind him and calmed down. She became aware of a slight moistness on her mouth where Gene's rather papery lips had touched hers. She rubbed them dry. It was only then that she wondered how he was getting back to his hotel. She sure as hell didn't want to drive him back lest he try to kiss her again but she could at least call a taxi for him. She yanked open the door and clattered down the stairs, intending to catch him on the street, but there was no sign of him. She realized that she didn't even have a number for him. Then she heard her phone ringing in her apartment and she bounded back up, thinking it might be him.

She answered breathlessly but it was only Steelie, sounding shocked.

'Are you just getting in now?'

'No,' Jayne puffed. 'We were here and then I just came back in again.'

'Wait. You let Gene come over to your place?'

'Yeah, why?'

'My God, Jayne. Do I need to remind you? The guy's an ignorant… superciliant!'

'Is that even a word? And he's mellowed a little.'

'People like him don't mellow. And have you forgotten that night at the Cadillac?'

'He wondered if you were still holding that dance against him.'

'That would be a yes. But what's the deal? Are you seeing him again? And what was he doing in LA?'

'He was out here on business and all we did was a have a nice reminiscence session. Talked about life – post-mission life. He's still supercilious at times, which was grating but not impossible. He did kiss me, though.'

'Ugh! Did he consider this a *date*? Because if he did, he should have sign-posted that!'

'I don't think so. He invited you too, remember?'

'And now I have another point of validation for not coming. Getting kissed by India Tango One.'

'Yeah, it was kind of fourth-grade school yard.'

'Like when no one knows what they're doing and a tongue ends up in someone's left nostril?'

'God, no. There was no tongue, but there was something behind it… I don't know. Something.'

Steelie was unmoved. 'Who cares what was behind it, so long as it wasn't a tongue?'

DAY THREE

Thursday

9

As Scott pulled into the curb in front of the final body shop on his list, Eric looked at the sheet he was holding, checked his watch and almost suppressed a yawn. 'Sepulveda Body Shop.'

Scott caught the yawn. 'I shouldn't have skipped lunch.'

They got out of the car and walked into the gated concrete yard. It was packed with cars that were reflecting the light and heat of the summer afternoon, while all four bays in the building were occupied with vehicles up on raised pallets, mechanics working beneath them. Scott and Eric threaded their way past the parked cars and walked into the small office. An unattended desk whose trays were filled with papers was jammed into what appeared to be a closet but a larger desk had prime real estate close to the window-mounted air conditioner spewing frigid air.

Behind this desk was a young man wearing a blue shirt streaked with grease. His nametag read *Javier* and he was on the phone. 'If you bring it here before eight in the morning, I can get someone to have a look at it same day. But if it's rotors, it's gonna take a day to get 'em in.'

When he hung up the phone, the agents opened their badges, announced themselves and asked for Javier's surname.

'Ruiz.'

'What's your position here?' Eric asked.

'I'm the manager.'

'Okay. Were you working Tuesday?'

Ruiz took on a wary look. 'Yes?'

'You get a van in here that needed body work to the rear doors?'

'Yeah.'

Eric restrained himself from looking at his partner. 'You note the license plate?'

'Well, I don't know if—' Something out the window caught his attention and he hurriedly got up from the desk, moving to the side just as a heavy-set man charged through the front door. The man hardly glanced at Scott and Eric as he made his way around the desk. He only looked up after he'd sat down and put his head in line with the air conditioner, rolling his neck around to expose all the folds to the air.

'What do you need, folks? Ruiz taking care of you?'

Before they could answer, Ruiz said, 'Mr. Malbandian, these gentlemen have a government vehicle that needs looking at.' He shot a nervous glance at the agents.

'Well, help them, Ruiz. Help them. Out there.' The heavy-set man shooed them out with his hands.

Scott caught Eric's eye and they didn't pull out their badges. They followed Ruiz out into the hot forecourt. The young man went to a narrow area between two black SUVs liberally adorned with chrome accents and halted. It was like standing in a toaster oven.

'Look,' he said desperately. 'That guy's my boss. He doesn't know about this and he'd fire me in a second.'

'Because of something you did with this van?' Scott

102

wasn't following.

'No, because I took a tip that maybe should've gone to the shop.' Ruiz looked over Scott's shoulder.

'Take it from the top, Javier,' Eric encouraged.

'Okay. This guy came in with a van. Looked like he'd been rear-ended. There was a lot of damage to the lower part of the back doors and it was stopping the handles from latching right. Nothing weird about it until he said he just wanted me to spray the van and do all the work from the outside. Under no circumstances could I touch the handles. I said, don't you want me to fix the lock, but he said that the padlock he'd put on was just fine. He had a chain through it too. He paid me six hundred dollars extra to do everything the way he said. And it wasn't easy. He was real particular.'

'Describe the van.' Scott had pulled out his notepad.

Ruiz closed his eyes before recounting. 'Light blue Chevy. Old. Maybe a pretty old Astro but it didn't have its model on the outside. Um... good tires, I noticed that.'

'And what color did you spray it?'

'Gold.'

'License plate?'

Ruiz looked embarrassed. 'That was part of what he paid me to not notice. But I know it was Georgia.'

The agents exchanged a look. 'Georgia?' Scott said. 'You're sure?'

'Yes. But I didn't look closely at it.'

'You can't remember anything else about it?'

'No. Honestly. I see a lot of plates and they don't mean that much to me anymore. Especially from out of state because they're a different layout to California plates.'

Eric cut across Scott's emerging exasperation. 'What about the man, Javier? What did he look like?'

'He was Anglo. Kinda tall. A light-colored beard. But he was wearing a baseball cap and sunglasses, so I didn't see much more.'

'What was his voice like?'

'I guess you could say it was soft. I mean, it was American and all. Just... he didn't speak loud. You'd do better asking Margarita about him.'

'Margarita?'

'Yeah, she does the filing. She's not in today but I know she had some kind of problem with him.'

'They spoke to each other?'

'I don't know. She just came walking back into the yard here and said something, like, about the guy being weird.'

Scott had his pen poised. 'Where can we find Margarita?'

'Um, I know where she lives. Over by Birmingham High School.' He gave Scott the address.

'Let's go back to the man,' said Eric. 'What time did he get here?'

'He was here when I arrived to open up at six-thirty.'

'Just parked outside?'

'Yeah, like he was waiting.'

'Was anyone else with him?'

'Not that I saw.'

'And what'd he say to you?'

'Just said hi and that he needed some work done on his van, right away, and he was going to pay extra to put a rush on it. My boss wasn't coming in for two days, so...' He shrugged. 'My boss wasn't coming in for two days, so I just decided to take on the job myself.'

'He say anything about where he'd come from or where he was going?'

Ruiz shook his head.

'Did he wait here while you finished the work?'

'No, the paint had to cure. He came back the next day, late in the afternoon.'

'But he just walked away when he dropped if off? Did he ask you for directions or anything?'

'No, he just walked. I figured he was going to the bus stop or something.'

'Is there anything else you can tell us about him?'

'I don't think so.'

'Okay.' Eric pulled a business card from his shirt pocket. 'Here's my card. If you remember anything more, call me right away, any time, day or night. Got it?'

'So I'm not in trouble?'

'No, but we may need to take a formal statement later.'

Ruiz put the card in the back pocket of his pants. 'And you're not going to tell my boss?'

Scott shook his head.

It wasn't until the agents were back in their vehicle, air-conditioner blowing, that Eric spoke. 'We're on to him, Houston. I can feel it.'

They drove directly to the address Ruiz had given them for Margarita, which was in a neighborhood of single-story ranch houses built in the 1940s and 1950s in the heart of the San Fernando Valley. The street they parked on was neat; dry lawns were cut short where only geranium and jade bushes held up against the heat. Margarita's house didn't have a car parked in the driveway but the swamp cooler on the roof suggested someone was home; its hum was audible to the agents as they walked up the front path.

The teenager who opened the door had a neutral expression. TV advertisements blared behind her.

'Yes?'

They identified themselves, established that she was who they were looking for and that she was eighteen years old. When they explained that they needed to speak to her as a witness and she had the option to have a parent present, she said that she didn't mind describing the man who had brought the van to the garage.

'Javier dealt with him outside. It was just that I wanted to make a personal call and the owner is real strict about that, makes me use the pay phone on the sidewalk just outside the gate. So I go to use the phone but the van guy was already there and he gave me a look that really scared me. I went away but I was pissed because it was an important call I wanted to make.'

Scott said, 'Did you hear him say anything?'

'Well, when I came over, he was speaking up so I heard him. It was like he was talking to one of those computer voices, y'know? Like an operator? He said, "Arizona" real loud.'

'Anything else?'

Margarita shook her head. 'No. Soon as he said that was when he realized I was there.'

'Can you describe him?' Eric said.

'Just a skanky guy. White.'

'How old, would you say?'

'I don't know. Forty? Fifty?'

'Hair color? Eye color?'

'He had a patchy beard that was kinda blond. I think

his hair was light. Blond-ish. But his hat hid most of it. I don't remember what color his eyes were. Maybe brown? He was wearing sunglasses.'

'What was his voice like? Any accent?'

'No. I just heard him say that one word.'

Eric pulled out his card and repeated what he'd said to Ruiz earlier about calling if she remembered anything further.

When they were back in the Suburban, Scott said, 'You might just get that gold star, Ramos.'

Eric started to reply but then Scott's cell phone rang. He picked up, listened and said, 'We're on our way back now.' He looked at Eric. 'Tony's got a name to go with the surgical plate Thirty-Two One found.'

Eric slapped the dashboard in excitement. 'Hot damn!'

'She's an Eleanor Patterson. No word yet on whether she's ever been reported missing.'

'I told you, Houston. We're on to this guy.'

'We've got to track him down yet.' Scott started driving.

'Yeah, but if we're interpreting Margarita right, we know he's headed to Arizona. We know the color, the make, the potential model of the van.'

'But no license plate and no name.'

'I'm not letting that stop me,' Eric asserted. 'We need to issue a BOLO to Arizona.'

Scott glanced at him as he drove toward the canyon road that would take them back to their office. 'Let's do BOLOs for Arizona *and* California. He may not have made it to Arizona yet.'

'You're right,' Eric agreed. 'We'll ask LAPD to put it on their BOLO boards.'

Now his cell phone was ringing. He answered and then muted the microphone. 'The office is putting through a Detective Kragen from Carlisle PD, regarding the Patterson case.'

*

When the person who'd called the agency identified himself as a coroner from Alaska, Carol put him through to Steelie in the lab. Steelie brought the phone to the computer so she could have the digitized X-ray of Thomas Cullen's head on her screen, then she took the call.

'Chuck Talbot,' the matter-of-fact voice said. 'Anchorage ME's office.'

'Thanks for following up on the All Coroners Bulletin, Dr. Talbot.'

'Chuck's fine. Gotta tell ya, this whole situation with the John Doe bullet has caused a bit of a stir up here.'

Steelie couldn't read his tone but this sounded juicy. 'Oh?'

'It's probably for the best, I don't know. But that's not your problem. I'm calling to inform you of a positive ID for this John Doe as Thomas Cullen. We'll be posting it on the ACB network this afternoon.'

'This is great news.' Steelie jotted a note. 'Can I ask how you got the match?'

'Dental. It turns out the teeth were where the breakdown was. Or maybe I just want to blame the odontologist. We've been having a feud for years,' he chuckled. 'But I can't actually blame him.' He paused. 'Are we confidential here?'

'Absolutely,' Steelie replied quickly. 'All communications

108

between our agency and coroners are confidential.'

'Fine. So, at the time we got this John Doe, the odontologist gave us the dental chart and we submitted it to the police misper unit for them to put it on NCIC. Like most coroners, I don't have direct access to NCIC. Been trying to get a terminal in my office for, what, seven years? Ten? Anyway, I gave the dental to Missings. Didn't go anywhere, I've now discovered.'

'Well, you definitely can't blame the odontologist for that.'

'No, but I'm still tryin'.' He chuckled again.

Steelie smiled. She liked this guy.

Dr. Talbot continued. 'Seems that, on request, my autopsy tech had sawed out John Doe's max and mandible and couriered it to the odontologist for the dental report *before* starting the craniotomy. When I got round to doing the autopsy, I recovered the bullet no problem but I didn't have the mouth and I assumed the bullet was fresh. Figured the palate would show perimortem trauma since there was no sign of cause of death anywhere else and the tissue was too decomposed for toxicology. So the main result of the autopsy was that bullet. Case closed.'

'You've obviously got the mouth back now, though?'

'Oh, we've had the mouth back this whole time! It's been sitting in the fridge! But no one looked at it when it came back from the odontologist to confirm whether the trauma to the palate was peri- or antemortem, or healed or what. And it *is* healed. That is definitely old trauma, old gunshot. So, now we're all having to tighten our belts. My tech was hasty, I wasn't thorough, the odont only reported on the dentition itself and didn't bother to describe the palate, and our police unit didn't do the other half of its job with NCIC.'

Steelie found herself wanting to take the sting out of the ME's sorry but familiar list of the cracks in standard postmortem identification systems. 'The thing is, even without you ageing the bullet correctly, NCIC would have made this ID if only a cop had uploaded your postmortem dental info into the system. So I don't think you have too much to beat yourself up about.'

'You think getting cause of death wrong is nothing to beat myself up about? Huh.'

'I meant this was situational. It's not like you need to go back to med school. But speaking of COD, do you have anything there?'

'Now that the bullet's ruled out? No. I mean, there wasn't much left of this guy for me to work with. And no marks on the bones. It'll probably go down as undetermined, for both cause and manner.'

'And contact with the Cullen family?'

'I'll call them myself. I know a funeral home up here that can handle shipping the body back across state lines.'

Steelie looked down at the notes she'd been making. 'Well, Chuck, I guess I don't have any more questions.'

He cleared his throat. 'I've been asked by my highers and betters to reassure you that we are making some procedural changes up here so we'd prefer if you didn't go public with your role in making this identification.'

Steelie's cheeks burned. 'We don't do that. We're just trying to facilitate identifications. Quietly.'

'Sure. But you never know what you might set off.'

'What do you mean?' Steelie asked warily.

'Ever picture what it would look like if every parent of a missing person found out that a couple thousand coroners and medical examiners, between them, have tens of thousands of Jane and John Does sittin' on ice in this country? Just do the math. You've got a hundred thousand missing persons, at least. They've got one parent each, maybe two, and a couple of siblings. That makes for a heck of a march on Washington.'

Steelie had indeed pictured this but she wasn't prepared to admit it in this context. 'And that's a heck of an imagination you've got there, Chuck. But we're not a lobby group. We're not allowed—'

The coroner cut her off. 'What I'm also saying, Miz Lander, is that I'm not sure that would be a bad thing.'

He signed off and Steelie was left looking at the phone in her hand, wondering how many other coroners shared Dr. Talbot's positive take on that kind of pressure on the government from families. If she were still in graduate school, she'd do a survey. Maybe she could get someone else to do a survey. She walked to the front of the building, summoning Jayne from her office as she went.

Steelie came up to Carol's counter, knowing that their receptionist already had an idea of what she was about to say, since she'd put Chuck Talbot's call through and could now read Steelie's pleased expression. But Jayne had no idea. She raised her eyebrows at Steelie, who announced, 'Thomas Cullen has been positively identified in Anchorage.'

Jayne stood still, returning Steelie's grin, so it was Carol who started clapping first. It was a slow clap that skipped two beats in between, then gradually sped up to one beat in between. Jayne joined in, then Steelie, until they were clapping as fast as they could, like a sports team psyching itself up after a mid-season win.

*

Two men from A-1 Electrics delivered the generator to Agency 32/1 just after 4PM. As it turned out, they didn't need to spend much time inside the building, as the generator was installed just behind the building in its own security cage. Just before 5PM, Jayne heard Carol call out that Scott was holding on line one for her. She located her copy of the agency's report on the freeway body parts:

```
MNI:        2; 1 female, 1 sex
            indeterminate
Left arm:   Female, 40 years ± 15,
            possible Caucasian,
            healed fractures,possible
            antemortem defense wounds
Right arm:  Female, 40 years ± 15,
            possible Caucasian, mid-
            shaft surgical plate
            conjoining proximal and
            distal humerus
Leg:        Sex indeterminate, 20 years
            ± 5, possible Caucasian
Torso:      Sex indeterminate, 18
            years+, possible Caucasian
```

She half-expected him to ask why there wasn't more to

it, but Scott sounded buoyant.

'I've got good news.'

Jayne sat up straighter in her chair. 'Let me have it.'

'We've got an ID on the arm. Or I should say, arms plural, though that'll have to be confirmed by DNA later.'

'Oh my gosh. Was it the plate?'

'Yes. That was a great find.'

Jayne was energized by this fast result. 'It was just sitting there waiting for us, Scott! The hard part was not cutting the flesh off to expose the humerus right then and there.'

'You kind of scare me when you talk like that, Jayne.'

'Sorry. So is she one of your missing women from Georgia?'

'Unconnected. She's a Mrs. Patterson from Carlisle, Oregon.'

'Carlisle?'

'Outside Portland.'

'Was she in NCIC?'

'That's the interesting part. She was, but not listed as suspicious missing. And get this: she went missing two months ago. Eric's been trying to get details from Oregon. We'll be sending the arms to the coroner up there after we've got the results on whether the left arm goes with the right.'

Jayne looked at the report in front of her. 'And maybe you can run DNA on the torso? That's the other body part that could have been hers.'

'We're all over that.'

'I take it you won't be running DNA from the younger person's leg through CODIS, given that we couldn't even tell you what sex it was?' She was referring to the FBI Laboratory's Combined DNA Index System.

'Even if the Bureau would let me, it won't be worth it – not enough information. And the leg's not one of your cases?'

'Not enough information.'

'Tell me about it.'

She recalled Scott's desire to get around the backlog at the LA County Coroner's office when he'd asked Thirty-Two One to do the preliminary investigation. 'So you're okay with the leg and maybe the torso going to the coroner's office after all?'

'Identifying Patterson makes up for a lot.'

'Yeah.' Jayne smiled. She had said almost those exact words to Gene when he was looking at the Thirty-Two One filing cabinets. Gene had been negative but here was Scott, sharing her positive perspective. This was yet another reason why she liked the man. 'How's the search for the van going, if you can say?'

'Actually, we've got a lead on that and I've... gotta run.'

Jayne knew Carol had left for the day while she was on the phone, so she went in search of Steelie and found her in the kitchen, washing up the afternoon's accumulation of cups. She relayed Scott's call.

'That's fantastic news,' Steelie said. 'Mrs.? Sounds like he thinks she was married. I'll bet it was her husband who's responsible for those fractures.'

'Or maybe she divorced him and married a new guy.'

'You live in a dream world.'

'You live in a criminal lawyer's world,' Jayne retorted lightly.

'Which reminds me. Did you remember the raffle ticket books?'

'Oh, Steelie! I completely forgot.' Jayne picked up a tea

114

towel to dry the cups.

'Don't worry. I did, too, until someone from Legal Aid called to remind me that I'd volunteered.'

'You need them today?'

'Yeah.' Steelie put the last cup on the rack. 'The raffle's tomorrow morning. Can I swing by your place tonight to get them?'

'Yeah, I'll be in.'

'Not out with Scott then?'

'Ha, ha, and thank you – not – for telling my mother that he'd moved to LA.'

'Ah. Yes. Sorry about that. But I will say in my defense that I was trying to protect you.'

'How does telling her about Scott protect me? She came over to deliver the lecture in person!'

'Hear me out. She met Dario when he brought the pea gravel by my house—'

'Wait, Dario who switched over to the DA's office? With the eyebrows?'

'He's manscaping those now.'

'Great.' Jayne threw up her hands. 'Good for him.'

'Your mom established in short order that Dario is single—'

'As she does.'

Steelie gestured expressively. 'As she does. And Dario, who totally remembered you from my birthday party two years ago when you were still with that idiot Phil, was shooting me mean looks because I hadn't told him you were no longer with Idiot Phil, so I was forced to throw Scott's name out there. Ooo, your mother went dark on Dario so fast, he thought his eyebrows had grown back.'

115

Jayne snorted with laughter.

Steelie doffed an invisible hat. 'You're welcome and I'll call when I'm near your place tonight. Should be around eleven.'

'That late?'

'I have that thing with those people. Don't ask.' She made a theatrical exit.

Jayne rolled her eyes. Steelie had already told her where she was going tonight. But as Jayne placed the last cup on its hook, she wondered if Steelie's plans had changed.

*

The pinky-white flower heads waved high above the gaura plants as Jayne carefully lifted them out of her truck. Next were the two geums: absolutely shameless doubles in a clear red, swooning in front of anyone who came near, and sure to meet with Marie's approval. Jayne nestled them in the two terracotta pots she'd bought to replace the ones by her door. She was still debating about whether the damage had been inflicted by possums or raccoons; either had the strength to tip over cacti pots. She made her way up the stairs to her apartment, reached the landing and then stopped.

Three zinc washtubs filled with blooming white daisy bushes were displayed next to her front door. The tubs were different yet complementary sizes, their shine artfully worn off in places. Jayne thought the arrangement was gorgeous, like something from a magazine, and it made her doorway look hip and inviting. She stood back, admiring first the porch and then her mother, who had to be responsible for this transformation. She'd have to remember to call her after she'd potted and found a home for the other ridiculous flowers she'd bought.

116

10

The noise woke Jayne. She sat up where she'd fallen asleep on the sofa, pushing aside the open book on her lap and looking at her watch. It was too early for it to be Steelie, who said she'd be there at 11PM, and it was a scratchy sound that seemed too loud and definitive to be an animal poking around. It sounded like a person was out there, and now… were they gone?

Without a front window to look through, she only had a few choices: try to identify the sound, look through the peephole or open the door. The peephole was out; she'd seen a film where someone was shot through the eye doing just that. And she had seen too many people lying dead on autopsy tables after having let their killers in the front door.

So she waited to hear the sound again. She almost jumped out of her skin when her cell phone came to life, its vibrations creating a buzzing noise against the coffee table's glass surface.

'Hello?' she whispered.

'It's Steelie… are you okay?'

'I heard a noise outside.'

'What kind of noise?'

'Hang on. I just heard it again. Something on the front landing.'

'Human or non-human?'

'Can't tell. Are you on your way over?'

'I am and I'm less than a minute from your place. Keep your door locked.'

Jayne moved to sit on the floor with her back against the bedroom door, which enabled her to see the front door while staying hidden from anyone looking in the kitchen windows. She kept the phone cradled in her lap but didn't hear the noise again. When the phone vibrated with another incoming call, she didn't flinch but still answered quietly.

Steelie sounded confident. 'It's me. I've looked around down here but don't see anything. I'm coming up.'

Jayne got up with relief and went to the front door. She opened it just as Steelie exclaimed, 'Whoa!' That was followed by the sound of footsteps thudding down the stairs.

'Steelie?!'

Her voice came from the bottom of the stairs. 'Make some noise up there, Jayne. You've got a mother possum on your stairs with her baby. And the baby's big enough to have a name. I'll wait in the driveway.'

Jayne started clapping her hands and whistling. Then she walked forward until she could see around the corner. The possums were about halfway down the stairs, moving slowly. When they reached the bottom, Steelie turned on the flashlight she was holding and mimicked airport ground staff guiding a plane into its berth, raking the light across the lawn and away from the driveway. The possums obediently headed off into the darkness.

Steelie trotted up the stairs. 'That's probably who you heard.' She looked down at the plant tubs by the front door. 'And you got off lightly with the mess. At my place, they get in the dirt, then put their paws in the water I leave out

118

for the birds, wash their hands—'

She broke off and sank down into a crouch by the tubs, flicking on her flashlight again. 'Look at this. There's something in the soil.'

'Where?'

'You're at the wrong angle. Come this side.'

Jayne walked over and crouched down to look at one of the tubs. Something was glinting in the beam of light. It looked like the top of a metal plant marker.

'Has that always been there?' Steelie asked.

'I'm not sure.' She hadn't looked at the daisy bushes closely when she came home but thought she would have noticed the marker. She'd since forgotten to even call Marie to thank her.

'Mind if I pull it out?'

'No, go ahead. It's the sort of thing my mother would do. She's responsible for these things.' Jayne stood up and looked at the roofline of the duplex, where a telephone wire seemed to be hanging loosely.

Steelie said, 'It's punched with a series of dots. From the back, they feel like Braille.'

Jayne looked sharply at the metal tag in Steelie's hand. It was actually a flat rectangle above a sharpened stake, now studded with soil.

'You think your mother would have brought this by without knocking on your door to say hi? No way, Jayne; not Marie.'

'She brought the plants without telling me.' They stood for a moment in silence. 'Why don't I call her?'

She stepped inside while Steelie began poking around in the other plant tubs. While Jayne waited for Marie to answer, she took the book of raffle tickets from the kitchen counter and waved them toward Steelie, who pocketed them with a nod.

Marie answered after five rings.

'Well, hello, darling! To what do I owe this pleasure? It's late for you.'

'I wanted to thank you for the daisies and the tubs. Sorry I didn't do it right away.'

'Daisies?'

'Yeah, the ones in the metal washtubs.'

'By your front door?'

'Yes.' Jayne was relieved that her mother remembered them.

'Well, I'm glad someone replaced the *cactaceae* but it wasn't me, darling.'

'Oh, so you didn't leave a plant marker in them today?'

'No, but what a cute idea!'

'It's not cute if *you* didn't do it!'

'Jayne, what's going on? You sound frazzled.'

'Look, did you tell anyone about my cacti?'

'Why would I tell anyone?'

'You know, like one of your landscapers? Tell them to replace them for me?'

'No. What *is* this? Jayne?'

She didn't answer because Steelie had come to stand in the doorway and was making a throat-slitting motion, which Jayne took to mean, *Get off the phone NOW.*

'I'll call you later, Mom. Bye.'

She looked at Steelie, who now had a finger to her lips and was beckoning to her.

Steelie shined light into the plant tub closest to the

house. She had excavated more soil than the possums had and the landing was a mess. The root ball of the daisy bush was exposed and nestled beneath it was a plastic box. Steelie gently tilted the tub to expose its underside. A coated wire snaked out of the central drainage hole and ran under the landing. Steelie used the light to trace the wire along the inner edge of the floorboards until it disappeared into a small hole just under the threshold of the front door. The hair on the back of Jayne's neck stood up.

Steelie whispered, 'Get your purse and whatever else you want. You're coming to my place and we'll call for help from there.'

Jayne was filled with an overwhelming desire to get out of there and perhaps never come back.

Within minutes, she was driving behind Steelie, her overnight bag on the bench seat next to her, concentrating on the Jeep's taillights. She felt like she couldn't get her anxiety under control and that fact bothered her as much as the situation itself.

Her cell phone rang and Jayne jumped again. It was only Steelie, informing her that she was stopping for 'emergency ice cream' and confirming that Jayne had her spare key.

When she parked in front of Steelie's house, Jayne noticed a light was on inside but only sheer shades were pulled over the front windows. That wasn't like Steelie but the effect was nice. The glow emphasized the arches of the tall living room windows while the up-lights among the aloes in the garden picked out the interlocking curves of the clay roof tiles. Jayne's shoes crunched on the gravel path to the front porch, where she unlocked the door and stepped inside. The uncluttered comfort of Steelie's house was an immediate balm and Jayne felt herself start to relax.

*

Steelie waited for the left-turn arrow for the shopping center, feeling a little worried. She was used to Jayne's fears, which almost bordered on paranoia, but she knew where they originated. She also knew that it was usually better to address whatever had frightened Jayne rather than try to talk her out of being frightened. PTSD didn't work like that.

But this time was different. There was something man-made in the plant tubs outside Jayne's front door. Someone had put it there and Steelie couldn't come up with a ready explanation, which made that seem sinister even in her mind. She made the turn into the shopping center parking lot but was almost immediately blinded by light reflected in her rearview mirror. She put her hand up to cut the glare and heard the too-brief *wa-woop* of a siren behind her. It seemed to echo on the night air. Odd that she hadn't noticed a police cruiser before now.

There were plenty of parking spaces to choose from at this time of night and she navigated the Jeep into one. She locked the door, opened the window and got out her identification, using her side mirror to watch for the officer. She could barely see him because the spotlight on his vehicle had made a silhouette of his form but she noted his swagger and that he didn't appear to stop to take down her license plate number.

When he reached her window, the bright light slanted across his oversized, tinted glasses. It was impossible to see his eyes.

'Ma'am.'

'Evening, Officer.' Steelie scanned his uniform for his badge. The way he was leaning hid most of his nametag – 'Marron' or 'Marion'.

'Do you know why I stopped you?'

'No. Is there a problem?' She was looking at his mouth since she couldn't see his eyes. A light-colored moustache all but hid his upper lip.

'One of your taillights is out.'

'Oh, I didn't realize! Which one?'

'Step out of the vehicle, ma'am.'

'Don't you want to check my license and registration?'

'Please step out of the vehicle, ma'am.' He took a step back and crossed his arms over his chest. 'I can help you determine if it's a fuse or a bulb. It's a lot cheaper to fix if it's a fuse.'

Warning bells were going off in Steelie's mind but she couldn't tell how much was Jayne's paranoia infecting her and how much was her ex-Legal Aid bias against police. No matter what, she would follow Legal Aid's advice to its clients. 'Can I see your ID first, please?' She tried to smile. 'Never can be too sure these days.'

'No, ma'am, I guess you can't.' He came to the window and leaned his arm on the door. He used his other hand to flash a badge wallet.

Steelie just made out a photo with some writing next to it. It had *looked* okay. She told herself to stop being paranoid and moved to unlock the door. Then she noticed his fingernails. They were long. They seemed too long for a cop. Her pulse quickened.

'Sorry, could I see it closer, please?'

She wasn't ready when he tried to open the door and then reached through the window. He seemed to know that the Wrangler's lock was low and forward and his hand scrabbled for it, banging Steelie's knee. She squealed without meaning to and grabbed for the ignition. She over-started the engine, which whined, then roared to life. Throwing the car into first gear, she slammed on the gas, popped the clutch and peeled out, the window frame slamming the cop's elbow.

'God dammit!' he shouted, leaping back.

One of the Jeep's wheels went directly over the concrete bumper at the front of the parking space and Steelie momentarily drove on the passenger-side wheels until the vehicle dropped back down. As soon as all four tires gained purchase, she was at the shopping center exit in an instant. Only the Jeep's high clearance saved it from scraping heavily across the deep gutter where the driveway met the road but Steelie's head almost hit her soft top ceiling when the car bounced across the intersection. She raced down the nearest residential street, her heart pounding as she scanned her rearview mirror, looking for chasing headlights.

When she halted in her own driveway minutes later, she couldn't work out why her key wouldn't come out of the ignition until she absorbed the fact that she hadn't shut off the engine. Then a buzzer blared when she opened her door. She spun around to look at the street before recognizing the sound as her own car's warning that the headlights were still on. *The lights.* She walked to the back of the car to look at the broken one. But both of her taillights were working. Steelie squeezed her eyes shut for a second and then took a last look around the street before turning off

124

the lights, pulling a car cover over the Jeep and running to her front door.

*

When Jayne saw the look on Steelie's face, she knew not to ask about the ice cream. As Steelie double-locked the front door and whipped the living room curtains closed, Jayne sat up on the sofa. Steelie kept moving fast toward the rear of the house and Jayne heard the slap of Venetian blinds in the kitchen. Next was the sound of the fridge or freezer, followed by the microwave starting. When Jayne heard the bolt at the back door slide into place, she got up. She'd only known Steelie to throw that bolt when she was going out of town. She arrived at the kitchen at the same time as Steelie. The microwave dinged.

Jayne said, 'I'd just managed to relax. What's up?'

Steelie shook her head mutely as she pulled a parcel out of the microwave. She ate what Jayne identified as a defrosted Krispy Kreme donut in three bites.

Trying for levity, Jayne said, 'If you get out another donut, I'm calling the police.'

Steelie swallowed. 'Don't do that. I'm probably about to be arrested for assaulting one of 'em.'

'Um, *what*?'

'Or I might've just escaped being kidnapped by a total nutcase.'

Steelie recounted the incident at the shopping center while peering out through a chink in the curtains. Then she said, 'At first I thought he was legit. But then there were those fingernails, and I couldn't see anything! And he didn't want my ID! I mean, that's so not like them. God,

125

this sounds stupid now.'

Jayne didn't think it sounded stupid but she was also relieved this had nothing to do with the wires at her apartment. 'I don't blame you for getting a bad vibe. Cops are supposed to identify themselves properly, not stick their hand in your window. It's not like he stopped you after a high-speed chase.'

'I should have known when he got out of the cruiser right away. Don't they usually sit there for a couple minutes while they run your license plate through NCIC?'

'But this was a taillight stop.'

'Except it wasn't. Sorry, I forgot that part.' Steelie glanced out the front window again. 'I checked. My taillights are fine.'

'Ohhhh.' Jayne came around to sit on the sofa. 'So what the hell was this? Why would a cop tell you to get out of your car to look at a broken taillight you would immediately see was just fine?'

Steelie inhaled thoughtfully. 'Well, it would get me out of my car, wouldn't it? And once there, I'm just another victim he can overpower.'

Jayne was shaking her head. 'But if he assaults you, you could ID him later. It's so risky.'

'Maybe it was a carjacking.'

'Seriously?'

'Why not? Late at night, deserted parking lot, some guy with a decommissioned police cruiser painted a dark color just waits for someone to pull in. Uses a fake uniform picked up at any Hollywood costume shop to get the person out of their vehicle on the fake pull. Once they're out, he hits 'em on the head or whatever and he gets to go off in their – presumably nicer – vehicle. Parts will be sold to a dozen shops all over town by the time you can call the real cops.'

'Do you really believe that?'

Steelie was silent for a moment and then came to sit next to Jayne. 'No. It's an awful lot of trouble for your typical opportunist. So if he was a cop, he probably already has my license plate and *will* come and get me...'

'I hear an "and" in there.'

'And... I was thinking about your place. The wire. What if it's connected?'

'How, though?'

'I don't know! It's just weird that we find some black box on your porch, in plant pots delivered by someone unknown. Wire is drilled into your house. We leave, and I get pulled over by a fake cop who's followed me into the parking lot.'

Jayne grabbed her arm. 'I've just remembered! I saw that car pull in behind you. He was behind me!'

'From where? How far back did you notice him?' Steelie searched her face.

'Um, let me think. He was there when we turned onto Los Feliz.'

'By Griffith Park?'

'Yeah. I definitely remember him being there after we crossed the river, because I was looking behind me for anyone merging off the 5.'

'You're going forwards. Did you see him *before* we turned onto Los Feliz?'

Jayne thought. 'No.' She exhaled. 'I don't remember anything from before then.'

Steelie walked to the telephone hanging on the wall in the kitchen. 'I'm going to call Bud Reese. I'll bet his wife hasn't let him retire yet.'

'Doesn't he work out of Downtown?'

'He'll know who to call over here at Northeast Station.'

Jayne listened as Steelie greeted Reese, one of the LAPD officers she had had a lot of interaction with while working at Legal Aid. Steelie described what had happened to her that evening and then described the wire in the plant pots. She listened for a while and took notes. She laughed once, saying, 'Give me a little credit, Bud.' Eventually, she thanked him and hung up.

Steelie threw the pencil down on the pad. 'Bud says I have grounds to make a complaint because the guy probably was a cop – a bad one. He gave me the number to call and said I needn't worry I've been followed to my house. Too much effort. He doubts it was an attempted carjacking, though they just picked up two guys for impersonating cops while shaking down undocumented immigrants who keep stalls in the Garment District. So it's not unheard of. But the wire in your pots is another story. He asked if we'd ruled out a self-watering system.'

'He thinks this is funny?'

'No,' Steelie smirked. 'He thinks *he's* funny. The wire he takes seriously. He said wires going toward thresholds "scream" tapping to him.'

'Tapping? Like bugging?'

'Like that. He didn't want to touch it with a ten-foot pole. Said it was very unlikely whatever's going on will end up in LAPD's jurisdiction so he recommended we go direct to the FBI.'

Jayne scrunched her hair. 'God, Steelie. I really, *really* don't want to call Scott.'

Steelie gave her a wry smile. 'I think Bud meant their main number in Westwood but, since you bring up Scott...' She flopped onto the sofa next to Jayne. 'Why wouldn't you want to call him?'

'Because he'll think I overreacted to a noise on my porch!'

'It wasn't an overreaction for someone with PTSD.'

'Argh! How many times do I have to tell you? I do not have PTSD!'

'Yeah, I got that memo. Anyway, it's not about you hitting the floor because you heard a noise. There's actual stuff on your porch that needs looking at by the Bureau.'

'But we only found it because some noise made me hit the floor. And hide. And whisper.' Jayne frowned at Steelie. 'How did you know I hit the floor? I didn't tell you.'

'I know you.' Steelie waved this off. 'You've never told Scott about Benni, have you?'

Jayne thought about dodging the question but suddenly didn't have the energy. She shook her head.

Steelie regarded her. 'Have you told him about anything else?'

'Of course! We've known each other for five years.'

'Down a phone line.'

Jayne sighed. *Here goes.* 'He knows about everything except Benni.'

'Well, well, well.'

'Don't say it.'

'I have to. I really do. Because you're my best friend and I like you better when you're happy. Jayne—'

'Is this the lecture?'

'This is it, so be quiet for a second.' Steelie took Jayne's hand in hers. 'It is categorically not your fault that Benni died. You shouldn't hide something this important to you – to your psyche – from Scott. And I'm going to tell you right now that, eventually, you're not going to be able to hide it. The man can see you.'

Jayne held Steelie's gaze but couldn't stop her voice from wavering with emotion. 'That's just it, Steelie. If I tell him, he'll see me as damaged goods and that'll be the end of it.'

'Why on earth would you think that?'

'Other guys have. Phil did.'

'But we've established that Phil is an idiot. The problem isn't how anyone sees you, it's how you see yourself.' Steelie squeezed Jayne's hand and then let it go. 'Plus, Scott probably knows about trauma. He was in Kosovo when the bombs were still dropping.'

Jayne pounced on this. 'Exactly! And he's never mentioned having repercussions from that.'

Steelie shrugged. 'Maybe he hasn't had any. And if so, lucky him.' She looked at her watch. 'I'm going to call him and Eric first thing tomorrow to ask for help with the wires on your porch. In the meantime, you're staying here. Get up so I can make the sofa bed.'

Jayne went to the kitchen in search of something sweet to eat in lieu of ice cream. Moving her limbs was breaking the hibernation mode she went into whenever she thought about Benni. 'I wasn't planning on leaving you here to get attacked by the rogue cop-carjacker who probably has your address.'

'I never actually showed him my license!'

Jayne opened the fridge and leaned down to examine its shelves. 'You got anything to eat in here? What *is* all this stuff? Looks like pressed cardboard.'

Steelie came in with bedding in her arms. 'That's Tofurky. Trader Joe's special.'

'Why did you give up meat only to eat false meat?'

'You want me to short-sheet your sofa bed? No? Then I suggest you shut up and be glad when I serve it up for breakfast tomorrow.'

DAY FOUR

Friday

11

Eric drove fast into the parking lot beneath the FBI building on Wilshire. He forced himself to slow down once in the dark, cramped space but undid his seatbelt even before he'd turned off the car. The elevator seemed to be running slower than usual this morning. When he hit *4*, nothing happened. He hit the *Close* button several times in quick succession. The doors crawled shut.

When they opened again, Eric turned sideways to get out shoulder-first before the doors had finished their slow retraction. On their floor, Lance, the office administrator, wasn't in yet and neither was Scott. Inside his office, Eric's eyes immediately went to the printer. Nothing. He sat down at the NCIC computer just in case something had come in from an Arizona police department or the California Highway Patrol responding to the BOLO on the gold van. Nothing.

'Damn.'

His cell phone rang. When he answered, he could hear the road noise in the background and greeted his partner. 'Yeah, Scott.'

'Anything?'

'No.'

'Okay, I think I have something. As far as we know the perp's got a freezer in the back of an old van, right? Driving out to Arizona at this time of year, he'd have done

135

it at night because of the daytime heat. Now, unless he had a generator, he would have needed an electrical hook-up for the freezer if he stopped along the way. Following me?'

Eric was pulling a notepad toward him. 'Oh yeah.'

'We should check out campgrounds with hook-ups between here and Arizona, see if they had a visit from this guy during the week.'

'Going along I-10?'

'Let's start with that. It would make a long drive even longer if he was using blue highways and they're less likely to have places for hook-up. So, you on top of this?'

'Uh-huh. What's your ETA?'

'Twenty minutes.'

They signed off and Eric started looking up campgrounds along Interstate 10. The phone on his desk rang and he glanced at the caller identification. It was a Los Angeles area code but he didn't recognize the number. He picked up and identified himself.

The voice said, 'Hey, Eric. It's Steelie Lander.'

Eric relaxed and his eyes went back to the computer screen. 'Hey, Steelie. Where are you calling from?'

'My house. Why, can you see the number?'

'Yeah. How you doing?'

'Not bad, but I wondered, would you and Scott have some time for me and Jayne today? We'd like to run something by you.'

Eric was scrolling down the list of campgrounds on the screen.

Steelie added, 'In your professional capacity.'

'That shouldn't be a problem. It might be late in the day. Can I ask what it's about?' He clicked on a web link.

'Bugging, speaking generally.'

Eric's eyes fixed on the information that had just come up on the screen. 'Well, that sounds mysterious enough. I'll call you as soon as I can.'

Eric barely registered Steelie's thanks before he signed off from her and began dialing an outside line.

*

Sitting next to Steelie in the lab, Jayne felt groggy from stress and lack of sleep. Steelie's sofa bed was not the most comfortable and she had stayed awake too long thinking about the wire in the plant tubs. She increased the speaker volume on the conference call that she and Steelie had just started with Thomas Cullen's parents.

Donald and Patricia were each talking over the other and Patricia's sniffles were audible.

Donald was saying, 'We've heard from a coroner in Alaska – here, dear, take the whole box. And they said that—' He was interrupted by Patricia, who seemed to have regained her composure.

'They said that some information you sent up to them about Tom was what made the difference and we wanted to thank you.'

Steelie and Jayne looked at each other. The 'information' was the X-ray of the bullet lodged in their son's head.

'And we wondered if the doctor told you how Tom died?' Patricia sounded hesitant and hopeful.

'Wasn't he able to tell you anything?' Steelie had to tread carefully, unsure of how Chuck Talbot would have worded things. The bullet was an artifact of Thomas Cullen's life, not his death, as far as they knew.

'Well,' Donald began, 'he said they couldn't tell how he died. Now, we didn't think that was possible, but we get most of our information from TV. Is it possible to just not know?'

Jayne answered, 'Yes, sometimes it can be difficult to tell the cause of a death, when the body hasn't retained enough traces. You *can* have a second autopsy done by a private pathologist. They're expensive and may still not give you any answers but it's an option available to you.'

'Yes, well, I don't know if we'll go to those lengths,' he said hurriedly. 'But we'll make a decision before the funeral.'

'At the minute, we're just glad to have Tom back.' Patricia sounded on the verge of tears again. 'Thank you so much.'

Jayne watched Steelie thank the Cullens, hang up and write a note about the call to add to the Cullen file. Feeling like a sleepwalker, she followed Steelie to the front of the building where Carol was gathering her things for her usual early departure on Fridays.

Steelie said, 'Carol, did you speak with the Cullens before you put their call through?'

'Yes...' Carol put her bag back down.

'Thanks. They seemed to be in a good place, despite the fact that they'd just learned their son's been dead for years.'

Carol nodded. 'I'm glad to hear that. We talked about moving past things we can't change, whether it's related to anger at the police for not finding Tom sooner or anger at themselves for not being able to prevent what happened.'

Jayne turned from where she was staring absently out the front window. 'Did you get a sense of how they're going to cope with not knowing exactly how he died?'

'I think Patricia is finding it difficult. She told me that she's a statistician and is used to mining information for as long as it takes to turn it into meaningful data but...' Carol waggled her hand from side to side. 'She can't really apply that to this situation. I think it's shaking her entire foundation for life, work, everything.'

When Carol left, Steelie handed Jayne all her notes related to the Cullen case. Jayne stood at the window a minute longer, listening to Steelie walk away, and then she turned into her office. She filed the notes in the folder labeled 'CULLEN, Thomas (Tom)' and then took the whole folder to the cabinet that held closed cases. Opening the drawer reminded her of Gene's visit to the office and how unimpressed he'd been by the agency's completion numbers.

So far, every missing person who'd been found using an Agency 32/1 profile had been found dead even though theoretically their profiles could identify someone in a coma or with amnesia. There was no way of telling how many of the missing people's bodies had been hidden by killers in the hope they would never be found. She wondered if the killers realized that they harmed countless others by this practice? That it was a further injury?

As she slotted Thomas Cullen's folder in the drawer, she found herself thinking about the bodies she'd helped to exhume from the mass graves near Srebrenica, the steep slopes of Kigali. She thought about the attempts made by the killers to hide the identities of the dead. How it stunted survivors' attempts to grieve, to move on through the healing rites of washing the deceased's body or a funeral followed by cremation or burial, or to engage in the therapeutic ritual of visiting their relative's grave for the rest of their own lives.

The lack of those rituals tortured survivors – individuals who perhaps never came into contact with their torturers. It was in this way that the killers planted seeds of disruption that would germinate far into the future. And in the meantime, bodies lay in the ground, mingled with friends and strangers, teachers, lovers, the person standing next to them when they were pulled off the bus and shot, the person they fell onto when they were hit across the forehead. Jayne saw them all in her mind's eye, the bodies they'd been unable to identify. She'd never known whether subsequent teams had identified them.

Yes, it was torture to not know.

She knew where these thoughts could take her but she was still surprised to hear the sob escape. It came from so low down that she clutched her abdomen, thinking she could stop the next one. But it erupted, always stronger than her will, and caught her breath, forcing tears. She wiped them away impatiently and looked at the open drawer of closed cases. The dark recess of the empty portion felt like a reproach and now the tears were back. She slammed the drawer shut.

'Pull yourself together,' she muttered. Then, louder, 'And stop talking to yourself.'

'Hey, that's my line.'

Jayne whirled. 'Steelie! Did you have to creep up on me like that?'

'Oh, please! Most of LA heard that file drawer slam shut. I was just the one who pulled the short straw to go

140

investigate.'

Jayne wiped her eyes irritably and went to sit at her desk.

Steelie came in. 'Look… we just helped get one person home. Right? Focus on the positive.' Her cell phone rang.

As Jayne listened to Steelie greet Eric, she decided to follow Steelie's advice. She tapped out a short email to Gene, almost boasting that the agency had closed another case. She pressed *Send*.

Steelie was consulting her watch as she finished up with Eric. 'Yeah. Can we make it Café Tropical on Sunset? Do you know it? 'Kay, see you there.' She hung up and turned off Jayne's desk lamp. 'Come on, let's get some food in you.'

12

Driving along Hyperion toward Sunset Boulevard, Jayne kept checking her rearview mirror. 'Another dark Chevy or maybe a Lincoln Town Car.'

'You've got to look for a spotlight on the driver's side.' Steelie turned around to look out the window behind the truck's bench seat. 'I think whatever you just saw turned into that parking lot at the bank.'

'You say you're not scared by what happened last night and yet you didn't want to put your car on the road today.' Jayne glanced at her. 'I think maybe you are a little scared.'

Steelie jerked a thumb out her window. 'You just missed the shortcut to Sunset.'

'Oh, damn.'

Forty minutes later, they were finished with a dinner consumed under a patio umbrella outside Tropical. Inside, the Cuban café was busy with diners crowding around varnished pine tables after moving potted spider plants to windowsills to make more space.

Steelie had just gone inside to order coffee when Jayne saw Scott and Eric's Suburban pass by in search of parking. She ducked inside the door and told Steelie to increase the coffee order.

When Scott and Eric eventually walked up the street, Jayne noticed that they were still wearing their office clothes: dark pants and white shirts, the latter now open at the neck. They'd removed their jackets and ties but still didn't quite fit in with the Friday evening crowd at the café with its mix of sandal-wearing academics, kids wearing Che Guevara T-shirts, and people who were either too cool or too broke to go to the west side for entertainment. As she watched the agents advancing, she realized they'd probably never fit into café culture because they were too watchful; they took in rooflines and parked cars, and walked in step with each other without looking like they meant to do it.

Steelie came out just as they arrived. 'How you guys doin'?'

Eric blew out his breath. 'Glad it's Friday.'

Scott said, 'I'll second that.'

Jayne addressed Eric, thinking that he'd be less likely than Scott to discern that she'd been crying recently. 'Long week?'

'Oh yeah. But next week's going to be a doozy.'

'Why's that?' Steelie asked.

'We're going to Arizona, and as if it wasn't bad enough to lose a day driving there, we're on stake-out for a couple of days.'

'And nights.' Scott waved his index finger. 'Can't forget the nights.'

Jayne swallowed the disappointment she felt on hearing this news and stole a look at Scott over the top of her mug. 'What's in Arizona?'

'Ironically, it's where the Georgia license plate takes us.' He told them about tracking the van through a body shop in the Valley all the way to a campground west of Phoenix. 'The old guy who runs the ground doesn't hold much stock in keeping records of license plates but told us that a van

143

matching our description hooked up there just last night for a couple of hours. Seems this old guy had a nice chat with the driver.'

Eric tapped his temple. 'Old guy reckons he can learn more about people from talking to 'em, not taking down their ID.'

'Turned out he was right because he learned that the driver was heading over to Mesa,' Scott said. 'We put out a request for Phoenix PD to look out for the vehicle and it seems they've found it parked in a residential area. The van's the right make, model and color, and has a padlock on the back door handles.'

'That sounds like the one, right?' Jayne said.

'It does – except it's not wearing a Georgia plate. Thing is, it's easy to flip a plate so there's enough to warrant us checking it out.'

'I hope it's the right one.' Jayne had to avert her eyes when she had a sudden vision of the body parts by the freeway: a leg, a midriff, Mrs. Patterson's arms. She pictured the van in Arizona leading to the rest of her.

Steelie pushed her chair back. 'Anyone for more coffee?'

'Let me get it,' Eric said, hopping out of his seat to follow her inside.

Jayne hoped that by looking upwards, the tears welling up in her eyes would just slide back to where they came from. Music from the café's outdoor speakers suddenly seemed louder; Rubén Blades in call and response with his cheering audience on a live recording of 'Buscando América'.

'Hey,' Scott said gently.

Jayne chanced a look at him. The tiny movement gave

144

a waiting teardrop its big break and it scudded down her cheek before she could brush it away. But something in Scott's expression made her feel like she might be able to leave the wet trail; that when it was dry, it would be as though it had never happened.

'Hey, yourself,' she replied. It was their traditional phone greeting and the fact that he'd used it now comforted her.

'Thinking about Mrs. Patterson?'

Her lips parted in surprise. 'How'd you know?'

'Because I was thinking about her myself. Or I should say, talking about this case with you and Steelie always makes me think about the victims, not the perps.'

He put his elbows on the table as he looked toward the traffic stopped at the light on Sunset. 'Y'know, when I was sent to Kosovo, I was only thinking about killers – people who burned their victims alive after locking them in a house – what their psychology was. But once I'd been in one of those houses, trying to work out if my eyes were tricking me or if the ash on the floor was actually a person reduced to a... to a fucking shadow...'

His voice had dropped almost to a whisper. Jayne felt her arms come out in goose bumps.

He shook his head and then looked back to her. 'Well, I came out thinking about bodies. And I guess that's how it is for you all the time.'

Jayne was stunned into silence. Any time they'd talked about Kosovo before, he'd never described this, just as she'd never described seeing Benni blown to pieces by a mine when on their way to a gravesite... that day in northern Kosovo, that day of blood and sweat but no tears. Those

145

came later, when she was home, jumpy and demoralized, not sleeping well, the type of person for whom an empty filing cabinet could now produce an outpouring of pent-up grief: mingled grief about victims and killers, graves and booby traps, life and loss. These were her reasons for omission with Scott – and with others. And now she knew he'd omitted things too.

She examined his face, his features softened in the glow of lights strung along the café's umbrellas, looking for physical traces that he was damaged goods like she was. But he only looked rested, excited and engaged, his fingers twirling the salt shaker on the table between them. She sensed his anticipation to get to Arizona and thought that maybe this was why he seemed so balanced. The same phenomena might demoralize them both but where she got stuck or felt overwhelmed, he pushed through, powered on and closed the case. He could be future-oriented like that because it was his job to catch perpetrators who were still out there, not stop at digging up evidence of their past deeds, as she had done, as she had had to do with the UN.

Scott had stilled the salt shaker. Jayne wanted to pull his hands to her lips and thank him for caring about people reduced to shadows, especially when he needn't because that wasn't his job; when he needn't look back, only forward.

Steelie's voice came from behind her and the moment was gone.

'Here you go. Long line but worth the wait.'

Eric put a mug down in front of Jayne. 'Steelie tells me you've got some kind of situation at your place?'

Scott said, 'What's this?'

Eric was coming around the table. 'Looks like maybe someone planted a bugging device outside Jayne's apartment.'

Scott's eyebrows lifted. '*This* is what you wanted to talk to us about? When Eric said bugging, I figured you meant legals or clearances. If you'd said something, we could've brought sweeping equipment.'

'We did bring sweeping equipment.' Eric took in Scott's look of surprise. 'That's why they pay me the big bucks.'

'Tell me what you know, Jayne,' Scott said.

Jayne still didn't want to tell him all the gory details. 'I don't really know anything. There's a wire coming out of a box on my porch.'

Steelie exclaimed, 'You left out the relevant details! The box is hidden inside potted plants left there anonymously!'

Before anyone else could chime in, Jayne said, 'But my "situation" is probably nothing compared to Steelie's.' She enjoyed watching Eric frown at Steelie.

'You didn't mention anything.' He sounded almost accusatory.

Jayne continued. 'She didn't say she was pulled over on a fake taillight stop by a cop who maybe wasn't a cop and tried to drag her out of the car?'

He looked concerned. 'Give me that again.'

Steelie described the events from the Atwater Village Shopping Center the night before.

Scott had the first question. 'You drove off while his arm was in the car and he didn't follow you?'

'Yeah. Stupid, right?'

He smirked. 'More like gutsy. You report it to the LAPD?'

Steelie shook her head. 'I just called an old friend at Parker Center. He said I had grounds for a complaint, which I can file even if I don't know whether he was an officer or just pretending to be one. I guess the ombudsman, or whoever, will work that part out. But let me ask you, do you think a cop would act that way?'

'Hm. Some aspects don't sound right. The fact that he was riding solo, him not letting you get a good look at his badge, grabbing the lock on your door. And, of course, not following you. A lot of cops would track you down if only to save themselves from being a laughing stock back at the House.'

Eric said, 'If he was a cop, you'll be getting a summons in the mail any day. If he wasn't… you maybe got a lucky break in getting away from a real piece of work. And you should watch your back.'

Steelie looked discomfited. 'What do you mean?'

'You live in your own house, right?'

She nodded.

'Alone?'

Steelie jutted her chin upwards slightly. 'At the moment.'

'Got a dog?' Eric asked.

'No.'

'Got a gun?'

'Hell, no!'

'Well, ma'am.' Eric had assumed a southern drawl. 'What *do* you have?'

Scott rolled his eyes. 'Don't listen to him. You don't have to get a gun. Just stay alert. And maybe curb your late-night ice cream runs.'

Eric added, 'Seriously, though, you should call us –

either of us – if something like that happens again. I'm in Hollywood and Scott's in Downtown. Only a few minutes from either of you.' He saw Steelie's expression. 'You didn't know we lived so close, huh?'

She recovered, 'No, I just didn't realize government agents *had* homes. What do you guys do there, anyway? I'd find that interesting from an anthropological perspective.'

Looking at Jayne, Scott said, 'It wouldn't be more interesting than finding suspicious boxes hidden on your porch. Where're you parked? We'll follow you over.'

*

Jayne drove more carefully than usual, aware of Scott and Eric behind them. It made the drive hypnotic as the narrow road wound gently uphill from Sunset.

Steelie said, 'The reservoir looks calm tonight.'

Jayne looked across the water, catching glimpses between trees. 'In a dark way.'

'Maybe I should get a dog.'

'Maybe I should, too.'

They lapsed into silence. Jayne turned into the driveway of her duplex and saw the Suburban in her sideview mirror, pulling to the curb.

Eric came up the driveway holding a case. 'Lead the way.'

Jayne went up the stairs first. What she saw as she rounded the corner of the landing surprised her so much that she came to a sudden halt. Scott collided into her back and put a hand on her waist. Behind him, Eric grunted but was able to stop in time and put out a warning hand to Steelie, who called up to Jayne.

149

'What is it?'

Jayne looked past the others to Steelie, her eyes wide, the porch light casting a hazy glow across her face. She spoke through clenched teeth.

'They're not here.'

The landing was clean. No pots, no soil, no wire.

13

Scott could feel Jayne start to tremble and knew she wouldn't be aware that she was trying to back down the stairs even though he was right behind her. As nice as it was to have her moving against him, he would enjoy it more if she intended to do it. He could only see the back of her head but with his hand firmly on her waist he sensed he was reading her right: she was experiencing a fear made more intense because it was brought on by the absence of something.

He slid his hand over hers and moved it to the railing, forcing her fingers to curl around it by using pressure from his own. Then he twisted around to Eric and gestured upwards with his head. Eric nodded and squeezed past them to reach the landing.

Scott saw that Steelie's usual wry-tough expression was gone, replaced with something taut and far away, like she was speed-thinking through a million topics. He knew he had to get her to lock down on something. 'Steelie.' He watched her focus on him. 'Keep an eye on her, okay?'

When she spoke, her voice had its usual clip. 'No intention of doing otherwise.' She came up the stairs.

Scott joined Eric, who was crouched in front of Jayne's door with a flashlight. Eric was running a gloved finger across the wood siding on the wall just above the floor of the landing. Then he stopped. Holding his finger in place, he passed the flashlight to Scott, who kept it steady on his partner's hand while Eric selected a tiny metal tool with a curved end from the open toolkit beside him. He dug at the wall gently and a plug of material softer than wood but well-camouflaged came away on the tool and left a small hole.

He glanced up at Scott, who returned the flashlight and turned to Jayne. She was looking at the doorway, brows knitted and chewing her bottom lip. Scott wanted to make her stop and kissing her would have been his preferred method.

He asked, 'When were you here last?'

Steelie spoke when Jayne didn't respond. 'Yesterday. She stayed at my place last night.'

'Can we open your door?' He was still directing the questions to Jayne.

She was watching Eric thread a wire into the hole he'd exposed and nodded.

'Just need your keys,' said Scott.

She didn't lift her eyes from Eric. 'I'm not sure where they are.'

'I think they're in your hand.'

She looked at him then and he saw confusion and fatigue in her eyes. Steelie was the one who took the keys from her and passed them over.

When Scott unlocked the front door, he opened it but didn't go in. Instead, he waited for Eric to continue threading his wire through the hole on the outside. When Eric depressed a switch, light glowed weakly from under the metal threshold plate. After a bit more threading, the wire and its bright headlamp came out through a hole where one of the screws on the threshold plate should have been, but wasn't.

Eric spoke softly to Scott. 'No doubt there was something here. Probably audio, though it's the right size for a fiberscope video package. Whoever set it up has done a nice clean-up job.' He began retracting the wire. 'I don't think we'll find anything inside but let's sweep it.'

Scott looked back at Jayne. 'We're going to check inside, and then you should come in and see if anything's missing or out of place.' The anxiety he'd seen on her face up until now was gradually being replaced by relief, as though exposure of facts – even facts she couldn't make sense of – was preferable to half-buried pieces of information.

When they entered the apartment, Scott was acutely aware that this was a step beyond the peculiar closeness he and Jayne had maintained over the years. Turning on the lights revealed a large room that seemed like two due to the placement of the living room furniture: two yellow sofas made an L under a beam bisecting the ceiling. The seating functioned as a room divider because the L was backed by console tables set with large lamps and neat stacks of magazines whose white spines Scott recognized as those of *Architectural Digest*.

When he turned from checking the lock on the sliding glass door to the deck, he pictured Jayne sitting on the sofa, feet resting on the glass coffee table and gazing at the corner fireplace. He realized with a start that the image had turned into one of him intertwined with Jayne on that sofa. He smiled inwardly; he'd moved himself in before even asking her out. It was beyond 'wolfish'. But it was also electrifying. He knew exactly what he wanted.

Eric came into his peripheral vision as he methodically moved the bug detection unit around a pine TV cabinet. So far, the unit hadn't raised any red flags.

Scott crossed the full length of the room, past the glass dining table and the front door where Jayne and Steelie were now hovering, and stepped into the kitchen. He checked all the locks on the windows. Nothing had been forced or tampered with so he moved toward the bedroom.

Over the years, Scott had imagined how Jayne's bedroom might look and he initially only peered around the door after pressing the light switch. He was surprised by how feminine it was compared with the rest of the apartment and he stepped inside fully. She'd draped a blanket at the foot of the large bed and placed numerous pillows against the linen headboard below a sizeable window. The arrangement was striking and the bed inviting. He would enjoy getting almost no sleep here.

To get at the window locks, he had to navigate a complicated set of semi-transparent curtain panels running on different tracks. His thigh jogged the dainty bedside table and he steadied it, noticing the small stereo unit, some books-on-tape, a slim silver pen and a pad of paper. The top sheet looked like a list. He registered a few words and then turned on the bedside lamp to take a closer look.

Kigali. Blocked road.

Genocide starting. Ripping shoulder joints.

Driving but no rides. Child with fever.

Embassy. Knowledge of ignorance.

He started to re-read it, hoping it wasn't what he thought it was, and then he heard a soft tread on the carpet behind him. He turned quickly. Jayne had come into the room, looking more like herself, if somewhat pale.

He faced her. 'I was just...' He couldn't explain why he was reading her private notes.

She walked toward him and looked down at the paper. 'It was just a dream.' She flipped the pad over so its cardboard back was uppermost.

He was looking at the top of her down-turned head. 'You're dreaming about roadblocks in Kigali.' He couldn't make it a question.

'Yep.' She met his eyes.

He was surprised to see that she looked angry and was even more surprised when she jabbed an index finger toward his chest and hissed, 'And don't you dare judge me.' She turned on her heel.

'Jayne, wait.' He couldn't believe she didn't think he knew what this dream was about.

She hovered by the door but didn't turn around.

'I know what the tapes are for.'

She turned toward him but spoke warily. 'They're just entertainment.'

'No, they're not.' His tone was harsher than he'd meant it to be, but he was trying to hold her there with his voice, desperate to stop her from putting up more defenses. 'You have them so that when you wake up from a nightmare so real that you think you're there, you can hit "Play" and know that you're here. Here, not *there*. And maybe you feel guilty about that.'

She looked stricken. He pinched the bridge of his nose and closed his eyes, determined to explain himself better. 'You know what? You're not the only one who sometimes needs a reality check to get through the night.'

155

The confession left a bitter taste in his mouth but he opened his eyes, hoping to see that Jayne understood now. But she wasn't there and he didn't know when she'd left.

Eric stepped through the doorway. 'I just told Jayne that I'll check this room and then we'll do the outside.' He did a double-take at Scott. 'Everything alright, man? You weren't shouting at her, were you?'

'No.' Scott sat down on the bench at the foot of the bed.

'Okay, maybe not shouting, but that thing you do that sounds like shouting to everyone else.' Eric swept the bug detection unit around the walls and closets but kept an eye on Scott.

'Maybe my voice was raised.'

Eric stopped in mid-sweep and looked him over.

Now Scott felt defensive. 'I just don't want to be misunderstood on any of the stuff that matters.'

Eric turned back to the sweeping. 'Houston, I have never known you to care what other people think about you.'

'Yeah. Well, I care what Jayne thinks about me.'

Eric came to the end of his circuit and rested a hand on his shoulder. 'My friend, at the rate you're going, you'll be lucky if that woman thinks about you at all. Ever.'

Scott knew exactly what Eric was doing and it had worked: he wanted to punch him. His blood was flowing again, the bitter taste gone.

He exchanged an amused look with his partner and said, 'Get your hand off my shoulder.'

*

Steelie stood next to Jayne in the doorway of her apartment, watching the beams from Scott and Eric's flashlights move

156

around the garden as they checked the outside of the building. The two agents came closer and then went under the stairs that led to the front door. Jayne went back inside and dropped onto the sofa. Then she kicked off her shoes and turned to lie down.

Steelie came to perch on the arm of the sofa. She tried to see Jayne's expression but her hair was obscuring her face. Steelie pushed it back from her forehead and noticed Jayne's freckles were standing out. Usually they were almost invisible against her skin but she was decidedly pale this evening. Steelie pulled up her shirtsleeve and pressed the inside of her wrist to her friend's forehead. 'You're warm. How do you feel?'

'Kind of cold.'

'Hm. I think you need a hot shower and a hot drink.'

'My shower's probably bugged.'

'They said the place is clean.'

'Feels dirty.'

Steelie recognized the stubborn tone and got up. She went to the kitchen, put on the electric kettle and started rummaging in the cupboard that held tea and coffee. She straightened up as the agents came inside. Scott walked to the living room and sat on the sofa next to Jayne while Eric detoured to the kitchen. He was using a folded surgical glove to hold a small box.

He put the item on the counter, resting it on another glove.

'What is that?' Steelie was curious.

Eric kept his voice low. 'A radio frequency transmitter. It's a type of wiretap.'

'Where was it? I mean, is it something to do with Jayne?'

'It was on the exterior part of her phone line.'

'Jesus. But who…?'

He shrugged and looked over to the living room. Steelie followed his gaze and saw that Jayne had sat up. She was shaking her head in response to something Scott was saying.

Eric said, 'He'll be asking her some questions about her phone before we say anything about the tap. Listen, you said she stayed with you last night? Can you keep her over there for a couple more days?'

'I can but she's already complaining about my sofa bed.' Steelie stopped the kettle before it came to a boil and emptied packets of powder into four mugs. She used a small whisk to vigorously stir the drinks.

She pushed a mug toward Eric and indicated the wiretap. 'How serious is this?'

'I don't know, but we're in "better safe than sorry" territory.' He took a sip of the steaming, frothy drink and then looked at it. 'What the hell is this?'

'Matcha au lait.'

He raised his eyebrows.

'Instant green tea with milk. Chinese,' Steelie spelled out. 'Very popular.'

'Got anything stronger?'

She smiled. 'I hear you, but Jayne doesn't drink so, no, we don't got anything stronger.'

She took a sip from her own mug and made exaggerated noises of satisfaction. 'Think Scott'll dig it?'

'I think you'll be lucky if he put the safety back on his gun,' he joked. 'That'll buy you some time to get away.'

They carried the drinks to the living room, leaving the transmitter on the counter. Jayne looked like she'd been in a wind tunnel, hair pushed this way and that, her eyes watery. One of Scott's sleeves was rolled up, the other down, and he looked like he'd come in contact with some dust. *Same wind tunnel*, Steelie thought.

'So, what's your professional opinion?' Steelie asked.

Eric put his mug down. 'We clearly found a place where a wire could have been inserted into the floor of the apartment. That's not to say a wire *was* inserted there, but I gotta say that the location makes it likely. It's common practice to install a listening or video device in a threshold segment because it can be easy to access without entering the premises.'

Jayne covered her face with both hands.

Scott compressed his lips and shook his head at Eric, who got the message and rushed on. 'As I said, this is only an indication. There may never have been any device. But the reason I mentioned video is that we found a tap on the phone line—'

Jayne splayed her fingers so she could see Eric with one eye.

He spread his hands. 'All I'm saying is that whoever put on the tap could already hear you. No need for another audio bug in the threshold, which just leaves video.'

Steelie swallowed her drink. 'Sounds like Big Brother to me. How do we know it's not some other arm of your office that put this in?'

Scott sounded impatient. 'Why, because that racketeering thing Jayne's been developing has finally taken off?' He shook his head. 'Look, this stuff wasn't government and it wasn't sophisticated. The person who did it had some knowledge but no experience.' He turned

159

to Jayne. 'Do you use your landline for work-related calls?'

She dropped her hands but looked unhappy. 'No. I mean, occasionally Steelie and I might mention something while on the phone.'

'How many people have the number? Are you listed in the phonebook?'

'I'm in the *White Pages*, sure. Last name, first initial.' She paused. 'What are you getting at?'

'Well, one interpretation of what we've found is that the person who planted this stuff may know you but not well enough to get invited in. Doesn't stop him from wanting to get closer to you and maybe he doesn't mean any harm. You'd probably never even notice the guy. And he'd have to be nearby to pick up the low signal this transmitter would've given out. Who lives downstairs?'

Jayne answered. 'Luke, but you're not seriously suggesting—'

'How well do you know him?'

'Like, to say hi and bye.'

'What does he do? Do you know?'

Jayne stood up and went to look out the sliding door. 'Something to do with computers.'

Scott and Eric exchanged a glance.

Steelie noticed it. 'This is crazy!'

Eric put his hands out in a calming gesture. 'You won't know what it is until you get more information. And, Jayne, until you do, you might want to stay somewhere else.' He twisted to look at her. 'Your place is fine; we've checked everything and disabled the tap outside, but that could also draw him back, to see why his transmitter's not transmitting. And you should have what we found tonight evaluated by professionals.'

He faced Steelie again. 'In case this isn't just a Peeping Tom, get the agency premises checked, including your phones.' He pulled out his BlackBerry. 'I'll give you some names of people. Reputable sweeping companies, ex-Bureau tactical ops guys. Tell 'em we told you to call.'

Steelie eyed him. 'What, so they'll charge us double?'

*

Jayne opened the sliding door and went out to the deck. Her table looked bereft without the white cloth and the glassy surfaces of the candle holders were dulled by dried wax. She walked to the railing and looked down into the driveway. Her neighbor's car wasn't parked in its spot. She was trying to recall what kind of car he drove – a station wagon of some kind – when she realized that Scott had joined her.

He handed her a mug, drank from his own then looked at it in surprise before taking another, more tentative sip. 'Steelie thinks you should go to your mother's until you know what's going on.'

She felt annoyed. 'Why can't I just go to Steelie's?'

'Because *she'll* be at your mother's.'

His mouth twitched and Jayne smiled reflexively. Suddenly, she felt almost normal again.

After a minute or two of standing side by side, drinking matcha, Scott put his mug on the table and returned to her. 'Do me a favor,' he said softly. 'Call me if you learn something while I'm in Arizona? I might not be able to pick up but I'll get back to you.'

'No, Scott, I appreciate what you've done tonight but I

don't want to involve you any further.'

'Maybe I want to be involved.'

'In this mess?' Jayne nodded toward her apartment.

But Scott wasn't looking at the apartment. He was looking at her.

'In everything,' he said.

He walked away before Jayne could formulate a response. Indeed, she didn't know what to say. She only knew what she hoped.

DAY FIVE

Saturday

14

Scott caught the mayonnaise just in time as it squirted out of his sandwich. He looked to see how Eric was doing. His partner had the Suburban's steering wheel in one hand and his sandwich in the other. On his first bite, barbecue sauce dripped out in a fat droplet. Part landed on his pant leg and part on the fabric seat but, to Eric's credit, the vehicle's speed remained steady as it hurtled east along Interstate 10.

'Shit,' Eric mumbled while he chewed. Then he noticed Scott. 'What's so funny? You won't be laughing if you bring this vehicle back to Supervisory Special Agent Turner looking like a minivan after a trip to Disneyland.'

'I got the impression from SSA Turner that he couldn't care less if we brought it back at all, so long as we secured a suspect.' Scott balanced a paper napkin on Eric's leg but forgot to keep an eye on his own food and mayo got on his shirt. 'Dammit.'

Eric looked pleased. 'Did you get the impression that Turner got a call from our old boss?'

'From Franks? He didn't say as much.' Scott was dabbing at his shirt.

'But he was concerned we were on a wild-goose chase?' He caught Scott's nod. 'Did he actually use those words?'

'No, but you know Craig Turner; he can be a diplomat. A nice quality in a boss.'

'For a change! Man, when I think about how SSA Franks held us back on this case in Atlanta! Who knows how many leads we missed.'

'It's not like we stopped following leads.'

'Yeah, but we didn't have the resources to do proper surveillance to generate the high-quality leads. We were slowed down by only getting intel the sex workers could *remember* to give us—'

'Don't remind me.'

But Eric was on a roll. 'And thanks to SSA Franks, we couldn't do what was needed to rule suspects in or out. And now we're tracking the same perp out here. He's probably killed again, too.'

Scott balled up his napkin, put it in a paper bag, then balled that up and threw it in the footwell. 'We don't know that it's the same guy. Our perp's stomping grounds are in Atlanta. Right now, we're...' He looked out the window just as they passed the sign for the Arizona state line. 'Fifteen miles shy of Quartzsite. What's our perp doing out west?'

'I don't know,' Eric admitted. 'But it's the same guy. Maybe he wanted to take a road trip. He took the northern route, killed Patterson in Oregon on the way down south, got rear-ended in LA—'

'The van was going north when it was hit, Eric.'

'So he was lost. He gets back on the road and goes to Arizona to get some sun. Or, wait... he could be from Arizona originally and it was time to come home. Things getting too hot in Georgia the past few months. I mean, you were on the news and in the paper, what, every couple of weeks for a while? Appealing to the public: "We're looking for a van that might be driven by a man abducting women in Atlanta." *I'd* get out of town if I had you on my tail.' Eric put the last of the sandwich in his mouth and held out the trash to Scott. 'You still think it's the same guy, too, right?'

'Yeah. But I'll tell you what I didn't tell SSA Turner: I think it's the same guy because I want it to be him.' Scott sighed. 'The evidence only says it's some perp with a Georgia license plate hauling body parts around.'

'Okay, so what *did* you tell Turner?'

'I just told him there was no need to hand off to Phoenix police, wasting time bringing them up to speed. At the very least, we'll get forensics that relate to the LA body parts and we'll get the van's owner, who is either the perp or someone who's helping him. We can tie up the LA end of the case no matter what.'

'And Turner doesn't care about what happened with us in Georgia?'

'I sure as hell didn't bring it up. If SSA Franks *has* called him from Atlanta, then Turner already knows that when it comes to that case, I'm... what did Angie say Franks called me?'

'An ego-driven maverick who can't see the forest for the trees.'

'Right.' Scott looked at the instrument panel. 'You're over a hundred, Ramos.'

Eric glanced at the speedometer and eased up slightly on the accelerator pedal. 'It's thinking about Franks that does that to me.'

'Remember, he's our *old* boss.' Scott reclined his seat and closed his eyes.

'Not if he's calling SSA Turner with bedtime stories,'

167

Eric replied, an edge to his voice.

'Turner's too smart for that kind of game. And if you're going to be thinking about Franks while I'm getting some shut-eye, put it on cruise control.'

Eric focused on the road. It was still another couple of hours to Mesa, so he turned the radio on with the volume low. He'd just missed the news.

*

An hour later, Scott woke suddenly and then oriented himself. He brought his seat back up and cleared his throat. 'How far out are we?'

'Thirty miles.'

'You need to switch?'

'No, I'll take us to the location and get in some rest when we change vehicles.'

Scott drank from a bottle of water and then pulled a file folder from the seat behind them. 'You get a chance to look at this fax from Phoenix PD before we left?'

Eric shook his head. 'Not in any detail. The detective who I spoke with, Czuzak, is up to her neck on a drug bust so she sent a couple of rookies to babysit the van.'

'She sure the van's associated with that address?' Scott was pulling papers out of the file.

'Well, it's parked in front of that address. The rookies have seen one man emerge from the van and go into the address but not by the front door. He went down the side. Could be a side entrance, could be nothing. Could be a shortcut to a neighbor's place.'

'Right. Says here that the house at that address is owned by a couple in their seventies by the name of Spicer. Been there since '99. Previous address is Burbank, California. No arrests, no convictions. No problems with property taxes or mortgage payments. No van registered in their name or associated with the house.' Scott paused.

'They could know the perp. Let him park at their place.'

'I see you're presuming Mr. Spicer isn't our perp.'

Eric gave him a look. 'He's too old for the description we have. Plus, how many seventy-year-old *active* serial killers you heard of? What about the people who live on either side of that address?'

'Uh, let's see.' Scott flipped through some pages. 'To the west we have a Mr. Knox, the owner since '98, unknown to police, but resident with him is one Alice Elizabeth Smith whose priors include possession, dealing, and acquiring goods through deception.'

Eric raised his eyebrows. 'Possession of what?'

'Ah... pot. Same for the dealing.'

'Interesting.'

'Maybe.'

'She could be someone who crossed paths with the perp.'

'Possibly.'

'And on the other side?'

'Neighbors on the other side are tenants. Phoenix hasn't run down the info on them yet but the owner lives outside the US and that's confirmed.'

Eric said, 'Let's give Phoenix PD a punch list of backgrounds we need when we get there.'

Scott yawned and then twisted to look in the back of the car. 'We got anything else to eat in here?'

*

169

Steelie watched Marie snip the thin branches of the mint bush and held the trug out for the cuttings. Marie moved on to a rose bush whose flowers grew in bunches, some buds yet to open, others just past their glory.

'I think we'll have some of these, too.' She started cutting off little bouquets.

'You're putting roses in the mint tea?'

'No, dear, these are for the table.' Then she peered at Steelie over the top of her vintage sunglasses. 'You're teasing me, aren't you?'

'Hey, I found rosemary in my scone this morning so I had to check.'

'I would have thought that you experimented with all kinds of herbs and spices, Steelie.'

'What, 'cause I'm a vegetarian? As someone pointed out, we don't just go and eat a fistful of the nearest bush. Like you don't pick up the nearest squirrel and throw it on the grill just 'cause you eat meat.'

Marie laughed. 'It is always such a treat to have you around, my dear.'

They walked up the sloping lawn to the Cape Cod-style house shaded by two old oaks. The weather-faded shingles contrasted with a particular shade of blue on the window shutters to give the effect of country retreat rather than beach house. The back porch was screened in and the wooden screen door slammed gently behind Steelie as she followed in Marie's perfume contrail past the lunch table, which was set with tulips. Marie picked the vase up as she swept into the house.

They passed through the formal dining room, its long table flanked by ten chairs, and into the bright white kitchen with its woodblock counters and island.

'Right, give me the mint and I'll leave you the roses. Here's another vase.' Marie handed Steelie a pot-bellied ceramic jug and the pruning scissors and pointed her over to a section of counter by a second sink.

After a few minutes, Steelie turned around with the jug. 'How's that?'

Marie looked at the rose arrangement, head tilted. 'There's hope for you yet.'

Steelie hoisted herself onto the counter to watch Marie make salad dressing. Her eyes traveled around the room and came to rest, as usual, on the large watercolor of Marie tending flowers with a four-year-old Jayne.

'Tell me the story behind the painting again.'

Marie looked up. 'Again? But you know it!'

'Again!'

Marie shrugged elegantly. 'Elliott painted this in our garden in Caracas. Nothing like this.' She glanced out the kitchen windows. 'Much smaller but *wonderful* soil. I was planting seeds I'd been experimenting with. Jayne had watched me harvest them and then decided to help me plant. I taught her how to hold the trowel and she was very good. No seeds too deep, nothing tamped down too hard.'

She smiled at the memory. 'The plants began to grow. Everything was fine. Elliott finished this painting. Then one day, I went to check on their progress and discovered that Jayne had excavated their roots. Not dug them up – no, no. She wanted to see what was going on underground so she had simply *exposed* them, poor things. It was quite clinical. They never recovered.'

Steelie smiled. 'Just think, you were the one who taught

171

her to use a trowel. Little did you know.'

'That's what Elliott says.' Marie began tossing the salad. 'Little did we know that our baby was going to grow up to be a forensic anthropologist. We'd never heard of such a thing.'

Steelie jumped down and came over to rescue a piece of cucumber that had fallen onto the counter. She popped it into her mouth and crunched. 'How is your other half? It's been, what, a couple of months since he was last home?'

'You say "home" like this is home for him.'

'Well, he is *from* here, Marie.'

'But he's been doing his best imitation of an expatriate since in Venezuela 1967! An academic, a painter, a professor.'

'He loves Caracas because,' Steelie stole another piece of cucumber, 'it gave him you.'

Marie looked shocked. 'Who told you that?'

'He did, of course!'

'Well, well. Let me add poet to the list of his talents.'

Steelie munched happily. 'You wouldn't move back?'

'My home is here, my dear. I am a true *emigrante*.' She handed the salad bowl to Steelie and directed her toward the front porch. 'Besides, how would the listeners of *Weekends with Prentis* manage without me?'

'As your lawyer,' Steelie called back, 'I'd have to advise you take the title with you at the very least.'

Marie joined her on the porch and put the roses on the table. 'Now, do you think Jayne will be here soon or shall we begin lunch without her?'

Steelie glanced at her watch. 'I'm actually surprised she's not back yet. Did you see her this morning?'

172

'No, but she left a note in the kitchen that she was going to Carol's.'

'Yeah, I know.' Steelie pulled out her cell phone and dialled Jayne. 'Her phone's off.' She started to dial Carol's home number. 'Let's go ahead; I'm sure she'll be here soon.'

*

Jayne walked out to the back porch to find Steelie and Marie at the table with the remains of lunch. Half the quiche was just crumbs and the salad looked picked over. She sat down at the third place setting and reached for the salad.

'How'd she take it?' Steelie's tone was eager.

'You know Carol. With equanimity. I tell her my apartment's been bugged and we need her to call some TSCMs—'

'TSCMs?' Marie cut in.

Jayne spoke while examining the salad. 'Technical surveillance counter-measures. I can tell Steelie's been here because there's no avocado left and yet I can see smears of avocado stuck in the crenulations of the lettuce.'

'They do say that it's trace evidence that gets you every time.' Steelie didn't sound remorseful.

Marie ignored their asides. 'Couldn't you have just called Carol on the phone?'

Jayne had too much salad in her mouth so Steelie answered. 'Eric said that it isn't always recommended to do what they did at Jayne's apartment last night; I mean, to dismantle the bug. In a business setting, it's sometimes recommended to leave it in, plant disinformation in it, and then see where that comes out to find the source of the

173

spying. So, just in case this is all to do with the agency, we're not using any phones to discuss this or make the appointments with the TSCMs. If there are wiretaps at the office, we don't want whoever planted them to take them away before a professional finds them.'

'It all sounds rather sinister. I can see why you converged on me for the weekend. And you're welcome to stay longer.' Marie went inside the house.

Jayne regarded Steelie as she cut a generous slice of quiche for herself. 'You're having fun, aren't you?'

Steelie threw her arms wide. 'Why wouldn't I? Great company, a comfy room, delicious food. *My* mom's idea of lunch is tuna and potato chips on white. Followed by Jell-O on a bed of Cool Whip. And if you ask her what flavor the Jell-O is—'

'I know: red.'

'Yeah! I mean, that's not a flavor!'

'She's just speaking a different language.'

'You never say that about your mom when she's talking to you about, oh, your choice in clothing.'

'That's not just another language. It's another planet.'

'She loves you just as you are, Jayne.'

'You know she wishes I was a bit more... vah-voom.'

'You're wrong about that.'

Jayne polished off the last of her quiche and looked at Steelie. 'This is why I don't like leaving you two alone together. What part of my life was discussed?'

Marie arrived holding a cake on a stand and a coffee pot. 'Your childhood, darling. And I don't need to seek permission to do that seeing as I was there for it, too.'

She began cutting the cake, which was iced white with a coating of coconut shavings. She put a slice in front of Jayne.

'What's that?' Jayne was poking at a dark line between the two layers of sponge cake. 'Looks like blood.'

'Raspberry jam, as you well know.'

Steelie sniffed her own slice appreciatively.

'Now, this particular cake,' Marie said, 'is ideal for a garden party. Say, when you want to introduce a special someone to your parents.'

'But you already know Steelie.' Jayne almost kept a straight face.

'Layered, this cake could even work for a garden wedding,' Marie mused.

'Good God,' Jayne muttered.

Steelie chimed in. 'You'll have to ask Scott if he minds your maid of honor wearing pants on the big day.'

Jayne glared at her but it didn't land because she was trying so hard not to laugh.

DAY SEVEN

Monday

15

Prickly Pear Close, Phoenix: high noon. The beeping of a digital watch alarm woke Scott and he quickly pressed a button to silence it. He swung his legs over the side of the fully-made bed at the rear of the motor home. His ankle-high boots were already on and he was dressed in combat pants and a T-shirt, so there wasn't much more to do besides a few stretches, preferably avoiding banging his hands against the ceiling. He walked the few paces to the foot of the bed and pulled back the accordion door that separated the bedroom from the main room.

Eric momentarily turned his head from monitoring a video screen. 'Mornin'.'

'Anything happening?'

'Nope. All quiet on the western front. No nosy neighbors either.'

They had parked the motor home on Sunday without any real concern that its arrival would arouse suspicion among nearby residents. Prickly Pear Close was a dead-end street where front yards had been turned into off-street RV parking for extended family who had moved in during economic hard times and never left. Some of the RVs were hoisted up on bricks, curtains closed against the heat as people lived in them full-time. The sunshades on the agents' deceptively aged motor home, however, obscured a powered surveillance station trained on the gold van parked farther down the block.

'Got my breakfast?'

'Your latte's right here.' Eric waved a packet of instant coffee.

Scott turned into the bathroom. It was too small for an adult to close the door and still be comfortable, so he left it open. He and his partner had been on enough long stakeouts to get over privacy issues. But the holding pan had been filling inexorably, as the only thing that broke surveillance is sleep or a bathroom break.

After washing up, Scott emerged feeling like he'd woken up properly but he still decided to make coffee to go with some energy bars.

He sat down next to Eric at the monitoring station. 'Nothing on the audio either?'

Planting the listening device the night before had been a quick operation that hadn't afforded an examination of the van itself because some joyriding teenagers had chosen that moment to park in Prickly Pear Close to smoke marijuana, car windows open, listening to music in the dark. The teenagers had stayed until 4:30AM, by which time the agents had deemed it too close to daylight for them to try for an undetected examination of the van without knowing the movement patterns of the street's inhabitants. They would try again that night.

'Just that same hum,' replied Eric. He turned a dial on the audio receiver next to the video screen. A medium pitch, uninterrupted hum became more audible.

'No fluctuation whatsoever?'

Eric shook his head and turned the volume dial down to its previous position.

'And no sign of anyone? Not even the homeowners on either side?' Scott moved on to a second energy bar.

'No, but it's summer in Phoenix. If they didn't get out first thing in the morning, they know better than to come out now.'

Eric pushed himself up from his seat in front of the monitoring station and made a note in the log they were keeping of their hours in the hot seat. Scott moved into the chair, downing the last of the coffee, his eyes already glued to the screen.

Eric walked to the bedroom but halted before closing the accordion door. 'You made the bed for me. I'm so touched.'

Scott held up his middle finger in Eric's direction.

Eric chuckled. 'Okay, I'm setting my alarm for 1900 hours unless a party starts.'

Scott settled into the seat, preparing for the challenge of maintaining alertness. He was always surprised that it was hard to sustain energy on a stakeout even though, in terms of physical activity, it wasn't all that different to his usual job behind a desk: sit at a screen of some sort all day, get up every now and then. There were fewer phone calls on a stakeout. Maybe that was it. He contemplated calling Jayne. He told himself it would only be to find out if she'd arranged to have the agency checked for bugs.

But he knew he wouldn't call. It was one thing to think while watching the surveillance screen; it was something else to talk with an outsider while on stakeout. Especially with this case. They didn't even have confirmation this was the right van so they were still hunting those body parts. This just got him thinking about Jayne again.

He was comparing how she seemed now compared to

181

when they'd first met at Quantico. Back then, her confident belief that inefficient processes could actually be improved had seemed naïve yet liberating from his vantage point inside a bureaucracy that was trying to fight crime. He'd watched her talk about starting a non-profit so that she could prove her point; he had noticed how her face and body had displayed the last traces of youthful roundedness, as though her figure represented a tightrope between gullibility and mistrust and she was still working out onto which side she would dismount.

Now, she looked like she'd tried both sides and found each problematic, perhaps deciding that it was easier to negotiate the tightrope, arms out to the side, inadvertently keeping people away as she waved and balanced. Scott knew his interpretation was self-serving since he felt on a tightrope himself and he hadn't met anyone else along it, besides Jayne. He'd known for a long time that he wanted to take hold of her but he hadn't known if that was for the sake of her balance or his. That uncertainty had been at the heart of why he'd never tried to move things to the 'next level'.

But being around her again was making him even more aware of the reality of his attraction to her. He had no intention of leaving things to his imagination forever. Ever since she'd backed into him on her stairs Friday night, he'd been thinking about the inward curve of her waist and the outward curves above and below… He shook his head. He'd have to save that train of thought for after the stakeout. There was no way he could watch the screen, listen to the audio feed and think those particular thoughts of Jayne all at the same time.

*

Although Carol had warned Jayne and Steelie that they would need to meet the bug-sweeping technicians from Jeppsen, Inc. outside the agency's four walls, it was still strange to take a meeting in their own parking lot. But Jayne was soon at ease with Lex Jeppsen, a big man in his sixties who introduced himself as the 'brains' while his somewhat younger colleague, Michael Eagen, was the 'hands' of their technical surveillance counter-measures operation. Their clothing reminded Jayne of what she'd have worn on an exhumation. Both men had on cargo pants and tool belts that featured an array of small gear, some electronic, some more recognizable like pliers. Lex also wore a headset around his neck while Michael had on kneepads and was supporting a lightweight, telescoping ladder that was clearly in regular use. Their toolboxes were at their feet.

Jayne liked that Lex complimented Carol on using a phone outside the agency so as not to alert anyone who could be listening in. 'You'd be surprised how many folks don't think that through,' he said and Carol thanked him.

While the technicians handed around their business cards, they asked how the agency had found them. Jayne explained that Agents Houston and Ramos had put Jeppsen on a list of recommended sweeping companies run by ex-FBI tactical ops.

Lex gave his colleague a look. 'A *list*?'

Michael smiled. 'No holiday basket for Scotty this year.'

'Or next,' Lex chuckled.

Amused, Jayne said, 'Do you know Scott from Atlanta?'

'Dallas,' Lex said. 'But we tried to recruit both him and Eric out of Atlanta more than once. We can't offer better pay than the Bureau but they'd get more flexibility, less paperwork. But these young guns, can't tell 'em anything. They're busy saving the world.'

'Eric might just do it, too,' Michael said, jutting his chin toward the transparent bag in Steelie's hand that held the bug from Jayne's apartment. 'Did he dismantle that tap for you?'

'Yes!' Steelie sounded impressed and gave him the bag.

'Recognize his trademark. Likes to kill 'em twice. Where's it from?' He lifted his eyes from the bag and scanned the building behind them.

'My apartment, actually,' Jayne said.

'Okay,' Lex said. 'We'll take it into account along with whatever we find here – if anything. We'll need access to the whole building, the phones and the exterior on all sides. Feel free to accompany us if you wish but we won't discuss anything inside until we know it's clear. Once we start talking about the issue, you can too.'

Jayne led the way into the building and joined Steelie in showing Lex and Michael the different rooms. She felt like they were in capable hands with Jeppsen but when she tried to work on an agency file, she found she couldn't concentrate. She was mostly listening to them taking apart phones and shifting ceiling panels. She ended up going to sit with Carol in reception, only to be joined by Steelie, who looked equally preoccupied.

They watched as Lex finished running a machine a few inches out over the walls and then moved onto another room. At one point, he returned to ask if they had a key to the cage surrounding the generator outside. Jayne gave him the key and listened to him whistle as he went out the back door again.

When the two technicians returned, Michael was holding an object. The women exchanged a worried glance and stood up.

Lex began. 'First question: you have three phone lines here?'

'Yes,' Jayne replied.

'You get any wrong numbers or hang-ups in the past couple of months?'

She shook her head. 'Carol?'

'No.' Carol was pointing at the object. 'I'm sorry, but is that a listening device?'

Michael nodded. 'I should have said. RF transmitter, just like what Eric found at the apartment.'

Lex asked, 'How long you been in this building?'

Jayne waggled her hand. 'About a year.'

Lex looked at his colleague, who shook his head and said, 'Hasn't been there that long.'

Lex said, 'It was on the phone line outside but within the cage for the generator.'

Jayne said, 'We only just got the generator.'

'It could pre-date it but we'll check it out. When we find this type of wiretap at a business, it's usually at corporate headquarters or an office where corporate secrets are discussed.' Lex looked around the modest room, taking in the aloe tree in the corner. 'You're running a charity here?'

The women nodded.

Lex continued: 'You got a competitor? Or have any proprietary methodology – something not patented?'

185

Steelie said, 'Uh, competition's a bit thin on the ground in our line of work.'

He looked around the room again. 'What is it you do here?'

'Forensic profiles of missing persons.'

Michael raised his eyebrows. 'You do anything to piss off the cops?'

Jayne refrained from offering up the possibility that Steelie broke a policeman's arm on Friday night. 'What we do complements law enforcement. And we have contacts with the LAPD. If they want anything, they just ask.'

Michael shrugged and started to pack up his gear. 'Might not be LAPD. Could be any cops anywhere, if I'm correct in assuming your profiles go national.'

'Or since you're dealing with data on missing persons,' Lex said, 'it could be someone who wants to get stuff for identity theft while the owner's AWOL. Whatever it turns out to be, we know your outside line was tapped and whoever did it didn't need to gain entry to put it on. They'll know you've disabled it. Ideally, we'd come back and sweep in a month's time.'

He'd been filling out some boxes on a clipboard. 'Here's the invoice for this location. Payment address at the bottom.' He ripped off a carbon copy and gave Jayne the top sheet before holding up the Ziploc bag with the tap inside. 'Now, about the apartment location. Carol here said that this tap was found on the outside phone line under the stairs?'

'Yes,' Jayne said.

'Alright, well, it's identical to the one we found here, so our opinion is that whatever you're dealing with is related to your work somehow as it's unlikely a Peeping Tom wants to hear your work calls. And it's someone nearby or a person who can get near to you. This little sucker isn't going to be useful for anyone at a great distance. You had the inside of the residence swept?'

Jayne nodded. 'By Eric and Scott. They said it was clear.'

'Then you're good to go. Talk freely here or at home. Can't speak for the rest of the world.' He smiled and passed the Ziploc to Michael. 'One thing you might consider is getting more security for your property.'

Michael added, 'Alarming the building isn't enough when people don't need access to plant a device.'

Steelie huffed. 'I think we're getting that picture.'

He gathered up his equipment and held up the bag with the tap in it. 'You want these or you want us to take 'em?'

'Please take them,' answered Jayne.

As soon as the two men had left the building, Steelie said, 'We're going to have to tell Scott and Eric.'

'That they inadvertently broadcast confidential case information? Absolutely,' Jayne agreed.

'You couldn't have known,' Carol said.

Steelie was matter of fact. 'That doesn't matter. Those two agents are in the middle of a homicide investigation and they passed a victim ID that they'd strategically withheld from the public over an open line.'

*

At eight minutes past seven on Monday night, Eric had resumed watching the surveillance screen in the motor home. Scott was in the bathroom when Eric said, 'Someone's coming to the party.'

Scott emerged quickly, tucking in his shirt. He saw Eric turn up the volume on the audio feed and press *Record* on both the video and audio screens. On the video screen, a tall man dressed in sweatpants was doing something at the back of the van. The audio relayed the sound of a key being inserted into a lock.

'Which house did he come from?' Scott asked quietly.

'Garage of 1501.'

On the screen, the man pulled a thick metal chain from between the rear door handles, opened the doors and jumped in. The doors closed before they could see the interior of the van and then they heard the sound of a padlock being closed.

Eric put on a headset to focus on the audio while Scott tried to monitor both stations. The video screen remained static. They heard someone moving around, another lock being turned and then a hydraulic sound. A voice came through, somewhat muffled. Scott glanced sharply at his partner, brow furrowed. Eric shook his head. He hadn't caught the words either.

The audio feed hummed, then the sound of locks again. On the video, the man emerged from the rear of the van and bent down by the corner of the rear bumper. Scott couldn't see what the man was doing until he twisted to look under the van. Something narrow and dark was dangling down to the ground. It hadn't been visible on the surveillance screen before because the bumper camouflaged it.

'What the hell is that?' asked Scott, pointing at the screen.

'He's not saying anything,' Eric said, his voice slightly raised.

Scott leaned in closer but that didn't help. The man replaced the chain through the van's door handles, locked the padlock and walked back to the garage. He didn't look around and his gait was unhurried. As soon as he was out of the frame, Scott said, 'What'd he say when he was inside?'

'It sounded like "Good for my pincers".'

'Go over that again until you can confirm it.' Scott sounded edgy. He noticed Eric's raised eyebrows and lightened his tone. 'And make it make sense.'

Eric smiled grimly and rewound the audio.

Scott sat down and used another screen to run the video back. He enhanced the image until it was just pixels and then zoomed it back out again, considering and rejecting conclusions as he did so. Suddenly, he pushed away from the counter and swiveled in his seat to look in a file sitting on the shelf behind him. Inside the file were eight sheets of smooth fax paper. Scott flipped the pages over one by one, quickly scanning the top of each sheet. When he got to the final sheet, he swore.

Eric had turned around to look at him and now pulled off his headset. 'What?'

'This fax from Phoenix PD?' Scott waved the sheets in the air. 'It's got pages one through eight of a nine-page document.'

'Shit.'

Scott stood up and tried to pace in the small amount of space available.

Eric asked, 'What do you think was on page nine?'

'How about, "Your gold van's out here and guess what? It's got an electrical extension cord running out its back end and into number 1501"?' He threw the papers onto the monitoring station and took up his seat next to Eric again.

Eric stared at the screen. 'Extension cord. That's probably what it is.' He glanced at Scott. 'About the fax. I should have checked it when I grabbed it on Friday. Lance told me that machine is notorious.'

'Yeah, but I actually read it Saturday and still didn't notice.'

'We could have gone straight for a warrant.'

Scott slapped him on the shoulder. 'Not if page nine only said, "Drive safe, boys". Let's just confirm the extension cord tonight.'

Eric nodded as he rewound the tape. 'I've cleaned up the audio. Take a listen.'

He pushed *Play*. The man's voice came through more clearly this time. Now it sounded loving and triumphant: 'Gold for my princess.'

16

It took Frank Spicer a full minute to get to the front of his house at 1501 Prickly Pear Close. Whoever was pounding on the door didn't stop the entire time, which was aggravating, but he could only move so fast given that he'd been in bed and was slower getting up these days. Slower at everything, in fact. He turned on the porch light, looked through the peephole and was relieved to see people in Phoenix Police Department uniforms given how late it was. He pulled back the deadbolt and the pounding stopped.

When he opened the door, an officer holding up what looked like some kind of federal badge handed him some papers. The front page had *WARRANT* typed across it in letters big enough for Frank to read without his glasses. He did need glasses for the rest of it, so he invited the authorities into the house. After all, he had nothing to hide.

As it turned out, the law enforcement officers did not want to search his house. It had all been a mistake, as Frank was sure it would be. They wanted to search that old van parked near their house, a vehicle that had nothing to do with them. Frank told them that and his wife, Sally, seconded him, now that she'd joined them in the front room.

'That's right, the van isn't ours. We have a Saturn.' She smoothed down her pink terrycloth muumuu. 'It's in the driveway.'

'Ma'am,' one of the agents who'd identified himself as FBI said. 'The van has an extension cord running into your garage.'

'I beg your pardon?' She pulled Frank with her when she crossed to the window. 'Had you noticed that?' She looked at him with wonder.

Frank felt tired. 'No, I sure hadn't.'

Sally tried to explain this. 'We've been out of town for a few weeks. Maybe someone was trying to steal our electricity while we were gone?' She broke off and looked at Frank again.

But Frank could only stare at the four people standing ramrod straight in their living room. They seemed as large and immoveable as statues.

*

Scott regarded Frank Spicer. He didn't fit the image of the man he'd seen climbing into the van earlier this evening. 'Mr. and Mrs. Spicer, does anyone else live here with you?'

'Our son, Wayne.' Sally sounded puzzled.

'We'll need to speak with him to determine if he's the owner of the van. Where can we find him?'

'But it's not his—' she began.

'Let me get him,' Frank interrupted. 'It'll be easier that way. He doesn't like to be disturbed,' he said over his shoulder as he headed for the hallway. One of the police officers followed him.

Scott stood across the room from Sally Spicer. She no longer looked concerned about the unfolding events, only befuddled. She fluffed her short gray hair and then smiled self-consciously at him. He maintained a polite expression.

192

The person who followed Frank into the room was a very good match for the tall man Scott and Eric saw on the surveillance video. He was still wearing dark sweatpants but now had on a white vest. His body hair was long and stuck to his skin in rivulets of sweat, as though he had come from a room without air conditioning.

Scott turned to the newcomer as the two police officers quietly moved to block the doorway. 'Are you Wayne Spicer?'

'Yes.' The man seemed surprised that anyone knew his name.

'Do you own the van sitting in front of this property?'

'Yes. It's mine.'

Scott noticed Sally grip Frank's arm.

'We have a warrant to search your van, sir.'

Eric came to stand next to Scott, holding a second copy of the warrant papers they had had issued.

Wayne's eyes darted between Scott and the window.

'Why? It's not parked illegally. I didn't do anything wrong.' Wayne's voice became louder with every phrase.

'Sit down, sir.' Scott indicated the flowered sofa. 'Here's your copy of the warrant.'

Eric handed the papers to Wayne. Scott expected the large man to resist in some way but he looked like he no longer heard or saw them.

Sally pleaded, 'Wayne?'

He didn't respond.

A police officer remained in the living room with the Spicer family while Scott, Eric and Officer Perez walked outside.

Perez went to her cruiser, which she'd parked to block

the Spicers' driveway, and put her spotlight full beam on the back of the van. Eric brought a camera out of an equipment bag and, using the flash, photographed the entire vehicle. Then he took several detail shots of the padlock securing the rear doors.

Perez arrived with a bolt cutter and Eric photographed her actions as she cut through the padlock and removed the chain from between the door handles. She then carefully opened both doors to their widest position while Eric photographed. Scott flicked on a flashlight and surveyed the scene before him.

The extension cord traveled up from under the bumper and into the van's floor via a rusty hole partially ringed with short pieces of black electrical tape. Scott's eyes followed the cord. It met another, this one white and protruding from the back of a white chest freezer. A gray rubber strap ran like a belt around the front of the freezer and was bolted to the wall with shiny screws that looked new. It was clearly an aftermarket, DIY job to hold something bigger than a stack of TV dinners while on the road. There was barely space for a path between the freezer on the right and an army cot on the left. At the far end of the van, a tarp hung from the ceiling and obscured the front seats.

Eric photographed the van's interior. Perez then climbed in to cut through the padlock securing the freezer's clasp. Eric traded places with her and lifted the lid. He lowered the camera without taking a photograph.

'What is it?' Scott asked.

Eric took three flash photographs in quick succession. 'You gotta see this.'

Scott climbed into the van and shined light into the

194

freezer. There was a dead woman tucked inside. She was resting on her back, held in a crouch with her head against the left wall and her chin tucked down. Dark hair curled about the young face and across shoulders pushed slightly inwards by the front and back walls. Her arms were extended and crossed over her body, which was clothed in a bra and underpants. Her hands lay palms-down over her abdomen. Her appearance was innocent and peaceful, preserved intact by the cold.

Scott locked eyes with Eric. 'We got him. We finally got the bastard. Perez, get us hooked up with a flatbed. We're impounding this vehicle.'

Wayne Spicer remained silent throughout his arrest. He nodded to indicate that he understood his Miranda rights and looked dully at his parents before being led out of the house in handcuffs. Scott glanced at Frank and Sally Spicer as he left their living room. They looked as though they had fallen into the sofa and weren't getting up any time soon. He closed the front door quietly behind him.

Eric stayed with the van. He would maintain continuity of evidence for the transport crew from the medical examiner's office after they arrived to formally confirm death and he would wait for the police tow truck that would take the van away on a flatbed.

Wayne sat in the back of the police cruiser as Officer Perez drove out of Prickly Pear Close and through the quiet streets of Mesa. He looked out of the window, taking shallow breaths and sweating. Sitting next to him, Scott was thinking about how they would be able to use the body in the freezer against the suspect during interview. He couldn't imagine this guy didn't know he was going down.

They would make him cough up the locations of the other women he'd killed and then he and Eric would finally close the cases in Atlanta.

DAY EIGHT

Tuesday

17

While Wayne Spicer was still being processed, Scott and Eric had made a brief stop at their hotel to shower and change and were now en route to get the coroner's preliminary report on the freezer body. Scott was aware he hadn't yet returned Jayne's call from the previous day and vowed to do it that afternoon when he hoped he'd be less wound up from tension. He re-checked his folder for the name of the forensic pathologist at the Maricopa County Medical Examiner's office who had agreed to come in early for them: Dr. Bodell.

When they arrived at the ME's office, a staff member showed them into a viewing room that overlooked the large autopsy suite, explaining that the agents could forgo protective gear by watching from there and using the intercom to communicate with the suite. The observation window was massive and Scott felt as though he was in the same room as the pathologist. He felt surprise to hear her voice come from a speaker in the wall.

'I'm Dr. Bodell.' She was directing her chin up to a microphone hanging from the ceiling above the autopsy table. 'Can you hear me alright?' An autopsy assistant pulled the microphone closer.

The agents nodded.

'I understand you found the body in a freezer,' she stated. 'Any idea how long it had been there?'

When the agents shook their heads, Dr. Bodell continued. 'Well, I'll be able to give you more information when the body's thawed and we can do a full post, but for now I can tell you that your Jane Doe is Caucasian, in her twenties, five-feet-six-inches tall, with a slim build. X-ray shows a COD of broken neck.'

Dr. Bodell paused to give the agents time to take notes. 'I thought you'd like to know that we've got good material for an ID. Take a look at your screen.'

The screen was black at first but then an image appeared, blurry and full of motion. Scott glanced at Dr. Bodell, who was manipulating a pen-sized tube around the body's mouth. The autopsy assistant moved to the nearside of the table and immediately but unwittingly blocked Scott's view. He looked back to the screen and saw teeth as the camera moved around the mouth.

Dr. Bodell's voice came through the speakers again. 'There. You see the filling in the canine?'

He and Eric replied, 'No,' simultaneously but then Scott remembered to activate the intercom and he repeated the reply.

The pathologist's assistant passed her an implement. 'Look at your screen again.'

They watched as a dental pick came into view and traced an oval on the outside surface of the canine.

'See how it's slightly whiter there on the labial surface?'

They could barely discern it and said as much.

The pathologist said wryly, 'A very expensive dentist somewhere would love the answers you two are giving.' Her assistant chuckled and the pathologist continued. 'This is a high-quality synthetic filling. Plus, there's some bonding between the canine and the lateral incisor.' She looked up at the two visitors. 'That kind of work isn't the norm for most of the Jane and John Does we get through here, so if she is in the system, the haystack just got smaller, gentlemen.'

She looked back down at the body. 'I can see why such good work was done on a mouth like this. Look at the teeth, the smile.'

She was now running the camera slowly across the front teeth. Scott mentally agreed that the teeth seemed unusually uniform in size and color.

Dr. Bodell said, 'If you've got the money to preserve a smile like that, you spend it.'

Scott looked from the screen to the pathologist. At that moment, the autopsy assistant stepped to the side, affording him a view of the body again. Scott's eyes automatically went to its mouth, where metal clips now held back the corners of the upper lips. The dead woman appeared to be smiling.

*

Jayne came down the stairs from her mother's guest room and followed the voices to the kitchen. Marie was wrapping sandwiches in wax paper while Steelie sat on the counter.

Steelie looked up at Jayne. 'Your mom wants to help "cleanse" your apartment.'

Jayne gave a slight shudder. 'Thank you. I'd love to paint it, Mom. Make everything feel fresh and new.'

'That's a wonderful idea,' Marie said as she put the wax parcels into a paper bag. She handed this to Jayne. 'Here. For the agency lunch today. The vegetarian's for Steelie,

201

of course, and I want you to ask Carol how she likes my wasabi mayonnaise.'

Jayne suddenly gave her a hug that lasted so long, Marie looked over Jayne's shoulder at Steelie and raised her eyebrows. Then she kissed her daughter on both cheeks. 'Does this mean you'll stay here a few more days?'

Jayne smiled but only said, 'Come on, Steelie; at this rate, Carol's going to get to the office before us.'

As they got into Jayne's truck, Steelie said, 'Did you try to reach Scott again?'

'I did and again it went to voicemail but this time I left a detailed message.'

'How did you phrase it?'

Jayne started the truck. 'I said that Lex and Michael checked the office, found a similar item as at the apartment, and it would have been there when he notified me of the identification of Mrs. Patterson, should he need to take any steps in mitigation.'

'Hm.' Steelie looked out the window as they rolled down the winding driveway. 'You didn't mention that he's not getting a holiday basket from Jeppsen this year?'

'Oddly enough, I did not add that into a message about his multi-state federal homicide investigation.' Jayne exhaled a deep breath. 'I wonder what's going on out there? I mean, did the stakeout turn into a shootout or what?'

Steelie glanced at her. 'It may be Arizona but it's not the Wild West.' But she gauged Jayne's mood and added: 'Look, bad news travels fast, so if you haven't heard anything, then he's fine.'

*

Eric and Scott had been questioning Wayne Spicer for two hours in an interview room at the Phoenix police station. Wayne had waived his right to a lawyer, so Scott had started by asking about the body in the freezer, her rigid smile coming into his mind as he looked at Wayne across the table. The suspect hadn't spoken except to ask for a soda, which he was still nursing, wiping spills from his chin with the inside edge of the shirt he'd been given to wear when the police took his clothes as evidence.

'She was a pretty girl, Spicer.' Scott leaned on his elbows and tilted his head at the man, whose eyes closed against his voice. 'Where'd you meet her? Were you watching her for a long time?'

Wayne's eyelids flew open but he didn't speak.

'What'd you do with the rest of her clothes? You keep those? Hmm, Spicer? You wear 'em?'

Wayne cupped his large hand around the soda can, swigged quickly and wiped his chin.

'Not really your size, her clothes. She was just a tiny thing. What'd you do? Trick her to come with you?'

There was a flicker of a response in Wayne's face, but he still did not speak.

When Eric took over questioning later, he returned the focus to the gold van. 'That really is a nice van you got, Wayne, with the cot in the back. Like going on road trips?'

No response.

'You like going north? Need to get a taste of rain every now and then, eh?' Eric chuckled and put his hands behind his head in a relaxed manner. 'You like Portland? You've been up there, right, Wayne? How about Georgia? Savannah's the real thing, isn't it?'

203

Scott watched from the wall. There wasn't even a flicker in Wayne's eyes as he looked directly at Eric.

Scott spoke without lifting his head. 'When were you going to cut her up?'

Wayne jumped up, sending his chair to the floor. Eric got to his feet, preparing to fend off the big man, but Wayne was stumbling backwards, toward the wall behind him, and pointing his finger at Scott, who was now at the ready across the room.

'I would *never* do that to her!' Wayne's voice cracked. 'She... I...' He faltered, his face suffusing with blood. 'I would never do that.' He righted the metal chair before the agents told him to do it and sat back down, wrapping his hands around the soda can.

Eric glanced back at Scott, who nodded. Eric asked, 'Want another soda?'

Wayne contemplated this for a moment and then nodded mutely.

'Okay, we'll get you a soda.'

The agents called the police officer standing outside to come babysit the suspect. Once Scott closed the door, he stopped in the hallway, ran his hands through his hair and then smoothed it all down again. Eric crossed his arms and leaned against the wall. Police officers and administrative staff passed by but took no notice of them.

'Well, at least you got a reaction,' Eric began.

Scott puffed out his cheeks. 'The dismemberment triggers it.'

'Let's push him on it, then.'

Scott nodded. 'This guy has been under the radar according to NCIC. No criminal record, no voting record, no parking tickets. Where's he been putting the bodies? And why go back and forth between Georgia and Arizona?'

'I'll get the drink.' Eric went down the hallway and returned a few minutes later with a can. They re-entered the interview room and the police officer left.

This time, Scott sat at the table. He waited for Wayne to start the next soda before speaking.

'Let's talk about the cutting.'

Wayne's eyes flashed but he didn't speak.

Scott continued. 'We know you like to cut them up.'

Wayne frowned but remained silent.

'After all, that's what you did with Eleanor Patterson. And the others.'

Wayne only gripped the edge of the table.

'Yep, we found your stuff on the side of the freeway. Thought you could hide Mrs. Patterson by cutting her into pieces, didn't ya?'

Wayne started breathing heavily. He looked first at Scott and then at Eric, who was standing by the door, then back at Scott.

'Well, she's getting her own back,' Scott said. 'Her finger's pointing at you, Spicer. The others will too.'

Wayne wiped sweat from his upper lip.

'Where's the rest of Eleanor Patterson, huh, Spicer? I'm sure her family would like to know. Where'd you put the rest of them? The other girls?'

Wayne looked panicked for a moment but then wiped his face all over. 'Uh… I need a break.'

Scott rolled his eyes toward the ceiling.

'I need a break,' repeated Wayne. 'I need to go to the bathroom.' He tried to smile at Eric. 'Can I get something to eat, too?'

'Okay,' Eric replied.

Wayne looked up at him gratefully.

'Someone will bring you breakfast and take you to use the head.'

The agents left the room and sent in the police officer.

'You rattled him,' Eric said.

'Let's get on to the ME; see if she's got a hit off of those teeth yet. If the woman in Spicer's freezer is from Georgia, this case will have a bow on it.'

But Scott's call to Dr. Bodell was re-routed as soon as he identified himself. She had directed the receptionist to put the agent through to Cliff Lockwood, one of their three medical investigators. Scott had already learned from Dr. Bodell that two of the MIs were former detectives and one was a forensic anthropologist turned investigator. They went to the scenes of all unattended deaths, tracked down identifying material on every Jane and John Doe in Maricopa County and notified next-of-kin for any body processed where the family was not already aware of death.

Cliff Lockwood was one of the former detectives and had been at the ME's office since – according to Dr. Bodell – the year dot. When he came on the line, his voice was as gravelly as that of a life-long smoker.

'Yeah, we got an ID on your girl already.' Lockwood broke off to cough and brought up mucus that Scott could hear being spat out somewhere.

'I'm ready,' he replied impatiently, raising his voice over Lockwood's hacking.

'You've got a Katherine Ruth Alston.' He cleared his throat. 'Date of birth: 9 January of '79. Caucasian. Five-

206

six, 125. Brown and brown. Missing from Los Angeles, California on 5 December of '99.' Scott immediately started calculating. Not missing from Georgia. In fact, her disappearance pre-dated the cases of the missing sex workers in Atlanta. Had she been Spicer's first kill and he'd kept her body as a prize? 'NCIC number?' he asked.

Lockwood rattled off the number.

'Circumstances?'

'You got suspicious missing – suspected abduction. She was an adult whose car was found on a freeway, but no sign of a struggle. She was reported missing by her parents. I'll be making contact today.'

'Which freeway?'

'Says the 101. One more thing, SA Houston. We ID'd her through dental records on NCIC and there's a note that they didn't come direct from a doc. Some shop out your way was involved. An Agency 32/1. You know it?'

Scott's ears pricked up. 'You could say that.'

'What the hell do they do?'

'Forensic profiles of mispers.'

Lockwood let out a low whistle. 'Leave it to you Californians to find a niche market. They been around long?'

'No, but your MEs will have heard of them.'

As soon as Scott was off the call, he picked up a second voicemail from Jayne. Then he turned to Eric, relaying first the Alston identification details and then Jayne's description of the results of Jeppsen's search of the Agency 32/1 offices for bugs. He didn't convey his other thought: he was relieved at how quickly the agency's premises had been cleared. Making Jayne feel safe in her office was the only thing he could think of that could mitigate residual anxiety she'd have after discovering that her home had been bugged. Scott wasn't dedicating time to thinking about who had planted the listening devices or what threat they might pose to Jayne. He would be back soon and planned to protect her himself.

Eric was thoughtful. 'The bug's gotta be about one of their cases.'

'Agreed, but Jayne was flagging up that I gave her the Patterson ID while she was on the agency landline.'

Eric made a dismissive noise. 'It's not like you recited Patterson's social security number. And the ID will be public in a matter of days. Is Jayne worried?'

'Probably.'

'We can take a minute for you to call her now.'

'No.' Scott looked at his partner. 'I want to get in that interview room with our new ammunition against Spicer so we can close this case and get back to LA.'

'Fine. Let's wrap him up.'

18

Eric had resumed his position near the door inside the interview room. Scott sat across the table from Wayne, who appeared to have perked up after eating. His hands were clasped loosely on the table as though he was about to close a business deal and he looked like he was trying to suppress a smile.

Scott opened the thin manila folder he had brought into the room. It held a single typed sheet of paper, the font small and in all capitals, difficult to read upside down. From Wayne's position, it could look like a printout of a police document. From Scott's side of the table, it looked like a printout of turn-by-turn driving directions from his and Eric's hotel to the Maricopa County Medical Examiner's office. Scott looked down at the sheet of paper and spoke.

'We know where you picked her up, Spicer. The girl in your freezer.'

Wayne's smile faltered.

Scott looked at him. 'The 101 a favorite of yours?'

Wayne jerked his arms off the table, putting his hands out of sight.

Scott looked at the sheet of directions again and then stared at Wayne. 'She must have been different from the other ones.' He watched a bead of sweat develop on Wayne's upper lip. 'We figured she was different because you didn't cut her up.'

Wayne suddenly bared clenched teeth and pounded his fist on the table. 'Stop saying that word!'

'But once you had her in the van—'

'It wasn't a van!' Wayne almost yelled. Then he spoke softly. 'It was a car.'

They didn't have a record of him owning a car. Scott remained silent.

Eric spoke quietly from his position by the door. 'Your car, Wayne? You have a car as well as a van?'

Wayne smiled at Eric's gentle tone, and directed his reply to him, ignoring Scott, who was now leaning back in his chair. 'No, I *had* a car. The van's mine but it wasn't always mine.'

'When did you get the van?'

'A little while ago.' Wayne's eyes looked beyond Eric, toward the door. A smile still played on his lips. 'I was going to go away in it.'

'Who sold you the van?'

'I don't know his name.'

'What'd you pay for it?'

'It was a trade. I traded him my car for his van.'

'That's pretty unusual, Wayne. Most people like cash. Sounds like you're making this up. It's always been your van. You've never had a car, never sold a car.'

'I did have a car. I kept it in my parents' garage. And I told you, it was a trade. That nosy hag across the street will tell you. She saw the whole thing.'

Scott tensed. If Wayne had a witness, then this was a different ballgame. He waited impatiently for Eric's next question.

'When?'

'End of last week.'

The answer was vague but Scott's mind was already running with the implications of this. If Wayne Spicer was telling the truth, he was linked to the death of Katherine Alston but wasn't responsible for the body parts they had found on the freeway, so likely had nothing to do with the crimes in Georgia.

Scott's mind raced. The vehicle identification numbers on the dash and door of the van had been mutilated, which meant finding the registered owner would take time because the crime lab would have to dismantle the vehicle to locate the confidential VIN on the van's frame.

So if Wayne was telling the truth, they needed a description of his car and they needed a description of the man now driving it because *that* person was the real owner of the van. Scott glanced at Eric, who nodded and spoke.

'When last week, Wayne? Exactly.'

Wayne's focus came back to Eric but now he looked more petulant. 'Thursday night. He swore it was clean.'

'His name, Wayne. What's his name?'

'He doesn't have a name.'

'What do you mean, he doesn't have a name?'

'I know his screen name.'

Now Eric was pacing around the room. Scott assumed his partner shared his impatience. If this man with no name really existed, he had eluded them again and they were spinning their wheels by interrogating Spicer for so long.

'What are you talking about, Wayne?' Eric sounded tense.

'I met him on offthegrid.net.'

'A website?'

'*The* website. I've been getting tips there for when I go off… with Katie. No one will be able to find us. We'll just be on a road trip all the time. Lots of people are doing it.'

'Okay then, what's his screen name?'

'Tripper.' Wayne sounded like he was boasting. 'You won't find him. He's a Level Three. You never find those guys. They find you.'

'So Tripper's driving your car now, Wayne?'

He nodded.

'Describe the car.'

Wayne put his hands back on the table and looked back at Scott for the first time. He became serious.

'Only if you leave me and Katie alone.'

Scott looked at him. He tapped his pen on the tabletop as if he was considering opening negotiations but he was actually thinking about the fact that a serial killer was still on the highways. They needed to post a nationwide All Points Bulletin for 'Tripper' and the car without delay. He didn't convey this through body language, only shrugging and looking toward Eric to draw Wayne's eyes back there. Eric came over to the table, looking at Wayne curiously. 'Are you trying to bargain, Wayne?'

'Well, yeah. I mean, you need me.' He laughed uncertainly, seeming confused by the new edge in the agent's voice.

Eric rested his palms on the table and brought his face down to Wayne's ear. The angle was tight and Wayne couldn't turn his head to keep eye contact.

'That's where you're wrong,' Eric said directly in his ear. 'If you don't tell us, we're going to track it down in the California DMV archives and your old registration is going to be right there, which will lead us straight to your car. Give it up, Wayne. There is no bargaining.'

Wayne looked back at Scott and then closed his eyes. He started to rock side to side in his chair like a schoolchild who needed the bathroom.

'Look at me, Wayne.' Eric's voice was firm as he stepped away.

Wayne looked but his lips were moving, forming silent words.

Eric said, 'You're not getting out of this.'

Wayne kept rocking and looked at the door. He was smiling and rocking. 'Katie. Katie.'

As Scott watched him, he realized he believed Wayne. Tripper existed and Katherine Alston's body had been Wayne's most cherished possession. In fact, he'd kept it on ice to keep 'Katie' looking alive. Scott knew how to break him down. He leaned back in his chair and spoke.

'They've cut her up, Spicer.'

Wayne stopped murmuring and rocking and squinted hard at Scott.

Scott almost smiled at him. 'You knew that, right?' He kept his voice mild. 'She's not your Katie anymore, Spicer. She's Katherine and they've cut her down her middle.'

'You're lying!' Wayne spat out the words, saliva landing on the table in tiny, bursting bubbles.

Scott shook his head. 'We saw her. Right before we came over here this morning.'

Wayne shook his head, faster and faster.

'You know why they had to cut her up, right?'

Wayne looked at him, his mouth open in wonder.

'Because of you.' Scott shrugged. 'If you hadn't abducted and killed her, that never would have happened.'

213

Wayne shut his eyes tight and sucked in his lips.

'How do you think they worked out who she was? They had to cut her up, check her out. Had to look at her bones – all that pretty flesh was no use. Didja know that, Spicer?' Scott's voice grew louder as he continued. 'She's not your Katie. She's just a girl whose teeth are more important than everything else about her now. They took her teeth right out, Spicer. Cut 'em right out of her head.'

'NO!' Wayne shouted back, thumping the table. 'No!'

Scott stood up and leaned across the table, staring at Wayne's face, which was screwed up tight, tears and sweat mingling on his quivering cheeks. He opened his eyes as though the room was too bright.

Scott caught his gaze and held it, speaking rapidly. 'Her parents are going to pick her up. Ever think about her parents, Spicer? Huh? They're taking her back home. By tonight, you won't even be in the same state as her. Tell us about your car, Spicer. It's just you now. Katie's gone.'

Wayne looked panicked but couldn't tear his eyes away from Scott, who decided that Wayne was hungry for information and redemption. He softened his tone.

'Give us Tripper, Mr. Spicer. Give us Tripper and you're out of here for today. That means you can sit in the holding cell, which is right next to the morgue. Did you know that? You can spend one more night next to Katie. She'll be next door. All wrapped up for her big trip tomorrow.'

Wayne wiped his face with his shirt. He struggled to form one word through his chattering teeth. 'Please.' Once he'd uttered it, he couldn't stop. 'Please. Please. Please.'

*

214

By the time Scott and Eric were back in the hallway, Scott was holding notes of Wayne Spicer's description of Tripper, the alleged original owner of the van with the Georgia license plates. It didn't differ significantly from the descriptions given by the witnesses in LA.

They'd also obtained a description of Wayne's car and dispatched Phoenix Police Department uniformed officers to Prickly Pear Close to conduct interviews that could confirm or refute Wayne's story about his trade with Tripper. Their next job was to interview Wayne Spicer to get the details of his abduction of Katherine Alston from the Hollywood Freeway in 1999.

They started down the hallway, swerving around police officers making their way between ends of the building. Scott recognized the two rookies who'd initially been sent to watch the gold van on Prickly Pear Close. Mays and Green, he remembered. Both officers had appeared almost too young to be in employment. Neither had addressed the agents with any deference when they'd first met and that hadn't changed; Officer Mays was chewing gum that was visible when he hailed them.

'We're just finishing the report on the Spicer garage search. Do you want a verbal?'

'Yeah,' Scott replied. 'What'd you find?'

'Nothing.'

'What do you mean by "nothing"?'

'The guy's a computer freak. He doesn't own anything besides a huge chest freezer – totally clean – a fast computer and some clothes. And, oh yeah, we *deduced* that he's still into Halloween.'

He shared a laugh with his buddy.

Scott shifted on his feet. 'What are you talking about?'

Officer Green took over, gesturing with his hands. 'He's got this closet, right? Everything's all neatly folded: sweat suits, pants, shirts. Except for this one Halloween costume hanging up. What a joke.'

Scott's tone was flat. He was tired of having to extract each piece of information with a question. 'What kind of costume?'

'Police uniform.' Mays snapped his gum loudly. 'Pretty shitty imitation of an LAPD kit.'

Scott went cold.

Eric grabbed Mays' upper arms. 'Listen to me, was there a badge?'

The gum fell out of the officer's mouth in his surprise at being manhandled. He turned his head away as Eric's face came frighteningly close to his.

'*Was there a badge?*'

Scott pulled down on Eric's arms. He dropped them to his sides but kept glaring.

The rookie looked like he wanted to get away from both agents. He directed his response to Eric.

'No, man. No badge.'

*

Steelie answered her cell phone and was surprised to hear Eric launching into questions without so much as a greeting – and they weren't questions about the wiretap at the agency.

'I need to know if you ever got a summons after driving away from that cop.'

'No.'

216

'What did he look like?'

'I mostly remember his swagger—'

'Could you tell his ethnicity?'

'I'm pretty sure he was white. Light-colored moustache. Couldn't really see his face because of his glasses and the hat.'

'What about build?'

'Regular. Maybe slim.'

She heard him speaking off-mic. 'He wasn't heavyset, Scott. No way it's him.'

'What's going on, Eric?' she asked. 'Are you guys still in Arizona?'

His voice came back to her. 'We are, and a perp we've pulled in had a replica of an LAPD uniform. It made us think of what happened to you because this guy might have used it to get people into his car.'

'Shit!'

'But our guy doesn't match your description. Hold on; Houston wants you.'

After a brief moment, she heard Scott's voice. 'Steelie, we caught a Thirty-Two One case out here. Wanted you to have a heads up.'

After Steelie hung up, she sat trying to recall the cop – she'd convinced herself it had been a cop, not an imposter – who'd stopped her, when Carol's voice came through the intercom to say that she had Ben Alston holding on line one for either Steelie or Jayne. Line one's blinking red light went solid before Steelie could pick it up, so she trotted up to Jayne's office.

Jayne was clearly being told a string of facts because she was only murmuring, 'I understand,' or 'Okay.' Steelie read

Jayne's notes from upside down.

Call fr MI in Maricopa. Kate ID'd. COD broken neck.
No sexual assault. Liaise tomorrow—

Then Jayne said, 'Alright. Did the medical investigator tell you which medical examiner you'd be dealing with? Bodell? You'd be fine with her, she has a very comfortable manner... No? Of course, if you would like us to liaise, we will... Okay, Ben, thank you, that's very generous. We'll hear from you shortly then.'

Carol came into the room as Jayne hung up. 'Has something happened? I could hear it in his voice when I answered the phone.'

Jayne shook her head in consternation. 'He was completely worked up. Kate's been found dead but he can't understand why he got a phone call from a medical investigator in Phoenix. The police told the Alstons in '99 that there were no signs of a struggle in or around Kate's car when it was found on the Hollywood Freeway, so they're trying to figure out why she would have willingly gotten out of her car and gone with someone to Arizona.'

Steelie raked her hair back from her forehead. 'I think I know why.' She thought for a second then let her bangs flip back. 'I just had a call from Eric, asking me about my taillight stop last Thursday. He said they've picked up a suspect in Arizona who might be using a replica of an LAPD uniform. And then Scott told me that they've come across one of our cases out there. I'm betting it's Kate Alston and the uniform is related.'

Jayne pointed at her notes. 'Well, the Alstons are hell bent on finding out what happened. They're flying to Phoenix in the morning and asked if we could liaise when they go to the ME's office. They're picking up our flights too.'

Steelie said, 'If Scott and Eric's case does involve Kate, then someone may be able to tell her parents what happened.'

Jayne looked at Carol. 'You're the expert on this.'

Carol spoke without hesitation. 'The family needs to know. Give them the hard stuff and they *will* handle it.'

'But the detail about the uniform will be sub judice, so we can't tell the family about it but we can... what? Urge Scott and Eric to divulge it?'

Carol nodded. 'Yes, to help the Alstons deal with this. I haven't met Eric yet but I think Scott will understand that intuitively.'

'Okay.' Jayne looked at Steelie. 'Call them back. Tell them that we don't need confirmation on whose body they've found, but if it's Kate Alston's and if the suspect has actually stated that he used a uniform to get her out of her car, then they should give the parents as much consideration as they can. This has to come from them.'

'Works for me,' Steelie replied and headed back to her office.

*

As soon as Scott and Eric issued the All Points Bulletin for Wayne Spicer's car, they went down to the holding cells of the Phoenix Police Department.

When they identified themselves to the duty sergeant, he buzzed them into the small room beyond his station. The room had four cells coming off it like satellites and they could see Wayne through the bars of his cell to their left.

He was stroking the yellow-painted wall in the direction he believed the morgue lay, with Katie's body within.

Scott and Eric had already agreed to take a tender approach with Wayne, going down his Memory Lane while trying to get him to separate fantasy from reality.

Scott set a tape to record and re-cautioned him then Eric began with an admiring comment on the accuracy of the police uniform found in Wayne's closet. Wayne took the bait and was off, his words like a current of water rushing along a country brook.

He said he came up with the idea of getting a false police uniform after several people mistook his car, a black Crown Victoria, for a police cruiser and pulled over to let him overtake when traffic was badly backed up on the busy Los Angeles freeways.

After his parents moved to Arizona, Wayne stayed in LA, bought the patrolman's uniform from a costume shop and added a few details. When he wore it, some people waved at him, the kind of people who never gave him the time of day.

Then he purchased a swirling red light and rigged it up into his car's electrical system with wire and a control switch, using rudimentary electronics skills he'd gained while working at Radio Shack. But he'd never used the light, or even tried to stop and talk to anyone, until he saw the brown Datsun ahead of him on the 101 Freeway early in December 1999, its hazard lights flashing a distress signal.

He was wearing the police uniform that evening. He had the false badge on the seat next to him. At the last minute, he decided to pull over and see if someone would actually talk to him. He didn't care if it was a man or a woman, as long as it wasn't more than one person. He had thought that more than one person could be dangerous because 'you never know what sort of people there are out there'.

He pulled onto the shoulder, cutting off other cars, whose drivers glared at him through his rearview mirror, their faces softening when he turned on the swirling red light.

The young woman in the Datsun was beautiful. She smiled and rolled down her window when he walked up. She barely glanced at his badge and so he had put it in his pocket. He asked her, 'What's the problem, ma'am?' just like he'd seen police do on television. She explained that the car had broken down and she had been hoping a tow truck or a police officer would come along because she didn't have a car phone or a cell phone. She didn't give him the pitying expression he was used to seeing at his job or when he tried to talk to people waiting in line at the supermarket.

He wanted to talk with her more. He asked her to 'step into' his vehicle, on the passenger side, so that she'd be safe from the traffic hurtling past. But once she was inside, she looked uncertain. He forgot the 'cop routine' and she began to look panicked. She tried to get out of his car but the door handle on the passenger side had been broken since he'd bought the Crown Vic. She didn't know that so she had started screaming and kicking her legs and trying to get the attention of passing cars. He wanted to let her out. When he leaned across her, it was only to roll down the window so he could open the door from the outside handle. But she didn't know that either. She tried to climb past him, into the backseat.

She managed to put her thumbs into his eyes and, well, he couldn't see then, could he? He fell against her and

221

the weight of his body pulled them both down onto the front bench seat, his feet slipping on the loose floor mats and her small body half under him. He couldn't get any purchase with his hands so he wrenched his elbow up and it connected with some part of her. She was instantly still and quiet.

He didn't even know what had happened to her. He tapped her cheek; her head lolled loosely. He tried to make her speak; she wouldn't talk anymore. The police badge was digging into his thigh and he pushed himself up. He turned off the swirling red light. Looking at her, he knew he couldn't leave her there on the freeway by herself. He opened her handbag and found her driver's license. Next to the photo it said her name was Katherine. He looked over at her, the dark hair, her smooth skin. He knew she was a Katie. A car honked as it passed and its headlights caught his peripheral vision. In that flash, he knew she would be his Katie. But they would have to leave California. 'She's been the only one. She'll always be the only one.'

At that point, Wayne turned in the direction of the morgue and refused to say more. The agents left Wayne Spicer in his cell, his big body pressed against the wall in a flat embrace.

As they emerged from the police station, Scott checked his cell phone and saw he had two voicemail messages. He listened to them as he followed Eric over to the Suburban. The first one was from Steelie and didn't require a return call. The second was from Cliff Lockwood, the Maricopa County medical investigator. He had asked Scott to return his call as a matter of urgency, even if it was after-hours, and had left his home phone number.

222

Lockwood sounded somewhat less gravelly now that it was evening. Scott suspected a liqueur had lubricated his throat.

'I've got the parents of your girl flying out here from California tomorrow. They got a lot of questions I can't answer yet. But I figured maybe you could. Can you make it over here at 1100 hours?'

Scott thought for a moment and glanced at his partner, who was now driving them to their hotel where they would stay the night, due to get on the road for Los Angeles at seven o'clock the next morning. If he stayed to meet the Alstons, Eric would need to go ahead of him to coordinate the search for Tripper, an endeavor that would be headquartered in their office in LA.

Scott stalled for time with Lockwood by asking a question he already knew the answer to, thanks to Steelie's message. 'What kind of questions are we talking about?'

Lockwood sighed. 'Seems they want to know how their daughter ended up out here in AZ in the hands of some perp. I'll be telling them about the freezer before they view the body but that's about the extent of my knowledge as of tonight.'

Scott didn't want to be the one to explain what had happened and briefly considered just instructing Lockwood to tell the Alstons about the LAPD uniform replica. He could hear a television sitcom and canned laughter in the background on Lockwood's end of the phone. Scott realized he wasn't even sure about the MI's bedside manner, and besides, it was his duty, not Lockwood's.

'I'll be there.'

DAY NINE

Wednesday

19

Southwest Airlines Flight 597 from Phoenix to Los Angeles had arrived on time and Eric was walking into his office on Wilshire Boulevard by mid-morning. The first call he made was to the IT investigators on the third floor to get an update on the request the agents had phoned in from Phoenix to have the investigators monitor offthegrid. net for activity by the screen name 'Tripper'. They reported no activity yet, but they were pulling caches of old posts by that screen name. So, no leads on Tripper's identity.

Eric glanced behind him at the computer that was dedicated to NCIC traffic. He was waiting for a beep on it that would indicate a hit. There was no guarantee it would be a hit on their All Points Bulletin for Wayne's car because the system would beep for any report filed by the Los Angeles office on any case since the database had been in use.

But he was still waiting for that beep.

The phone rang and he picked up. It was the Phoenix crime laboratory. They had a preliminary report on the examination of Wayne Spicer's/Tripper's van: numerous particles of biological trace evidence had been located inside. Although the van's interior appeared to have been cleaned thoroughly, the criminalists had collected traces of blood, saliva and epithelial cells from its faults, joins and other surfaces. It was too early for the lab to tell if all

227

the biological material came from a single source or from multiple sources, or whether any of it could ultimately link Tripper to the vehicle. They told Eric they would need reference material from people known to be in the van – for example, the man behind the screen name.

Eric looked back at the computer. Nothing.

*

Scott's first thought when Cliff Lockwood opened his office door was that he could have been Kris Kristofferson's double. His barrel-like chest blocked the doorway for a moment before he invited Scott in, indicating a seat to the left that was turned to face two people who were rising from their chairs.

The room wasn't large and, with everyone standing up, Scott felt like he had walked into a closet that was already too full. But it opened up the moment Lockwood sat down behind his desk. He introduced Ben and Linda Alston, describing Scott as the law enforcement officer who had found their daughter.

Linda Alston had brown hair caught in a loose bun. Her eyes were a clear blue and she was looking at Scott with undisguised relief. Ben Alston had a close-cropped brown beard. He extended his hand to Scott and then folded his other hand over the handshake. Neither man spoke. Linda smiled at Scott but didn't shake his hand. She was holding a sizeable piece of cardboard to her chest.

'Please take a seat, Mr. and Mrs. Alston,' Lockwood began. 'Special Agent Houston is here to answer any questions for you that he can. As I mentioned before, he may be limited by the needs of the ongoing investigation into your daughter's case but those limits will be lifted as soon as possible.'

Ben and Linda nodded.

Linda turned to Scott, still holding the cardboard tight. 'We wanted, first of all, to thank you for finding Kate.'

Scott nodded gravely.

She continued with more difficulty. 'We've seen her now and—' She broke off, her mouth twisting, and her husband put his long arms about her shoulders. She drew herself up. 'And we wanted you to know what a beautiful girl she really was.'

She turned the piece of cardboard around and Scott was looking at a large portrait of a smiling version of the woman he'd found in Wayne Spicer's freezer. He felt as though the color ink had flowed through her like blood, bringing her to life. And then he took in her smile. He would recognize those teeth anywhere.

Ben was saying, 'Kate was very bright. A bright, beautiful... good girl.'

Lockwood said, 'All of that is very clear to us, Mr. Alston. I hope you understand that.'

Linda had more to say. 'Mr. Houston, how did she end up out here?'

Scott knew from Steelie's phone message that if he said nothing else to the Alstons, he had to answer this question. He had been going over it with Eric the night before at the hotel, each of them fatigued beyond words, yet trying to put the known facts into more palatable terms, and failing. Eric had finally said, 'It won't be the words you use, it'll be the way you say them.'

Scott glanced at Lockwood, who was looking back at

229

him while reclined in his chair, his mouth obscured by his fingers, which were interlocked in a steeple. Scott was aware that he was about to tell the Alstons a story that was censored by his law enforcement training, one that protected the future prosecution of Wayne Spicer but was informed by his own sense of what the Alstons' image should be of their daughter's last moments. He tried to soften the edge of every word.

'Mrs. Alston, the person who abducted your daughter was wearing a replica of a police officer's uniform when he approached her sitting in her broken-down car on the shoulder of the Hollywood Freeway. It was by showing her what looked like a real police badge that he was able to get her to leave her own vehicle. He's kept her body with him since that time.'

Scott realized with a pang that although Ben Alston had remained motionless, tears were streaming down his face. He didn't wipe them away but kept one hand gripped around his wife's shoulder and the other on her arm.

Linda Alston smiled, her eyes bright. 'Kate always minded people in authority.' She patted Ben's knee as she wiped her eyes quickly with a tissue she pulled from under her watchstrap. 'She did what I would have done.' Her voice caught on the last word and her hand flew to her mouth, the tissue only half covering the pain hidden behind it. A muffled, 'Oh, God,' escaped and she collapsed against her husband, who tilted his face down into her hair. The photo of Kate smiled back at them from where it lay in Linda's lap.

Scott felt as though the Alstons were radiating a sorrow so raw that it was palpable. He found himself swallowing several times and looked back at Lockwood, who nodded at him slowly. Scott realized he'd just passed some kind of test and knew he'd underestimated Cliff Lockwood. He needed to go. He returned Lockwood's nod and left, not stopping until he was out the front doors. He was immediately assaulted by midday heat and a blare of nearby ambulance sirens. The morgue was next to the hospital, not the police station and its yellow holding cells. He had lied to Wayne Spicer on that point.

*

Dr. Bodell interrupted the story she was telling Jayne and Steelie to introduce two colleagues who were emerging from the autopsy suite at the Maricopa County ME's office. One of the men said, 'I understand you had a role in this freezer case?' He nodded back to the suite, where a technician was rolling Kate Alston's bagged body on a trolley back to the refrigerated storage room, now that her parents had finished their viewing.

Jayne replied, 'It looks like the full dental profile we managed to get added to the misper file helped with the ID.'

Steelie gestured at Dr. Bodell. 'If it wasn't for the dental worksheet Liz made for us last year, we wouldn't have known how to code half the synthetic restorations for NCIC.'

Dr. Bodell turned to her colleague. 'They're too modest.'

He smiled faintly, assessing Steelie. 'Well, it's good to meet you.' He looked at Dr. Bodell. 'Lunch, Elizabeth?'

She nodded and said, 'I'll catch up with you, Alan.' She motioned for Steelie and Jayne to head for the rear exit doors.

When the three of them reached the bay where two body recovery vans were parked, Steelie leaned into Dr. Bodell and whispered, 'Is there something we should know, *Elizabeth*?'

Dr. Bodell smiled but ushered her on. 'Go on around front. Your clients will be needing you. Jayne, come back to visit again soon. You needn't bring Steelie and her innuendos.'

As they rounded the building, Steelie said, 'That makes me sound like I'm part of a band. "Steelie and the Innuendos". But what would we play?'

Jayne smirked. 'Something heavy-handed.'

Steelie pointed at her. 'I set that basket up for you. I want you to remember that.'

They took up a position under the mesquite trees casting dappled shade at the front of the building. Their reflections were visible in the tinted double doors that led into this side of the structure, where relatives of the dead came and went. The reflection now showed someone emerging from a car behind them and then a voice called out their names. They turned around to see Scott next to a Suburban one row back in the parking lot.

Going toward him, Jayne said, 'Scott? What are you doing here?'

His mouth was a grim line. 'The Alston case.' He looked at Steelie. 'I got your message. I've spoken with them.'

'Thank you,' Steelie said.

'I didn't do anything.' His tone was sharp. He wiped a hand over his face. 'Sorry. Are you escorting them?'

Jayne nodded. 'Liaising.'

'Good. Well, I've got to get on the road. Eric's already

in LA.' He gave them a lopsided smile. 'It's nice to see you.'

When he turned away, Steelie nudged Jayne toward him while calling out, 'Um, Scott? Do you mind taking Jayne with you?'

He turned back and looked at Jayne. 'No. Why?'

'Because I...?' Jayne looked questioningly at Steelie.

'Because of the turbulence,' Steelie said. 'It was a bad flight out and you said you'd prefer to drive back if you could, remember?' She turned to Scott. 'She was ready to get a rental car, so this would be perfect.'

Scott appeared to accept the explanation and went to move something from the passenger seat of his vehicle.

Steelie murmured to Jayne, 'He needs back-up, Jayne, if only to keep awake. I'll stay with Ben and Linda.'

Jayne nodded and Steelie gave her a quick hug in parting.

*

It took six hours for the weight of the meeting with the Alstons to metastasize in Scott's consciousness, and then it hit him hard.

It happened in stages. The first stage made him feel like he couldn't breathe. As he gulped air, he hyperventilated. That was the second stage. The third stage made him think he was having a heart attack. His hands tingled where they gripped the steering wheel and his chest was tight. It felt like there was a direct electrical current between his heart and his hands.

He veered from the right lane onto the shoulder, the car's tires spraying loose gravel before he steered into the upcoming exit lane, and that was when he became aware of Jayne calling out his name. He automatically read the exit sign as he passed under it: *Calimesa*. Scott had never heard of it and didn't care. His eyes were watering and he needed to stop the car.

Partway down the exit lane, he pulled over to the shoulder and put the transmission into park. He didn't turn off the engine because he felt like his breathing was getting easier, even though it was made up of deep breaths that he couldn't control. Jayne was gripping the dash and he sensed that she was staring at him, but he was calming slightly, sure now that he wasn't having a heart attack. He closed his eyes in relief and that was when he saw her: Kate Alston. Preserved in the cold stillness of the freezer. Smiling at him from the autopsy table. Living in her parents' photograph. Her parents. Their devastation.

The sob was dry but shocked him into opening his eyes. He slammed the palms of his hands against the steering wheel and then gripped it tightly. He squeezed his eyes shut and the same physical sensations instantly tore through him, followed by an image of Kate Alston's teeth, disembodied, ruthlessly exposed. He didn't realize Jayne had opened a door until hot desert air filled the cabin with the scent of creosote. He tried to see what was going on and recognized Jayne's familiar wavy hair just in front of him as she reached under his arms to turn off the engine. But he couldn't speak.

'Come on,' she said. 'You need to get out of there.'

He felt like her voice was coming from a great distance away. She reached around him and undid his seatbelt, then pulled his hands from their hold on the steering wheel.

'It's alright, Scott. Come on.'

20

Tripper cruised the streets in one of his favorite Atlanta neighborhoods, savoring the familiarity of both the dark stretches and the residential blocks where elderly owners lived in the back at night, the volume on their televisions cranked up because Medicare still didn't cover hearing aids. He'd taken risks in Los Angeles, especially with the surveillance gear. Even though he'd got the answers he needed to allow him to move freely again, it had still involved risks. He'd mitigated them somewhat by retrieving the repeater from outside the brunette's apartment so that, if anyone ever found the wiretaps, they'd assume a Peeping Tom, not someone at a distance, had put them there.

Tripper considered the white hatchback he'd been following and looked at the street they were on. The only building on the block was an office complex under construction. Its windowless bulk was dark, the workers long since home for the night. It was time to get started. He needed new dump material. He turned on the red light on the dashboard and the hatchback dutifully pulled over ahead of him.

As Tripper walked up to the car, he missed his old method using the van. But the van had to go and this new method had potential. He leaned down to the driver's open window.

'License and registration, ma'am.'

The driver handed the two items to him without speaking.

Tripper stood up and perused them. Her name was Pamela Winton. Nice. He leaned back down.

'You sure were in a hurry back there, Mrs. Winton.'

'It's *Ms*. Winton.'

Even better.

'Step out of the vehicle, ma'am. I require you to complete a sobriety test.'

She sighed and got out of the car. Tripper smiled to himself. The new method had passed its test. *Ms*. Winton, on the other hand, had just failed hers. He watched her move to the sidewalk, which was disappearing under sand and gravel seeping out from the adjacent construction site.

He directed her in a friendly tone: 'Put your hands out to either side of your body at shoulder height and walk toward me, one foot in front of the other, with your eyes shut.'

As soon as the woman closed her eyes, Tripper moved behind her, clamping an arm around her body and a hand over her mouth. She raised both hands and tried to pull his hand off her face. He wrenched her to the side so forcefully that her feet left the ground for a moment. But when she came down again, she stamped hard on his right instep. It was pretty painful and he inadvertently relaxed his grip enough for her to get the purchase she needed to pull one of his hands down. She bit the soft skin between his thumb and first finger and that really was painful.

Now he was holding her with only one hand and she repeatedly jabbed her left elbow behind her in gawky, unplanned movements. He was aware that while the method he'd used had got the mark out of her car, it didn't get her *into* his car. It was always easier, and safer,

236

when they got in themselves instead of him fighting them first. He moved in to control her but this allowed a jab that ordinarily would've only bruised him to hit his solar plexus and he keeled forward uncontrollably, struggling to breathe. Then the woman seized him by the hair and pulled downwards. As Tripper's face thudded against her right knee, he was reminded of how little fat covers a patella once the leg is bent.

*

Pamela Winton whimpered as she stared down at the police officer. He was lying on the sandy pavement, face down and silent. Then he groaned. She cried out and leapt away. As she trembled in the beam of his patrol car's headlights, she watched him slowly pull himself to lie on his side, but then he collapsed onto his back. Blood flowed freely from his nose and across his face, only pausing at his earlobes to pool before the overflow dripped onto the gritty pavement.

Pamela Winton clutched her shirt about herself, now unable to stop her body shaking. She knew no one would believe that a policeman had attacked her unless she had some proof of her own. She looked up and down the street. It was deserted; not a single car or person was visible in the weak glow from the streetlights. She peered at the policeman. He was breathing but his eyes were closed. His badge reflected the swirling light from the dashboard of his vehicle. Pamela Winton took a deep breath and then lunged at him, screaming in fear as she ripped his badge off along with most of the shirt pocket. She continued to scream even as she sped away in her hatchback. Her distress trailed out her open window only to be trapped by the car's slipstream and stay with her.

21

If security guard Troy Purcell had rounded the corner a minute earlier, he might have heard Pamela Winton's tires leaving a rubber deposit as she cornered at the end of the street. But his scheduled perimeter check of the construction site was all out of whack that night, on account of someone throwing eggs at his car while he was inside the security trailer. He knew from experience that egg had to be washed off immediately, preferably with a clear soda. So he'd had to find his boss's stash of Diet Slice, clean the car and then make a careful note to replace the soda as soon as his shift ended at 6AM.

When Troy saw the prone body by gate five, he knew someone was having a worse night than he was. But he was filled with dread when he saw the swirling light making patterns on the dirty rear window of what had to be a police cruiser parked ahead with its headlights on. He pulled into the curb and looked to see if the cops were nearby, perhaps chasing down another bad guy. No one. He walked over to the body.

A man. Bloodied but breathing. Wearing a dark uniform with a hole where the left chest pocket should have been. Troy's adrenaline spiked. *A wounded officer!*

He whirled around in fear while simultaneously unclipping his baton and phone, finger already on speed-dial, only to bring the baton to his ear and thrust the phone out like a weapon. The dispatcher's voice was swallowed by the night air: '911, what is your emergency? Hello?'

The officer on the ground murmured something and attempted to sit up. But Troy was *not* going to have that on his head. The second he was done telling dispatch to raise the alarm at police HQ and send him an ambulance, he held the officer down in the recovery position and reassured him that paramedics and his brother officers were on their way. In the meantime, he, Troy Purcell of Premium Security Corp., would personally ensure his safety. When sirens were audible, the officer stopped trying to get up and Troy believed he'd lost consciousness.

*

Eric was frustrated. The evening was closing in and he hadn't had a single call about Wayne Spicer's vehicle. He had been hoping some fresh patrol officer somewhere would be enthusiastically monitoring APBs and then miraculously arrest Tripper during a routine traffic stop. Eric was just getting up from his desk to get a cup of coffee when his supervisor, Craig Turner, walked into the room, holding a single sheet of paper.

Eric had only been working under Supervisory Special Agent Turner for a short time but they had met at Quantico, where the Bureau veteran regularly ran seminars or flew in to do special trainings. So Eric knew that it was normal for the wrinkles on SSA Turner's forehead to be reaching up into his receding hairline. What wasn't normal was the resigned way Turner indicated that Eric sit back down.

'Where's your partner, SA Ramos?'

'En route from Phoenix, sir.'

Turner perched his lean body on the edge of the desk and fixed him with the unblinking stare that had earned him the nickname of 'Ice' among Quantico newbies – a devolution from 'IC' after Turner's original nickname: 'Iron Curtain'.

'Fine. Bring me up to speed on the freeway body parts case. In fact, take it from the top.'

Eric marshaled his thoughts and recounted the essentials of the investigation up to the discovery of the frozen body of a woman inside the suspect van.

Turner consulted his paper. 'This is Katherine Alston, missing from LA.'

'Yes, sir. On interview, the suspect confessed to the manslaughter of Alston in 1999 and stated that he has kept her body in a freezer on his premises, first in California and then Arizona. He was preparing to go mobile with her body in the van, which he had recently acquired from another individual. That individual is who we like for the body parts on the freeway.'

'Do you have a name for that suspect?'

'We have an alias. Tripper.'

'That's all?'

'No, sir. We've got a physical description: White, between forty and fifty, blond and blue, approximately six-four, clean-shaven—'

'Has that description supported or refuted your theory that this Tripper was driving the van when it was hit on the freeway here?'

Eric paused. Turner's use of the word 'theory' was setting off alarm bells. 'It backs up the description given by two witnesses who had contact with the driver of the

240

van after it was hit.'

'No variation?'

'Yes, but only in the areas that can be easily disguised.'

'Hair color, eye color?'

'We've got a match on hair color. It's the facial hair that varies.'

'So you're good on race, age, height and eye color.'

'We don't have corroboration on eye color because he's sometimes been seen only in sunglasses.'

Turned nodded and consulted his sheet again. 'In your last memo you indicated that there was a hold-up on ID'ing the previous owner of the van you located in Arizona because the VIN was mutilated?'

'That's correct, sir.'

'And what'd the crime lab out there tell you on estimated time to get to the frame VIN?'

Eric spread his hands out. 'I'm just waiting for the phone to ring.'

Turner fixed him with the stare again. 'So, in sum, you have no leads on this suspect's name.'

Eric looked at Scott's empty chair, wishing he was there to take a turn on defense. He was running out of plays. Worse, Turner wasn't wrong. 'Not yet, but I've got the IT guys working on getting the name of whoever registered the alias Tripper on the internet.'

'Okay, so tell me this: if you have no sense of who this guy is, why have you activated a BOLO to all the local PDs in the state of Georgia, stating the make, model and VIN of the vehicle you believe he just *might* be driving?'

Eric opened his mouth and then shut it quickly. He felt like he was on day one at Quantico, sitting in the front of the class, and Turner had asked him a question that not only was he unable to answer but he'd also clearly missed the summer reading.

He tried to make sense of this. He hadn't issued a BOLO to Georgia law enforcement and, as far as he knew, Scott hadn't either. If Scott *had* issued a BOLO but *not* told Eric, that would raise Turner's eyebrows. More to the point, if there was a special BOLO for Georgia police, how had Turner heard about it over here in LA?

Eric decided to hedge his bets. 'No matter who's driving that vehicle, we need to locate it ASAP. It's part of an ongoing criminal investigation into the death of Katherine Alston.'

He could tell that Turner knew he'd sidestepped the question and was deeply relieved when his supervisor just responded with a slow nod. But when Turner loosened his tie, his bony fingers working themselves into the knot, Eric knew he wasn't off the hook.

'I had a feeling you were going to say something like that, because I just got off the horn with SSA Franks. He wasn't happy.'

Eric thought, *I was posted under Franks for three years and the man was never happy*, but held his tongue.

'And now I'm not happy because this is the second call I've had to field from him since you and Houston got posted out here.'

'Sir—'

'Are you familiar with these allegations, Eric?' Turner snapped his sheet of paper straight. 'An anonymous complaint was lodged direct with SSA Franks regarding the conduct of SA Houston during the investigation into missing sex workers in Atlanta. The complainant alleged that Houston was "friendly" with sex workers who were part of the investigation, during Bureau hours and in a Bureau vehicle.'

'This is just SSA Franks—'

Turner cut him off with a look. 'No. SSA Franks protected Houston by not referring this to the OPR.'

Eric inwardly winced at the reference to the FBI's Office of Professional Responsibility. The image of those internal affairs agents competed with his thoughts on who the complainant could have been.

Turner continued. 'SSA Franks explained that he took an interest in you and Houston and gained evidence of your partner giving sex workers rides in his Bureau vehicle, which, as you know, is in itself against regulations. He purchased food and drink for them. He fraternized with them alone and after hours. SSA Franks pointed out that for all the attention SA Houston was giving these "streetwalkers", it was ironic that two of them later went missing.'

Eric shook his head in disbelief but had learned not to interrupt his supervisor.

'Now, in SSA Franks' estimation, the reason you two never cleared that case was because you developed the erroneous theory that there was a lone abductor who was the lone serial killer. At the time you were transferred out here, he described you both as "obsessed".

'I told him it was my practice to give experienced agents their reins. But as soon as your BOLO on this vehicle came across his radar, he called me to find out what you're working on. I only gave him an outline but it was enough for him to inform me in no uncertain terms that you and Houston are pursuing a dead-end theory that will now leave my office with a case that can't be cleared, taking valuable resources and man-hours. He advised me to take control of this case ASAP.'

Turner rubbed his fingers hard over the faint stubble on his chin, jutting his lower jaw out as if to stretch it. 'Now, I'm capable of drawing my own conclusions about you and Houston but I do have one more item that needs clearing up.'

Eric braced himself.

'What in Sam Hell did you think you were doing when you allowed two civilians into the crime scene at the freeway?'

*

Jayne recognized the symptoms. While she had accidentally fallen asleep like a baby in the passenger seat, Scott had not done the same at the wheel; nor was he ill. He was experiencing a flashback of some kind. She didn't know if it was about the Alston case or if the case had simply triggered something else, but she knew she had to get Scott out of the car. Long drives conducted alone, or, in this case, in silence, had a way of breeding meltdowns.

Steelie had once referred to this as Jayne's Law. Steelie had probably seen this coming when they were still in the coroner's parking lot in Phoenix, whereas Jayne had thought Scott was suffering more from fatigue than anything else. She had to get him out.

She said his name again. He turned his face toward her but his eyes were still staring forward, out the front

244

windshield. She was shocked by the vulnerability of his expression, the red rims of his eyes. She took his hands and pulled on them, urging him out of the car, and now he slipped down from the driver's seat. But when his feet hit the ground, he pulled away from her, muttering, 'Christ' as he strode away quickly, disturbing a ribbon of blown desert sand along the edge of the tarmac. Jayne let him go. He eventually stopped and she watched his back, seeing him apparently loosen his tie, then clasp his hands behind his head as he looked up at the sky.

After a minute, she walked over to him, purposely stopping slightly behind him but close enough so that he'd know she was there.

He turned his head, putting her in his peripheral vision. 'How do you guys do it?' His voice sounded choked, tired.

'Do what?'

He turned his head away, his hair catching under his fingers. 'It about killed me to meet the Alstons.' He paused. 'I kept picturing their daughter in the freezer. At the morgue. Those teeth. I've never seen such perfect teeth. She was dead but there they were, just like life. For *Christ's* sake!' He brought his arms down and crossed them tightly against his chest.

Jayne was reaching to touch him when his voice came out in a whisper.

'I feel inadequate.'

Shocked, she drew her hand back and looked at the back of his head. Could he really have said those words? Did he feel something she'd felt? She knew what he meant. The dead were still dead, despite everything you'd done – despite all the Good, all the Investigation, the Uncovering, the Recovery, the Holding Accountable – the dead were still dead and you couldn't bring them back. She *knew*.

He was talking again. 'I've never felt so glad to clear a case and then felt so... terrible.' His head dropped down as his shoulders started to shake.

Jayne reached for him then, turning him and pulling his head to her chest, feeling his exhalations, hot and damp, on her shirtfront. She automatically began rubbing his back and her words came out despite her defenses. 'I know, I know.' She said them over and over until she was murmuring them into his hair, which muffled the words into noises only for them to resurface as kisses that landed on his ear, his brow, damp cheek, and then his arms were around her, tightening when his mouth found hers.

22

A single glance was all it took for Chesterton Police Officers Cobb and Hayden to know that the officer on the stretcher was not 'one of theirs', as the security guard had announced when he had called the station minutes earlier frantically shouting, 'Officer down! Officer down!' But he could have been from another substation. The paramedics would not let them speak to the barely conscious man so Cobb had let the ambulance leave for the hospital after they had searched the man's pockets and not found any proof of identity.

While Hayden took a statement from the security guard, who was still sitting on the curb, Cobb searched the sedan for the officer's identification. There wasn't a single item in the body of the vehicle. He opened the trunk and looked in the dark interior. It was lined with several layers of heavy-duty clear plastic. This struck Cobb as unusual but not outside the range of possibility for what had to be an undercover unit. He went ahead and ran the license plate number through the NCIC hook-up in his cruiser.

NCIC listed the owner of the license plate, a private individual, but the plates were registered to a different car than the one illuminated in Cobb's spotlight. He would need the vehicle identification number to resolve the discrepancy so he pulled it from the sedan and ran the number inside his cruiser.

An All Points Bulletin immediately popped up. Cobb leaned in, wondering if this was related to the BOLO that he'd given scant attention to at the beginning of his shift. It was. And now this APB was specifying that the driver of this car could be armed and dangerous and must be detained. He'd just let the guy go.

Cobb's immediate thought was to race after the ambulance, but he couldn't leave his partner on the side of the road with the witness. So he radioed the station and hurriedly told the duty desk to dispatch a unit to Chesterton General to intercept the ambulance on the way to or at the entrance of the hospital's emergency room. Then he radioed a colleague on another floor of the station and asked him to enter an NCIC response report that the wanted vehicle had been recovered, along with an unconscious man who may or may not have been the driver.

*

Tripper had been careful to respond to the paramedics with enough vital signs to get them to relax about his condition but not so many that they were going to start asking him questions about his identity. They had correctly deduced that he'd suffered a mild concussion, which he was coming out of, but they had no concerns about a cracked skull or fractured ribs that could cause major complications. Tripper already knew all this because *Ms.* Winton had only been lucky, not a goddamned black belt. He only needed this ambulance to get him away from the cops and the paramedics were making it happen, driving with lights but not siren and not at great speed. He could hear the two of them up front, joking about the construction site security guard and discussing where they would eat on their break: fast food or an all-night place called Rick's.

Tripper lifted his head. His eyesight was blurred but the blood that had been flowing from his nose was drying. He could feel clots deep inside his nostrils as well as the symptoms of an approaching, massive headache. Squinting down his body, he could see the seatbelt-like straps crisscrossing the ruined police costume and keeping him attached to the stretcher as the ambulance moved. It was easy to undo the straps but leave them looking as though still clipped into place. What he did next would depend on where the paramedics pulled in at the hospital: the emergency room or a main entrance. He waited, fighting the desire to close his eyes against the headache and fall into delicious sleep.

The ambulance coming to a stop jolted him into full consciousness. He stayed prone until he heard both paramedics jump down from the front of the ambulance and walk to the rear. He knew they had arrived at the main entrance; otherwise emergency room staff would have already opened the ambulance doors. In one swift movement, Tripper sat up on the stretcher. Searing pain flared in his head, accompanied by flashes of white light in his eyes. He pushed the straps clear of his body and swung his legs down on either side of the stretcher.

The paramedics were still chewing the fat when they opened the rear doors and weren't ready when he catapulted himself out on to the ground and ran toward the darkest part of the street. He heard their startled 'Hey!' but knew he had the advantage of surprise. As he ran, he felt every sense in his body sharpen while his legs and arms began to pump in perfect time, the blood clots in his nose clearing as he breathed deeply, the pain in his head masked by the adrenaline released by his body for this very purpose.

*

Eric didn't immediately respond to his supervisor's query about 'civilians'. SSA Turner had to be referring to Jayne and Steelie, but who had told Turner that the women had even been at the freeway site? The Critters had no reason to tell Turner and the Highway Patrol officers wouldn't have gone around him and Scott. And what did their old boss over in Atlanta have to do with this? It didn't seem possible that SSA Franks knew about Jayne and Steelie.

SSA Turner looked up from his sheet when Eric didn't respond. 'I've looked into this, SA. These women were not only at the crime scene but here in the building. You authorized SA Weiss to log two scientists from an outfit called Agency 32/1 into the building as visitors, yet he took them up to the tenth floor. That's reading like a potential violation of chain of custody protocols. Clarify it.'

'Sir, those scientists assisted us with gaining leads on this case.'

'Dammit, Eric, those body parts were supposed to be en route to the LA coroner, not being pawed over by every Tom, Dick and Harry while in our custody.'

'At no time did the scientists come into physical contact with the remains. Sir.'

Turner looked surprised. 'Can anyone back you up on that? *Besides* your partner?'

'Absolutely. Tony Lee.'

'Good. Get him in here.'

250

Eric went to reach for the phone but the computer behind him emitted an abrupt beep. He whipped around in his chair, scanned through the green binary code on the old monitor and quickly interpreted it: there had been a hit on the APB for Wayne Spicer's car. The responding agency was Chesterton Police Station in Atlanta, Georgia.

'I need to make a call to a PD,' Eric said, reaching for the desk telephone.

'Put it on speakerphone, SA.'

Eric paused momentarily but he did it, and they heard the southern accent of the man who answered.

'Officer Lake, Chesterton PD.'

'Officer, this is FBI Special Agent Eric Ramos. I'm the originator of the APB you just responded to. Can you give me further details, please?'

'Sure, Agent Ramos, but it ain't such good news.'

'Just give it to me.'

'Well, we've got your vehicle alright, but the unidentified man who was driving it is AWOL.'

'Wait, your response said the driver was taken to hospital unconscious.'

'Apparently, the boys on the scene thought he was unconscious or as good as. Maybe he just regained consciousness. Either way, by the time our unit caught up with the ambulance at Chesterton General, the man had absconded from the stretcher and they'll be damned if they can work out where he went. He *was* wounded.'

'And no one got an ID?'

'No, but the vehicle was wearing plates registered to a male, name of King, DOB 1960. I'm faxing you the sheet now.'

Eric almost got goose bumps. He spoke rapidly. 'I need you to put out a BOLO for that individual with whatever descriptors you have and I need it to maintain that he is armed and dangerous.'

'You got it, Agent Ramos. I already had a BOLO underway. We sure are sorry about this but we're on top of it.'

Eric disconnected the call by lifting and replacing the handset but he kept his hand on the phone as he said to his supervisor, 'I need to call Scott.'

SSA Turner shook his head. 'First, Tony establishes for me that you two are not conducting this case like a bunch of cowboys. Call him now.'

What Eric really wanted to do was smash the telephone against the wall while picturing his old boss Franks' smug face, but he steadied his hand and dialed Tony Lee.

When the Critter arrived and saw SSA Turner was there as well, now sitting in Scott's chair, he looked at Eric. 'What do you need?'

'Tony, SSA Turner needs your chain of custody protocols for when Agent Weiss brought Steelie Lander and Jayne Hall up to Critter Central.'

Tony immediately gave a detailed and organized account. He concluded with, 'I handled the body bags, body parts and all the equipment.'

Turner had listened without interrupting. 'Photographs?'

'I took images and retained them at the lab. Later use of the images for the purposes of analysis was conducted by the scientists at our laboratory and in my presence.'

Eric thought Tony had gone over the top with his Spock style of delivery but Turner looked mollified. He was even

252

folding the sheet of paper he'd been carrying.

Turner spoke while he worked the fold into a knife-edge with his fingers. 'You're saying they never even touched the body parts?'

Tony crossed his arms. 'They barely breathed on them.'

The telephone on Eric's desk rang and he looked at the digital screen. It identified the call as coming from the colleague who took over his desk in Atlanta, Georgia. He pressed the speakerphone button before Turner could order him to do it.

'Ramos here.'

'Eric, it's Nicks. You got me on speaker or something?'

'Yeah Angie; you're broadcasting to SSA Turner and SA Lee. Go.'

She resumed, speaking fast. 'On the pin-to-pin from Houston this afternoon—'

Eric flinched. He hoped that, in light of SSA Franks' witch-hunt, Turner didn't find it suspicious that Scott had used his government-issued BlackBerry to send the new type of instant message that was more difficult to track than a text message.

Angie was still talking. 'He asked us to check the shortlist of suspects you drew up on the missing women before you got transferred out. He suggested that we use the APB you guys just put out on that vehicle, on the thinking that the driver might be our Georgia perp.'

'Tell me something good, Angie,' he said, trying to make it sound like he'd been aware of his partner's request all along while simultaneously trying to place when Scott had leapfrogged to a Georgia focus instead of sticking to the idea that they would find Tripper somewhere on the road

253

between Arizona and Georgia.

'We've got a lead,' Angie said. 'We've been checking through the shortlist since we got the search warrants, and all your suspects were home in the time period you're looking at for this guy being out west except for one. We're not clear if he wasn't at home then, but he's not at home now and we just saw the BOLO go out on him from Chesterton PD.'

'King?'

'Yep. He hasn't been seen for weeks but as soon as we saw that BOLO, we got a search warrant that would allow us to enter the property in his absence. House seems clean but his backyard reeks of decomp.'

'Yesss!' Eric felt victorious.

'Hang on, Eric,' Angie called out. 'The reason I'm calling is that we've just had the ME down there to take a look. The yard is apparently full of bones buried pretty shallow and the doc says he can't handle it. Can't tell which ones are human or animal and he thinks there's some of each. Says he's got some university students – volunteers – who'd probably be glad to go through all of it but it could take them weeks and they don't have a lot of experience. So we're in a holding pattern here. What do you want to do? It's yours and Houston's case.'

Eric looked over at his supervisor, who was leaning forward in the chair, elbows on knees. He liked what he saw in Craig Turner's eyes and liked the man even more when he stood up while crumpling the sheet of paper he'd been carrying with the notes from SSA Franks' phone calls.

Turner spoke, his tone authoritative. 'Call in Agency 32/1.' He turned to leave the office but then turned back.

'And get Houston's ass back here, present and correct.'

Eric and Tony exchanged a smile and then Eric said toward the phone, 'Got all that, Ange?'

'Ten-four.'

'I'll call you back ASAP.' His tone was jubilant.

*

Scott slid his hands up Jayne's back until they were on her neck, in her hair, pulling her to him. He wanted her even closer but they couldn't get any closer. Their kisses were turning into something else altogether and Scott's pulse was speeding up. But the roar in his ears wasn't related. There was a vehicle exiting the freeway and rolling too slowly toward them. He and Jayne surfaced simultaneously but he held her to him as they watched the off-road pick-up truck pass, then turn right at the bottom of the exit ramp. Scott became aware of other noises... cars on the freeway, a fly buzzing past, Jayne's fast breathing, her chest rising and falling in syncopation with his. And something else... his cell phone. He looked to the Suburban where the driver's door was wide open.

He started for the car and drew Jayne with him by taking her hand with a familiarity he didn't want to lose. She let him pull her into the confined space between the door and the seat, let him keep contact between them even as he reached for his phone in the center console. In the first seconds of hearing Eric's voice, Scott was still in the moment with Jayne, whose gaze was fixed on his mouth, causing him to look at hers, wanting to kiss – but then the import of what Eric was saying broke through. Scott tensed.

Jayne looked up at him with a questioning expression

255

but it was faster to simply hold the phone out to her. 'I need you to listen to Eric.' He activated the phone's speaker.

'Jayne?' Eric's voice sounded thin but audible. 'We've got a situation where we need the agency's help. We may have a multiple or mass grave in a residential area and the ME's out of his depth. We need you to assist us to get a lead by doing a day's assessment and some training up of the volunteers they've corralled to help the ME. No exhumation work on your part. This is urgent but it does involve traveling to Georgia, to the premises of a suspect who is still at large. I'm not going to pretend there's no danger quotient but you and Steelie would be under federal protection. Can you do it?'

Scott thought he read excitement, concern and then duty on Jayne's face before she said, 'I'd need to confirm with Steelie, but yes.'

'Good,' Eric replied, 'because Steelie's already on her way over here with your overnight bag. Scott, see you at LAX as soon as you two can get there. We're all booked on the red eye to Atlanta.'

DAY TEN

Thursday

23

FBI office, Atlanta: 9:45AM. Scott rolled his shirtsleeves above his elbows and leaned on the briefing room's long conference table. The lights were dimmed to allow a screen at the end of the room to take center stage.

Eric was contemplating the blurry portrait projected on the screen, while Special Agents Mark Wilson and Angela Nicks were looking at Scott from the other side of the table. Scott looked at his watch. 'Jayne Hall and Steelie Lander will be here in fifteen and I want to make sure we're all on the same page before they arrive.

'Starting with descriptors on our suspect, King: forty-five-year-old white male, six-foot-four, blond and blue. Holds the title to 1320 Mead Street and witness statements suggest he is also resident there. Eric and I put him on our list of suspects for the sex worker abductions about a year ago because he was alleged to have associated with some of the missing women. We never had any hard evidence on him, thanks in part to lack of surveillance, so we never got a search warrant for his property. Eric?'

Eric pointed at the screen. 'This image is the most recent photograph we have of him. It's the one on file at his work. The facilities contractor at Atlanta Airport employs him part-time, primarily cleaning floors; he alternates between employee areas and the arrivals transport section. Right now, they have him down as on vacation. He's had the job for a year and a half. No previous employment record.'

Scott used the remote to bring up the next image. 'This is the photo of King on file at the Department of Motor Vehicles. It's five years old.'

The man in the portrait hadn't smiled for the shot. His narrow face was pale and he appeared older than his age.

Scott continued. 'His appearance is a good fit for the man Chesterton police had contact with last night and it was his Georgia plate on Wayne Spicer's car. The address for the license plate is the Mead Street one. What's the latest from your house-to-house?' He directed the question to Angie.

She was pulling her thin braids into a ponytail, exposing a neck that was slender despite a well-known penchant for daily workouts. 'Usual story from the neighbors,' she replied. 'They don't see him that much, he's quiet, puts his trash out on time. We haven't tracked down any friends or social set and no one at his work has socialized with him or been to his house.'

Mark added, 'He doesn't own a cell phone – in his name, at least – so we can't track him that way.'

Eric tapped his notebook. 'He has used the internet, however. We've been following info we had from this website, offthegrid.net, where we believe King was operating under the screen name Tripper. If he is Tripper, he successfully masked his identity while online. The IT guys are monitoring the site but there's been no recent activity under that screen name. There are no leads there right now. Catch is, if King *is* Tripper and he's gone to ground, he probably knows how to stay there.' Eric looked to his partner.

Scott forwarded the image on the screen and a map came up. He used a laser pointer to highlight a street on the map. 'Here's where police recovered the Spicer vehicle. In addition to the car wearing King's plate, the man driving matches King's description on the basic levels. We are working on the assumption that the man, who was wounded and wearing a police uniform or replica, was indeed King.'

He pointed to another location on the map on the screen. 'Here's Chesterton General, where King escaped on foot. And here—' he pointed at another location two miles away '—is King's residence. At about the time he was jumping out of an ambulance at the hospital...' Scott paused to consult his notes.

Mark finished his sentence. 'We were breaking down his front door on the search warrant. If he's tried to come home, then he knows we're crawling all over it.'

Angie's cell phone rang but she addressed the room as she pulled it from her pocket. 'We've got surveillance at both ends of the street in case he does turn up. Nicks.' This last was said into her phone. 'Thanks.' She stood up. 'The scientists are here. I'll escort them.'

*

Jayne and Steelie still had damp hair from the quick wake-up showers they'd taken at the motel after the overnight flight from Los Angeles. But hot water could do only so much and they'd maintained a fatigue-induced silence during the ride in a government vehicle to the FBI office. The woman who met them in the lobby introduced herself as Agent Angela Nicks and they hurried to follow her to

261

the security station.

She glanced back at them as she walked. 'Motel fit the bill? You need anything?'

Steelie pulled her glasses from the pocket of her shirt and began cleaning them. 'Weirdly, I think I'm ready for breakfast.'

'We've got stuff in the briefing room. Muffins, bagels, coffee. Sound okay?'

'Sounds like I should come 'round here more often.'

They were passing offices that came off both sides of the hallway. Open doors revealed agents at work. Jayne half-expected to find their way barred by the infamous Supervisory Special Agent Franks about whom Eric had told infuriating stories last night at the airport. She was still smarting over the fact that SSA Franks had acted on an anonymous tip about impropriety between Scott and Agency 32/1 without vetting anyone who called in with such specific information.

'This is the office Agent Wilson and I share.' Angie pointed into a room as they walked past. Two desks were pushed up against each other, both relatively neat, with a potted plant right on the dividing line.

Jayne asked, 'Will we be meeting SSA Franks?'

Angie shook her head. 'He's at his crime stats meeting. Here's the briefing room.' Angie swung open the door that anchored the end of the hallway.

Jayne saw Eric bent over a projector, Scott at a table and a third man sitting at a computer to the side. When he stood up to greet them, Jayne saw how tall and trim he was, the brush cut on his thinning, reddish hair contributing to an air of neatness. He came over with a friendly smile and shook hands with a strong grip.

'Welcome to Atlanta. Mark Wilson. Good to meet you. How you guys feeling?'

Jayne replied, 'Been more awake before but we're ready to help out on this.'

'In that case, help yourselves to coffee.'

They put their bags on chairs and joined Scott at the refreshments table. He was spreading cream cheese across a bagel and winked at Jayne. She surreptitiously grinned back, noticing that he'd changed into a different suit.

She enjoyed seeing his left side after using the waking hours on the flight to study his right side, which was all she could see of him from one row back and across the aisle. She'd continually turned over how he'd acted after his meltdown on the drive back from Arizona. He hadn't been ashamed of the impact the Alston case had had on him, hadn't apologized for almost running off the road while having a flashback. He seemed to accept that there could be fallout from his work – had even told Eric what had happened. It had been so striking that Jayne felt she could even tell Scott about Benni and it wouldn't mean an end like she'd feared. The kiss they'd shared on the side of the road had certainly felt like a beginning, and she wanted more.

A bright light in the briefing room behind her brought her to the present and she turned to see a map projected on the screen. She followed Scott and Steelie to sit at the table.

Angie used a remote control and the map on the screen switched to a photograph of a smiling woman. Her face was full, her brown hair showing white roots, and she looked as though she was laughing at being teased. Her shoulders were visible around her flowered sleeveless top.

It was Eric who gave the photo a caption. 'Eleanor Patterson.'

Jayne and Steelie simultaneously sat up straighter in their chairs. It was a shock to see a photograph of the woman whose dismembered limbs they were so familiar with, whose surgical plate had led to her identification. Eleanor Patterson, of whom only her arms had so far been found.

Scott addressed the room. 'Patterson is the only identified victim we can associate with the perp's van so we need to do two things as a matter of priority: put her with him while she was still alive and determine if how they met will give us a lead on where he is now.'

Eric said, 'Starting with what we know about Patterson: the Thirty-Two One preliminary analysis suggests that she had likely been the victim of physical abuse but the misper report filed by her husband made no mention of any scars related to that nor was there any mention of the surgical plate we eventually used to ID her. So we had Carlisle PD talk to the husband. They've sent over their report.'

He held up a piece of paper.

'The husband admits to the domestic violence but said he didn't report her surgery because he didn't realize it would be helpful. Didn't expect her to be found dead because when she left, she didn't take any of her belongings or clothes and left behind her credit cards. He presumed she'd gone off to start a new life with one of the men he alleged she was having affairs with. Oh, and he told the Carlisle cops that he didn't want to have her body returned to him; that he'd only filed the misper report so she would come back and, quote-unquote, get her shit.'

Eric looked up at the group. 'Apparently, he's still got her "shit" kept perfectly in place in an upstairs room. Carlisle PD has no leads on how Patterson came to be outside of Oregon, let alone dead.'

Steelie cleared her throat. 'I know Jayne and I are here about the body parts at the suspect's house, but I've just had an idea about Patterson.'

Eric gestured with his hand, inviting her to continue.

She glanced at the screen. 'Okay, you said she left without belongings, not even credit cards, and that you have confirmation that her husband was the abuser?'

Scott said, 'Yes.' He was looking at her intently.

'Well, our sense from the healed fractures on her arm bones was that the injuries had been inflicted over a long period of time. So I'm thinking that maybe she finally decided to do something about it.'

'What do you mean?' Eric asked. 'She didn't file a police report.'

'I don't mean reporting. I mean she decided to get the hell out of Dodge. What about checking with domestic violence shelters? And not in Oregon. Patterson was probably trying to get as far away from her husband as possible. I don't know that she came out here to Georgia but you already know she crossed the suspect's path somewhere and he's primarily been here in Atlanta. You could start by looking at DV shelters here. Maybe?'

There was a brief silence and then Eric jumped up from his chair. '*That*, my friends, is what I call a lead.' He was at the end of the table in three long strides. 'Angie?'

Angie had pushed back from the table and was gathering her papers. 'I'm on it.' She flashed Steelie a smile and then

265

followed Eric out of the room.

Scott chuckled quietly.

'What?' Steelie asked, sounding taken aback by the activity her comment had triggered.

He tapped her on the shoulder. 'I was just wondering if you wanted a job.'

Mark got up from the other side of the table and headed toward the food. Jayne joined him so she could get more coffee. She felt good because the agents had made her and Steelie part of their team. She turned back to the room as Scott was advancing the image on the screen.

'Alright everyone. Here's our suspect: a janitor at Atlanta Airport.'

Jayne looked over and then had to grab the back of the nearest chair.

It was Steelie who spoke. 'Well, Jee-sus Christ. Or I should say, Gene King.'

24

Tripper understood the catalysts for the physical sensations breaking over his body like waves. One part was nerves and the other anger, but the zing brought on by the thought of Wayne Spicer's sedan going to a police yard before he'd ensured it was clean was fear, pure fear. He clenched and unclenched his fingers. He knew he had to control fear. He must repeat in his mind that there was nothing to fear as long as he wasn't Gene King.

Sure, that was King's license plate on the car but he would be Tripper full-time now. Indeed, he'd planned this day; it had just arrived sooner than he'd intended. That made him angry again. Who were the cops to dictate when he made The Transition? Which meant the real danger was that he left something of Tripper's in that car? *Zing*. No! Control the fear. Clench, unclench.

'You sure you want me to take Peachtree?'

Tripper looked up to see the taxi driver eyeing him in the rearview mirror. 'Yes, I'm sure.'

'The parkway will get you there in half the time.'

'I said I don't like that route.'

The driver shrugged. 'It's your dollar.' His eyes went back to watching the traffic ahead of them and he turned up the AM radio.

Tripper refocused. The taxi was working. It kept him off both the streets and the public transit system while the

267

cops might be searching for Gene King during the crucial hours while he was completing The Transition. They'd only search hard for him if they knew he'd impersonated a cop, and they'd only know about the assault if that bitch he'd pulled over had reported it already. In case she had, he had done three things: run until he put distance between him and the hospital, given his house a wide berth and waited several hours before hailing a taxi. There would have been no point in getting a taxi near the hospital, and at a time of night when the driver would remember him if questioned by the cops later. And he wouldn't take a taxi to the house. No, he was going to the storage unit.

The Transition Plan called for this, naturally, but it was supposed to be late at night when the front office was unattended. But current circumstances dictated that he go during business hours when the gate was already open. He would draw little attention to himself and, on the plus side, his code would never be used, so it could never be tracked.

The driver would never know his true destination because he would ask to be dropped off several blocks before the taxi reached the storage place. Then he would walk. Now that he'd discarded the uniform's shirt, he knew he was unremarkable in a white T-shirt and dark pants. If anything, he looked like a waiter who'd just come off a night shift.

Tripper dug his fingers down into his right sock and felt the money he'd hidden there when he'd dressed in the uniform at the beginning of the night. He was surprised to find the cash damp with sweat. He didn't remember sweating. As Tripper sat up straight again, he heard a police siren start up behind the taxi. It took extraordinary effort to not twist in the seat as he watched the driver's eyes looking in the rearview mirror to something behind his head.

*

Scott was looking at Jayne, whose coffee had sloshed out of the cup when she'd stopped to stare at the screen, mouth open. 'Yeah, Eugene Frederick King. What's wrong with you?'

She still didn't look over at him. 'What?'

'You know this guy? Steelie?'

Steelie replied, 'Yeah, we do. You should know him too. Gene was one of you guys.'

He looked at Mark, who was shaking his head.

Scott insisted, 'Not according to what we know about him. You sure about that?'

She nodded. 'He was FBI ten years ago, anyway. A criminalist in the DC lab. Worked with us in Rwanda for the UN. And Jayne can tell you where he works now; he's not a janitor, that's for sure.'

Mark gaped at Jayne. 'You're in touch with King now?'

'I saw Gene last week but I'm not—'

'Everything stops.' Scott pushed his chair back roughly as he stood up. 'Right now.'

Everyone watched him as he brought both hands to his face as though in prayer. Then he pointed at Mark. 'Find out why he's not in our system and go straight to the director of the lab to get *any*thing they have. Find out who worked with him and talk to them ASAP.'

Mark nodded, jerked his chair back and headed for the door, which banged shut behind him.

Scott looked at Jayne and then rubbed his lips hard with

269

his fingers. 'You have some explaining to do.'

'But… I hardly know him.'

'Let me be the judge of that.' His tone had a sharp edge. 'I need to pick up some equipment. Wait here.' He left the room.

*

Scott stood just outside the door of the briefing room, his hand still on the latch, thoughts and images colliding in his head. Jayne calling King – *their suspect* – 'Gene'. She knew him. She fucking knew this bastard. He envisioned King and Jayne together, the two of them – friends? This morphed into a vision of Jayne in danger, so he pushed it out to focus on King again. A former FBI lab rat; how could they have missed that? Was he such a smooth operator that he'd wiped his own government record, and if so, who were they dealing with? This was no longer a janitor who'd 'just been lucky' to get away with murder all this time.

And if King had been in LA last week, then that tallied with their belief that he was the one who had been driving the van when those body parts fell out. Could it be coincidence that he had seen Jayne that same week or had King known she was involved in the case? What had she revealed? He needed to know how she'd been involved with this sick fuck. Anger and disgust made Scott tense up, so he pushed off from the door and strode down the hallway.

*

Jayne fought the nausea, repeatedly swallowing the saliva that was welling up in her mouth. She stared unseeing, her mind skittering over the night she'd met Gene in LA,

270

recasting him as a murderer, hardly able to believe it, then fully rejecting it. *He's an* alleged *murderer*, she told herself, and then felt her stomach twist. *I spent an evening with him; he was in my apartment. I let him touch me! Was he sizing me up the whole time? No, no. This is just an allegation. They need proof. I need proof. Jesus, do I have some proof and don't even know it? What is Scott thinking? What is he... what must he think of me? It's over, isn't it? It's over between us and it had barely even started.*

*

Steelie watched Jayne and could imagine what she was thinking. Steelie herself had no trouble casting Gene as a killer, but she couldn't imagine him being creative enough to spend an evening weaving whatever false stories he'd told Jayne about his life. She also couldn't see him taking a janitorial job unless there was some benefit to him beyond the paycheck. Most of all, she had trouble picturing him pursuing any endeavor where he couldn't take the credit.

*

Eric stepped into the hallway to meet Scott as he returned from the supply room. He kept his voice low. 'Mark told us. They know King?'

Scott nodded, his lips tightly compressed.

Eric registered the recording equipment in his partner's hands. 'You're going to interview them?'

'Jayne saw him just last week.'

'Christ.'

'She could have told him something. Inadvertently, of course.'

271

Eric's eyes widened and he dropped his voice to a whisper. 'You are *not* thinking that, man.'

Scott gave a tense shrug.

'Let me do the interview,' Eric urged.

'No. I know she might be the best lead we have on where this asshole is right now – I'll have my kid gloves on.'

'That's not the reason to wear them, Scott. This is Jayne. Look, if King is Tripper, he's leading a double life and there's no way in hell he told Jayne. If she knows anything useful, she won't realize it.' Eric paused to watch Scott closely. 'Don't do an interview. Just ask questions. And make it clear they're not suspects.'

Angie approached. Eric abruptly stepped back from his huddle with Scott. She didn't appear offended by this, nor did she ask about the recording equipment. She held up a sheet of paper.

'With the help of Health and Human Services, I've got a list of DV shelters in the metro area. It's recommended that we go in person so we can show ID, otherwise, forget it.'

Just then, Mark got off the phone and called them all into the office.

'The lab confirms that King worked for the Bureau doing trace evidence and photography for seven years. He was loaned to the UN International Criminal Tribunal for Rwanda on a nine-month agreement in '96, going into '97. Official title: forensic expert. He resigned from the lab in 1999, stating personal reasons—'

Eric interrupted: 'Nothing precipitated it?'

Mark shook his head. 'Nothing disciplinary in his file. The only thing that stands out was a psych debriefing after the UN mission that came back with a recommendation for further appointments. He never made them but he wasn't required to, either. Speaking of his file, there's no explanation for why it isn't in the Bureau's general records because it's there in the FBI Lab's database at the administration level.'

Scott responded thoughtfully. 'That's smart. He doctored it so anyone who knew him from the lab would find his records as expected but he's not in the system that the rest of us use when we're running a name against government employee lists. Did the lab think he had the tech skills to do that?'

'The director of the lab didn't know King well – came on just before he resigned – but said King was known as a jack of all trades. He'd been in the Bureau long enough to gain some working knowledge of everything: blood spatter, geology, entomology, forensic accounting, you name it.'

'They got an address for him?'

'Same one we've got crime scene officers at right now. Mead Street.'

Angie looked at Scott. 'Are we going to have a problem taking Steelie and Jayne over there?'

'I don't know yet. Keep on the domestic violence shelters. Mark, see if you can get on to whoever was the director of the lab while King was working there. We need leads on friends, anything on what he was planning to do when he resigned. We need some hidey hole he might be at right now, nursing his wounds from last night.'

The team broke up.

25

Sitting in the briefing room, Jayne was anxiously thinking over any signs that Gene was a violent person. She said as much to Steelie.

Steelie offered, 'I do remember that time Gerrit called Gene combative, particularly in conversation with you. But it was verbal combat.'

Jayne thought back. 'Yeah. For whatever reason, Gerrit had my relationship with Gene down pat.' A movement caught her eye. Scott was in the doorway, staring at her, a frown on his face.

She started to get up. 'Scott, I—'

He launched into the room. 'Whatever you have to say about King is going on tape.' The case he was carrying hit the tabletop with a thud.

Jayne froze, half-standing, half-sitting.

He spoke again, less harshly. 'So just... hold that thought and we'll get to it on tape, okay?'

She nodded and sat down.

Steelie was eyeing the contents of the case he'd now opened. 'What's the deal, Scott? I'm getting the feeling that you're about to read Jayne her rights.'

He continued to busily pull out equipment. 'She's not a suspect.' He set up a microphone on a stand in the middle of the table. 'Neither are you, for that matter. You're material witnesses. I'm recording this because I need it to be available for the whole team. You're going to give us background on the suspect. You're not under oath.'

He yanked tangled wires free and bent down to plug into sockets on the table's edge. Looking at Jayne, he said, 'But it would be helpful if you told the truth.'

He turned on the recorder, pulled over a legal pad and looked squarely at her. 'Who is Gerrit?'

Jayne opened her mouth, closed it, then started again. 'Gerrit? Aren't we supposed to be talking about Gene?'

'Yeah, and it sounds like this Gerrit is a mutual friend of you and King so I'll want to talk to him.' Scott dropped his eyes to the pad, jotted something on it and added, 'For background.' He repeated his question, directing it to Steelie this time. 'So, who is Gerrit?'

Steelie calmly replied, 'He was the UN Tribunal's lead criminal investigator for the sites we exhumed in Kigali in '96, when we worked with Gene.'

'Surname?'

'Leuven.'

'Seconded or...'

'Seconded.'

'One year or two?'

'He was into his second year.'

'From?'

'Government of the Netherlands. *Politie*.'

'Do you know his current title?'

Steelie gestured at Jayne, who replied, 'Chief of Police.'

'You've got contact information for him? Either *Politie* or personal.'

'I have both.' Jayne pulled her bag from the chair next to her. She dug around for her cell phone while Scott pushed the legal pad toward her, a fresh page uppermost. She wrote down Gerrit's email and direct telephone numbers as stored in her phone, then pushed the pad back across the table. 'He continued working with Gene after we left.'

Scott turned to the next page of the pad. 'You stated that you saw King last week?'

'That's right.'

'Which day, what time?'

So much had transpired since that night, Jayne had to think for a second. 'Um, Wednesday evening. I picked him up around seven and he left my place at about eleven.'

She saw Scott's pupils dilate and the start of a frown in the millisecond before he looked down to write. It felt like an entire minute passed before he looked up from his pad.

'Did he contact you for the meet?'

'I wouldn't call it a meet. It was just dinner. He contacted me – us, really. Sent an email to the agency on Tuesday and—'

'Meaning last Tuesday, the day before you met?'

'Yes.'

'So you were in regular contact?'

'No – you don't understand.' She looked to Steelie for help.

Steelie's tone sounded conversational compared to Jayne's. 'Scott, we hadn't heard from the dude since we worked with him in Rwanda. This was a one-off.'

'Uh-huh. So you get this email out of the blue. What did he say?'

'Just that he was flying into LA the next day and could we meet up,' Steelie replied.

'Just Jayne or both of you?'

276

'Both of us.'

'But you didn't attend the meet, Steelie?'

'Gene was never my favorite person – even before you alleged he was a serial killer.' She gave him a thin smile.

He made a note. 'We'll get to that.' He looked to Jayne again. 'How many more emails did you have from him?'

'I wrote back, said I'd be meeting him, then he just wrote one more time to tell me that he'd be staying at the Omni and what time I could pick him up.'

'That's it? Nothing about what he was doing in LA?'

'No.'

'And you're sure he said he was flying in the next day, the Wednesday?'

'Yes, positive.'

'Flying in from…?'

'I presumed DC because that's where he used to live.'

Scott tapped his pen against the pad. 'We'll need to see the email traffic between his account and yours, track his account.'

Jayne bit back the words *I'm not lying*. 'Fine. We can get into the agency account from here.'

'Have you had any more emails from him since you met?'

'No…' Jayne paused, remembering the message she'd sent Gene on the day the half-empty filing cabinet had depressed her. She realized that Scott would probably see that message now.

'You sound unsure.'

Jayne noticed Steelie looking at her curiously, so mustered herself. 'I'm sure. He hasn't written again.'

The door opened and they all looked up.

Mark Wilson walked in and addressed Scott. 'You want this now?'

Scott nodded and turned off the tape recorder.

Mark barely needed to consult his notes. 'There's almost nothing on this guy. Two people say they were friends of his when he worked at the lab but they haven't been in touch since. They understood he was resigning to take care of his mother down here, who was getting sick; one of them thought it was dementia—'

'That's right,' Jayne cut in. 'He told me she died a few years ago, after living with Alzheimer's.' She looked at Scott but he only indicated with his pen that Mark should continue.

'King's friends only ever socialized with him at their local bar in DC or at professional conferences. He used to have a DC-area-code cell phone. I called it and also checked with the phone company. He dumped the number four years ago.'

'When his mother died?'

'Around the same time, yeah.'

'Find out if it was before or after and by how much time.'

'You want me to check on the Alzheimer's business?'

'Yeah.' Scott flipped back to another sheet on his pad, ripped it off and handed it to Mark. 'And get a hold of this guy in Holland; get him out of bed if you have to. He was the lead investigator when King was working with Jayne and Steelie in Rwanda. He may have worked with King even longer than they did. Find out if anything happened out there. And his name's pronounced *Herrit*.'

Mark nodded and left the room.

Jayne opened her mouth to speak but Scott was already restarting the tape recorder.

'Let's go back to Wednesday night. Did you ask for King at the desk inside the Omni?'

'No, he said he'd meet me where the taxis pull in.'

'Did you see him come out of the hotel, through the doors?'

'No...' Jayne felt sudden surprise. 'I was scanning the area but he spotted me first and met me at the truck.'

'What was your impression of him?'

'Like, his behavior or what?' She knew she sounded distracted.

'Is this too tiring?'

Jayne shook her head. In fact, her brain was busy fast-forwarding her memories of that night, now alerted to how much she'd taken for granted with Gene's visit to LA and how little she'd actually learned from him.

Scott sounded more solicitous. 'Just think back to the first moment you saw him. Close your eyes if that helps.'

Jayne dutifully followed his direction. She thought back to Gene jumping in the passenger side of the truck, the hug he gave her once in the cab. 'I didn't recognize him at first; he looked older than I'd expected even though we're all older. His skin seemed grayer and it was as though his cheeks were being pulled down by gravity but he was energetic, lively, funny, and it was... nicer to see him than I'd expected.' She opened her eyes and shrugged.

'Good. Okay. Was he clean-shaven? Moustache? Beard?'

'No. No facial hair.'

'What was he wearing?'

'All beige. A zip-up windbreaker, golf shirt, slacks. I

279

don't remember his shoes. No logos.'

'So he got in the truck. It's about 7PM, and then what?'

'I drove to Little Tokyo.'

'His choice or yours?'

'Mine, because it was close.'

'He pick the restaurant?'

'No, I'd suggested we see what looked good once we got there.'

'During the drive, what did you talk about?'

'Let's see… he explained that he'd left the Bureau years ago, didn't miss it and now worked for an electronics company that was expanding to the West Coast and he was the advance guard.'

'Which company?' Scott had drawn a line out from his notes and was circling something three times, the ink sitting in a groove on the paper.

'I don't know. Didn't ask.'

'And he didn't volunteer? At any point in the evening? Give you his business card?'

'No.'

'Did he say where he was based?'

'No.'

'So you park and walk into Little Tokyo. Where'd you eat?'

'Um, I didn't notice the name. We had stopped in front of it and the host just handed us a menu.'

'He stopped or you stopped?'

'I don't remember; we just stopped. No, wait. I stopped because he'd said something that pissed me off and I couldn't walk and respond at the same time.'

Scott's mouth twitched into a tiny grin but then he

became serious again. 'You were arguing?'

'No. He just made a typical Gene statement, sounding supercilious and sure of his facts as he said that our effort to link up mispers with unidentifieds was just a drop in the bucket.'

Steelie cut in, leaning toward her. 'You never told me this.'

Jayne gave her a quelling look. 'There was no point getting you riled up as well.'

Steelie's protest was cut off by Scott's follow-up question for Jayne. 'Why did that bother you so much that you stopped walking?'

'Because it's the sort of armchair-quarterback statement you might expect from a disinterested person, not a forensic scientist – or any kind of scientist.'

'Right.' Scott almost smiled again. 'So you set him straight. How did he respond?'

'He kind of backed off and we went into the restaurant.'

'Which you don't know the name of.'

'Look, I can describe it.'

'Later.' Scott consulted his notes. 'During dinner, did you learn anything about where he lived or his activities, if he had a rental car or some form of transportation?'

'No. We were reminiscing.'

'And how long did you stay there?'

'About an hour and a half. Something like that.'

'King paid for dinner?'

Jayne felt a ray of hope that Scott could be jealous, wanting to know if this had turned into a date. 'Yes, he paid.' She tried to see Scott's expression but his whole face was tilted down to his pad.

'Credit card?'

She deflated. He was just trying to find out if there was a financial paper trail the FBI could follow to locate Gene now. 'Cash.'

'Then you went where? To your place, you said?'

'First we went to the agency.'

Both Steelie and Scott's heads snapped toward Jayne. Scott held up his hand to stop Steelie from interrupting again. 'Was that *his* suggestion?'

Jayne nodded, beginning to see how strange it appeared. She wondered what Gene had actually been doing, if indeed he was the person responsible for the freeway body parts. She sat still and tried to think of anything he might have seen or could have discerned about the case while in her office.

'Jayne?' Scott sounded impatient.

'Yes. Yes, okay? He asked to see it.'

'And that seemed normal to you at, what, nine at night?'

She couldn't help but sound defensive. 'We'd been talking about some similarities between our work in Rwanda and what the agency does now. It was a relatively natural request in the context of the evening.'

'Fine. You went to the agency. What did you do there?'

Jayne rubbed her forehead. 'I showed him around. We weren't there very long.'

'Did you show him anything in particular? Any case files, photographs, notes—'

She glared at him. 'No. And I didn't say anything about consulting on an FBI case, if that's what you're thinking. I didn't mention the freeway body parts and he sure as hell didn't ask.'

282

'Did he show an interest in anything in particular?'

She thought for a moment. 'He seemed interested in the All Coroners Bulletin.'

Steelie's sharp intake of breath was audible. 'You turned on my computer in the lab?'

Jayne rolled her eyes. 'Of course not.' She took on an assertive tone, aiming to clarify these issues for the last time. 'Look, I didn't open anything, use any passwords in front of him, didn't let him see the alarm keycode—' She stopped abruptly. *Oh, shit.*

'What?' Scott leaned forward. 'You've remembered something. The alarm system?'

She shook her head. 'No, I just thought of something. A connection. I mean, Gene's the one anomalous person who's been at the agency as well as my apartment.'

'So what?'

'The bugging. The taps on the phones, dammit!' Her voice was rising. 'He said he was in "electronics"! Maybe that's what he meant. His little joke! He's been in both locations and I let him in myself! For Christ's sake, I let him *in*!'

She tried to stand up but the legs of her chair tangled with the straps of her bag, pulling it upside down to the floor. She bent over to untangle the mess, gave up and stepped over it, only to be confronted by Gene's face on the projection screen when she looked up. *No!* She made an about-face, directly into Scott, who'd come around the table.

He stopped her short by gripping her by the shoulders. She looked everywhere but into his eyes as she felt despair wash over her. Gene had manipulated her with ease, she'd possibly compromised Scott's case and maybe even Agency 32/1 itself. *What have I done?*

She was aware that Scott was telling Steelie to turn off the tape recorder. Jayne watched Steelie follow the instructions. Her usually irrepressible friend looked upset. *Oh, God, Steelie; I'm sorry.*

Scott dipped and weaved, trying to get into her line of sight and finally succeeding. 'The wiretaps were *outside* both buildings, not inside. I don't want you thinking about what could have happened or making connections right now, Jayne. Just tell me what happened that night. We'll deal with whatever comes up.'

26

Eric and Angie waited in a small office that was clearly a later addition to the rambling two-story house used by the second domestic violence shelter on their list, Percy Gale. The first shelter, Horizons, hadn't yielded results but they hadn't crossed it off the list because the manager there had simply refused to discuss any of her clients. At Eric's insistence, she had agreed to look at the photograph of Eleanor Patterson but had said she didn't recognize the woman. Eric hadn't been convinced.

He liked Steelie's theory that Patterson had come to Georgia to get away from her husband for good and it made sense that she would have started with a shelter. He wanted to follow every sniff of a lead and it was Angie who cut off the interview at Horizons by giving Eric a look he recognized from when they'd first worked together in Atlanta a year earlier: she was telling him to drop it. He only complied because he knew she wouldn't let anything go unchecked; that wasn't Angie's style.

On the drive to Percy Gale, she had suggested a new approach to the same theory: get the shelter to explain their methods so they'd understand how Patterson might have come into Georgia, even if they couldn't find the shelter she used. That would give them another kind of lead. They had agreed that Angie would start the next interview, so when the Percy Gale site manager walked into her office, it was

Angie who moved forward first.

The woman who introduced herself as 'just Dora' looked about sixty. She wasn't exactly heavyset but looked as though she had lost some weight and there was still enough skin to contain the old bulk. As she passed them to reach her desk, she left a fresh floral scent behind her.

She picked up a paper fan decorated with flowers and leaned back in the chair to cool herself with practiced flicks of the wrist. 'Please sit down, both of you. It's much too hot to stand.'

Angie began. 'Dora, we're looking for information on a woman who went missing while she may have been seeking assistance from a shelter for domestic violence survivors.'

'Is there a missing person report out on her?' Dora's eyes were shrewd.

'Yes.'

'Put in by the woman's husband?'

'Yes.'

Dora leaned forward and snapped the fan shut, placing it on the desk. 'Can't help you.'

Eric's impatience led him to fidget but Angie continued seamlessly. 'We believe you can, in fact.'

'We don't reveal information on any of our clients, not even to the police, unless there's a warrant out for their arrest. And it doesn't sound like that applies here.'

'She's not a wanted person. She's a missing person. And as I said, we believe she went missing while seeking shelter. It would be helpful to us if you could at least give us some information on how your clients find you.'

'We're in the phone book, we have fliers at libraries, we're listed with all accredited counselors. Women who

286

need our services find us.'

'What about women from outside of Georgia?'

'Same process. Now, I really must get back to the main house.' Dora got up from her chair.

Neither Eric nor Angie rose.

Eric spoke. 'The woman we're searching for information on has actually been found. She's dead.'

Dora looked away as she pursed her lips. She fiddled with some papers on the desk, then sat down. 'Husband killed her?'

'We're investigating that now.' Eric gave Angie a slight nod.

Angie continued, 'We're trying to trace her movements and we would appreciate it if you could at least tell us if she was a client you were expecting. Her name was Eleanor Patterson.'

Eric was surprised when Dora laughed. 'My dears, you could give me any name you like but I wouldn't recognize it. Didn't you know that shelters for battered women don't use names?'

'Wait,' said Eric. 'How do you know a client is who she says she is when she arrives here?'

'We use code names, for everyone's protection.'

'How do they work?'

Dora opened her fan and cooled herself again. 'When someone contacts us to seek sanctuary, we assign a code name to them, ask them to guard it safely and then use it when they arrive here.'

Eric looked at Angie with an expression of frustration.

Angie asked, 'Would you tell us if you recognize the woman in this photograph?'

Dora lifted some papers and retrieved a pair of glasses. She cleaned the lenses and put them on, their silver frames complementing her white hair.

Angie handed over the photograph of Eleanor Patterson and Dora studied it before removing the glasses.

'I don't recognize her. And I'll confess that I just looked at it out of curiosity. You see, we wouldn't know what any of the women look like before they arrive here. We've never seen them before and, as I said, we don't know their names.' She stood up, and this time she moved toward the door and held it open for the agents. 'I wish you luck and I hope you get the bastard.'

*

It hadn't taken long for Mark to get through to Chief Gerrit Leuven on the telephone. First Mark had had to leave a message at the direct number Jayne had given them, but while he was tracking his way back to a main number at Gerrit's station, Mark's own phone showed an incoming international number. Gerrit's accent was clipped and his tone open but Mark could barely believe his ears when he heard what the Dutchman had to say.

*

Jayne sat at the table, feeling jet-lagged, as she let Scott take her thoughts back to the minutes she had spent with Gene at the agency.

'You said he was interested in the All Coroners Bulletin?' Her voice was quiet. 'Yes.'

'Did he say anything in particular?'

She sighed. 'He said that it was something we could be

legitimately positive about. He said that he understood how I handled the work, that I'd broken the big problem down into little ones.'

'And you said you left him alone for a minute or two?'

'When I went to the bathroom, I left him in the lab, but when I came out, he was in my office, in my chair.'

'Did you notice anything disturbed or moved on your desk or anywhere else?'

Jayne shook her head.

'So you left and went straight to your apartment? What did you do there?'

'Um, he used the bathroom. I made coffee. We sat on the deck, talked a bit more.'

'Anything come up about your work or his?'

'No, it was more… personal topics.'

'Personal?'

Jayne fixed her eyes on the table between them. 'He was wondering whether I was involved with anyone.' She anticipated Scott's next question but none came. She looked up at his face. He was staring at the recording equipment, lips pursed as he rubbed his chin.

He didn't look at her. 'And you again left him alone at some point?'

'I just went to get a photograph from my storage room by the driveway. A photograph from Kigali that he wanted.'

'About how long were you down there?'

'A couple of minutes. Probably less than five.'

'And then?'

'We looked through a bunch of photos and he left.'

'How did he leave? He say anything about staying in touch? Give you his number? Talk about getting together again?'

'I never had his number. He said he'd keep in touch but he hasn't contacted me yet. I understood he was flying out of LA in a day or two. He left after giving me a kiss goodbye.'

Steelie snorted derisively and Scott's pen hovered over the page but he didn't write down what Jayne had just said.

Scott cleared his throat. 'You didn't drive him back to the hotel?'

'No...' Jayne now remembered how odd it had been at the time, that Gene had disappeared down her residential street into the night. 'I thought he got a taxi.'

'Did you actually see him get into a taxi or had you called one for him?'

'Neither. In fact, I ran out to get him so I could call a taxi but he was already gone.'

'You get a lot of taxis on your street?'

Jayne shook her head firmly. 'No.'

'Okay.' Scott leafed back to an earlier page in his notes. 'Steelie. You said Gene was "never your favorite person" and you didn't meet up with him last week. Why didn't you like him?'

Steelie assumed a more relaxed position in her chair, legs crossed and one arm slung across the back. 'Ten years ago, he was arrogant. Smart, but arrogant with it. Self-important. And he had a tendency to act like a white settler in colonial-era Rwanda, which is never a good look thirty years after independence. I thought he made the UN look bad.'

'Was there something in particular? How'd you manage to work with him for so long if you felt that way?'

'One: I'm a master at disguising my feelings – note my

witty banter despite the grilling you've just given my best friend here. And two: he was good at his job once he got over the fact that he wasn't in charge of everyone else's job as well. The straw that broke the camel's back was when he—'

'Guys.' Mark Wilson slammed open the door and crossed to the computer hooked up to the projector. 'Guys, listen up.'

*

Tripper pulled up the roller door and surveyed the storage unit in the sunlight slanting in around the corner of the concrete and steel building. He looked up and down the access lane he was in. No one. He'd chosen this particular unit when he'd signed the contract with an alias because it was at the farthest corner of the storage center. Most people didn't want to drag their belongings any further than they had to once they were in the front gate, so his comings and goings were usually unobserved.

He walked in, turned on the light and pulled the roller door down behind him, slotting into place a temporary lock. The items he'd left inside looked undisturbed: select pieces of his mother's faded slipcovered furniture, the pile of old curtains with their hooks still attached, the aquarium whose ferns now resembled miniature ocotillo, and, right at the back, the motorcycle. He went to the motorcycle first.

He prized off a spoke and inserted it into the left exhaust pipe to retrieve a plastic bag. Out of the bag, he brought a knife and went to the sofa. He pulled off its slipcover and began cutting through the stitching on its back. As soon as he'd opened a foot-long section, he dug within the stuffing and retrieved two more small plastic bags as well as a much larger padded one.

He pulled on the edges of the padded bag until it formed a box. He attached this to the motorcycle's rear rack, ensuring its label faced out: *Joey's Pizza – We Deliver!* He put the smaller bags in the false bottom inside the pizza delivery box.

He moved on to the slipcovers on the two easy chairs and repeated his actions, retrieving scalpels, tweezers, surgical gloves, telephone wire, twine and duct tape. From the bottom of the aquarium, he pulled out bags holding the false driver's license and insurance cards, license plates for the motorcycle, the cell phone pack and the one grenade. Then he cut the lining off the curtains and peeled out a change of clothes, several Tyvek suits still in their plastic covers, and his motorcycle leathers.

Tripper changed clothes, stuffing the remainder of the cheap cop costume into the back of the sofa before putting the slipcovers back on all the furniture. He put on the leathers and turned on the cell phone to check its charge. The manufacturers had been good to their word; it had held its charge since he'd last been at the unit. He typed in a text message and pressed *Send*. When he saw it had gone through, he smiled and put on his helmet. He lifted the door and began to wheel out the motorcycle.

27

Mark Wilson plugged the flash drive into the briefing room computer. He spoke as he tapped keys. 'I just got off the phone with Chief Leuven. I think I know where King got his inspiration for the killings. Check this out.'

The projection screen at the end of the room switched to an image of a streambed bordered by tall reeds whose color was washed out by bright sunlight. The clear sky above them looked almost white. Among the reeds was a black photo board. It looked out of place. Beyond it on the ground, a fluorescent orange plastic arrow pointed toward a plastic letter N.

Mark looked at Jayne and Steelie. 'After you two left Kigali in '96, Gerrit and King were called in by the Civilian Police to assist on a homicide investigation. At first, CivPol had thought it was related to the genocide but then they realized it couldn't be because the body was fresh. So then they thought it was a retribution killing; like, a witness for the Tribunal killed so she couldn't testify about the genocide. That was when CivPol called in Gerrit and he in turn asked King to photodocument. Alright, look at this. Here's the overall scene and the photo board's right near the body parts.'

'Parts?' Scott asked.

'She was dismembered.'

Scott muttered something but Mark continued: 'Hang

293

on. Look at this. I'm putting it on slide show.'

He pressed a button and the slide dissolved and was replaced by another, which stayed on the screen for a time before dissolving and being replaced. Each photo brought them closer to the reeds, but in the third shot, a body part was slightly visible. In the subsequent photographs, someone was holding back the reeds with a flat tool, exposing the body parts like eggs in a nest. Two feet, the brown skin marbled by decomposition and the soil beneath them darkened with dried blood. Two hands, each finger separated from the palm. Then a single body part that it took Jayne a moment to recognize as a neck.

Mark came to sit by Scott. 'Remind you of anything?'

'Yeah, the first body parts we found on the outskirts of Atlanta. The neck especially.'

'And I don't think it's a coincidence. I think that when King was called in to photograph these BPs, it gave him ideas.'

Scott sounded doubtful. 'But if he worked in the Bureau lab, he'd have seen all kinds of stuff during his career. Why this particular case? Did they ID the body? Did they find the head?'

'No, never. And they only made a probable ID – turns out there aren't that many new missing persons in Rwanda; not like here in the US. Most cases date to the spring of '94 when the genocide broke out. The list of new mispers was small and most of the women on it were sex workers – and most of them weren't even Rwandan. They came from elsewhere to cater to the peacekeepers and internationals. For this body, they liked a young woman from the Ivory Coast. She'd only been in Kigali for a short time but was already known to pick up Johns at a club called...' Mark consulted his notes. 'The Cadillac.'

He looked up interrogatively at Steelie and Jayne. 'Heard of it?'

Steelie addressed Jayne. 'Um, maybe now would be a good time to tell them.'

Scott's cell phone rang and he held up an index finger.

Jayne could tell he was talking to Eric and the news wasn't good. She looked back at the screen, where the slide show was progressing automatically. As she watched, she began to think, *Something's here... what is it?* She went closer, pulled by that familiar professional curiosity, which was quickly displacing the self-doubt that had put her on the back foot earlier. She only gave part of her attention to Scott as he relayed Eric's news that the shelters used code words for clients and, therefore, neither Patterson's name nor her photograph was getting them anywhere.

Scott concluded by asking Steelie, 'Now, what is it you were going to tell us?'

Jayne spoke without turning from the screen. 'Hang on a sec. Mark, can you run the slides back and pause the show?'

He got up and punched a few keys at the computer. 'How far back do you want to go?'

'Go back two.'

The photo she was interested in was a close-up of a foot but it hadn't been taken *in situ* at the streambed. It had been taken on a table covered with a green surgical drape. Lighting had been used to illuminate the cut portion of the ankle. A ruler was placed in the photograph for scale, along with a label that read *UNCP #7-0193*.

Steelie got up to join Jayne at the screen. 'Can we see

the others in this section? Did Gerrit say where they took these shots?'

Mark replied, 'He said that all the material came back to UN HQ and they did the detail shots there, at your guys' temporary morgue.'

They looked at the photographs: separate ones of each dismembered finger, then the group placed in rough anatomical position to the palm. There were images of all surfaces of the hand and each shot was lit perfectly to show the cross-section of the cuts.

Jayne reached up, pointed at one of the cuts and looked at Steelie, who nodded. They communicated silently like this twice more before Scott said, impatiently, 'Thirty-Two One, there are other people in the room. What are you seeing?'

Jayne replied, 'Gene wasn't inspired by these cuts.'

Scott sounded exasperated. 'You can't rule out that he photographed them, came back here and copied them.'

She shook her head. 'No, I mean... or at least, I think I mean that he wasn't inspired by them. He made them.'

Both agents stared at her and she looked to Steelie for back-up.

Steelie elaborated, 'We've seen these cuts before. We saw cuts just like this at Critter Central. Patterson's arms. Same going between the joints, same careful approach toward not nicking bone. Dismemberment with hand tools – fine tools – not just going in with a bone saw.' She drew breath to say more but Scott interrupted.

'Are you seriously telling me that King *killed* this woman in Rwanda and then photographed her for the investigation?'

296

Steelie appeared to be choosing her words carefully, sounding more like a lawyer than ever. 'All we're saying is that there's a strong possibility that the same person who was responsible for cutting off Patterson's arms also dismembered this woman in Kigali. We don't know who that person is and it could be that it's actually two killers... though they'd be two peas in a pod.'

'What, the woman was killed by some other perp King met over there, who then taught him how to do this kind of dismemberment?'

Steelie shrugged.

Mark had been flipping through his notes. 'This is making sense. Listen to this: Gerrit knew that the cuts were precise, particularly compared to the large-scale, high-damage trauma inflicted during the genocide with a machete or scythe. He said he later developed some suspicions about people with access to UN HQ in Kigali because when they went to open a new supply kit for the morgue, about half the blades for the scalpels were missing, plus a few handles. Let's see.'

He scanned a page and then pointed at it. 'Yeah. Here. He said he questioned the logistics guys but they confirmed that the supplies had arrived from the European Union boxed up on a pallet.' Mark looked up at Scott. 'But Gerrit stressed that his suspicion that someone had stolen from their supplies was just a personal opinion and he didn't have any proof.'

Scott questioned Jayne. 'Could King have accessed a pallet?'

'Easily. If you were UN personnel, you could get access to almost anything that would be legitimate. Of course, we had to sign in and out and list how much of whatever item we took.'

'Was someone guarding the pallets or controlling the sign-out sheet?'

She shook her head. 'The logs guys had way too much to deal with to be able to guard anything when we were there. The sign-out sheet hung on a clipboard at the edge of the supply area.'

Scott swung his chair toward Mark, putting his back to the women, and lowered his voice. 'What do you think?'

'I think we gotta get them over to King's house ASAP, Houston. They can see things we can't.' He gestured at the slide on the screen.

Jayne could hear them and called out. 'What's the problem with taking us to the house? That's why you flew us out here.'

Scott replied without turning around, directing his voice at the ceiling. 'The problem is that now we know that *you* know the suspect. We need to make sure our case isn't screwed by taking you to his house.'

'Oh.' Jayne threw Steelie a sheepish glance as she suddenly plugged in to concepts of tainted evidence but Steelie just rolled her eyes while shaking her head dismissively.

After a moment, Scott righted himself in his chair. 'Mark, check on whether it's going to be a conflict to have them over there. And if you find a conflict, make it go away.'

28

Eric felt like he was being garroted by his seatbelt as Angie brought the Crown Victoria to a lurching halt in front of a building in a suburb of Athens. He saw her grin as she put the car into park.

'Soft brakes,' she said, mock-defensively. 'Gotta stamp on 'em like that or they don't work.'

He released his seatbelt and twisted to lower its anchor point on the car's frame. 'I don't remember you doing any "stamping" earlier.'

'And I don't remember asking you to comment on my driving.' She leaned forward to see out of his window. 'Looks like this one has a security system at the door.'

Eric turned to look and saw that the only feature differentiating the façade of the brick row house from its neighbors was the discreet metal panel encompassing a doorbell and keypad alongside holes for a speaker and microphone. He got out of the car and looked up at the building, noticing the small camera mounted above the door but beneath the windows of the second story. Railings painted a glossy black flanked a staircase that led up to the entrance and down to a basement. The brick on the building looked clean, as though recently sandblasted.

They mounted the stairs together and Angie pressed the bell. A woman's voice came through the speaker.

'Yes?'

Eric instinctively looked up at the camera above them and Angie held her badge open toward it.

'Special Agents Nicks and Ramos, Federal Bureau of Investigation. May we come in?'

'Just a moment.'

They heard several locks turn and a person who reminded Eric of the nuns who had run his elementary school opened the door. This woman wasn't wearing any religious adornment but there was something familiar in the cut of her gray dress and her air of friendly rigidity. As she inspected their badges and identity cards, he noticed a streak of white hair just to the left of the midline of an otherwise very dark brown bob. When she looked up from their badges, he saw brown eyes that were neither impressed nor curious about why they were there.

'Come in.' She closed the door after them.

Eric knew that the front door of most row houses would let into a hallway that would run to the back of the house, but this one had been remodeled to put them into a reception room that prevented further entry. There was a window to an office-like room that could be reached through another door with its own access panel.

The woman in gray said, 'I'm Aviva Goldsmith, co-director of Sanctuary House. How may I help you?'

Angie spoke. 'We're trying to ascertain whether you, at any time, have had a resident or visitor by the name of Eleanor Patterson. She would have come to you from Oregon.'

Aviva Goldsmith shook her head. 'You may not be aware that at Sanctuary House we don't know the

300

names of the women who seek shelter. This is done for everyone's safety in case their abuser comes here looking for them.'

Angie resumed. 'Ms. Goldsmith, we're in the midst of a manhunt for someone we believe may have harmed Eleanor Patterson. Could you look at this photograph and tell us if you recognize this woman?'

'I can look at it but I won't be able to tell you if it's the person you're looking for.'

Angie brought out a copy of the photograph Eric had used in the briefing room that morning. Eric watched Aviva Goldsmith closely as she looked at the photo and thought he detected relief under her calm exterior.

She said, 'I don't recognize her.'

*

Jayne spent the duration of the drive from the FBI building to Mead Street telling herself to think of their destination as a site, not Gene's house. But when Mark parked the Suburban and she looked out the tinted back window, she just saw a house. It was a two-story Victorian building covered in siding that was supposed to look like bricks but didn't succeed, topped with a chimney and an attic window in the peak of the roofline. A small porch fronted the house above three concrete steps and a large police tent dominated the unkempt yard.

Jayne got out of the car and waited for Steelie to come around from the other side. She looked down the street and saw a television crew and a small crowd of people on the other side of some yellow tape. She and Steelie joined Scott and Mark to cross the street toward the house.

Inside the tent, a police officer and an FBI agent logged them into the site visitor books and then gave them protective gear to put on over their clothes and shoes. Once everyone was suited up, Mark led the way from the tent to the front porch of the house. He greeted a police officer stationed at the door and then he addressed Steelie and Jayne.

'The electricity was turned off here. We're working on having it restored, but take these flashlights. Use them. We'll be going straight through the house to the back; the side access is barricaded. You'll meet the medical examiner and it'll be easier if you don't make a reference to ever having met King.'

He handed them the flashlights and they entered the house.

On stepping over the threshold, Jayne felt like she'd walked into another climate zone. Where it was warm and humid outside, the house was cooler and damp and smelled of old carpet. Boxes and debris crowded a dark, narrow hallway that led past a staircase. Swinging the beam of her flashlight across the floor and up the walls, Jayne couldn't understand how Gene had lived here. It was nothing like what she'd pictured when he'd talked about living in his mother's house. A wood-splitting sound suddenly exploded above her head and she hunched her shoulders instinctively before Mark patted her elbow.

He said, 'It's just the evidence techs upstairs.' He took them through to the back door, out into sunlight and the smell of decomposing tissue.

The grassy backyard was narrow but long. Rangy bushes hugged the tall wood fence that separated it from

302

the neighbors on each side. There was a concrete path leading to a clapboard garage whose double doors stood open, and Jayne could see floodlights set up on stands, their extension cords running to the generator humming on the path outside. Scott was heading for the garage but the decomposition smell was coming from the open section of the yard.

Mark said, 'Let me introduce you to the doc and his team.'

Over by the right fence-line, there were four people working in different sections of a grid marked out by fluorescent pink twine suspended between stakes hammered into the ground. They were all wearing Tyvek protective suits and rubber boots. Beyond them were three more Tyvek-suited people standing at waist-high sifting trays suspended over plastic troughs. A table near the sifting station was laden with plastic and paper bags, evidence labels, photograph markers and other tools needed to document evidence emerging from the excavation.

A man was walking across to them by following forensic stepping plates placed to preserve evidence on the ground beneath them. He pulled down his mask as he approached, revealing a lined, olive-toned face. His protective suit was baggy and twisted off the mid-line of his slight frame but his voice was strong.

'You must be the anthropologists. I'm Leonard Penman, the ME.'

Mark introduced Steelie and Jayne to the chief medical examiner. They shook gloved hands.

'We're not behind the times out here,' Dr. Penman

said with a smile, 'but we're honest enough to say that we haven't had to deal with multiple sets of buried remains, let alone mostly skeletonized remains. Even our biggest recovery effort – the commuter jet crash last winter – was fleshed remains and we had DMORT's help on that one.'

Jayne nodded. She and Steelie had enormous respect for the regional disaster mortuary operational response teams that were made up of forensic scientists and dispatched to scenes of mass fatalities to provide immediate human identification services.

Dr. Penman pointed toward the yard behind him. 'As you can see, the criminalists have already put a grid over that area. We're working over there by the fence first because it's where the soil was recently disturbed – by a dog, most likely – which exposed the remains that are putting out the stink. We've got Dr. Greg Parker from the university here. He's the archaeologist and it's his grad students from the anthropology department over there sifting the soil. I've been told that you two can advise on strategy? If so, you've arrived just in time because we're reaching the bigger body parts now.'

Steelie said, 'I guess the best thing at this stage would be for us to have a closer look at what you're dealing with.'

'Follow me,' said Dr. Penman, with something like relish.

Jayne recognized the ME's enthusiasm as born from being out at the scene as opposed to stuck in the morgue, with a meaty (if you will) problem to tackle. It also helped that he hadn't recently been out to dinner with the person who owned this house, a fact that was weighing on Jayne more heavily by the minute.

Scott emerged from the garage and called out, 'Thirty-Two One. I need you.'

They looked to Dr. Penman, who said, 'Go on. We're not going anywhere.'

Scott held a clear evidence bag with something inside it. He tilted his head toward the garage.

'You see that cabinet against the back wall?'

Jayne saw a metal wardrobe. A criminalist was collecting and documenting items that were on the labeled shelves.

Scott continued. 'Next to it are some huge chest freezers where King probably kept body parts. But he used that cabinet for a different bunch of mementos. This was in there.' He held up the evidence bag to show the large cream-colored handbag within. 'There wasn't much in it, but one thing it did have was an Oregon driver's license for one Eleanor Patterson.'

Steelie let out a low whistle.

Jayne was speechless. This was proof. Overwhelming proof. And then, like clouds parting after rain, she was able to imagine Gene charming and then assaulting the kind of woman who'd carry a capacious handbag in a color that required regular care to keep it looking decent. She found her voice. 'What else was in the handbag, Scott?'

'Like I said, not much.' He glanced at it. 'An empty coin purse, an empty wallet, a powder compact, a tube of lipstick and a, ah, sanitary pad.' He hurried on. 'Looks like he kept belongings from other vics on the shelves.'

He started to go back inside but Jayne said, 'Wait.'

He stopped and looked at her.

Jayne was thinking about the contents of the purse

and about Patterson's arms as they'd seen them at Critter Central. She remembered the sunspots on the forearms. 'You told us you'd ID'd Patterson from the surgical plate on her arm. How old was she?'

'Fifty-one when she went missing. Why?'

She held out her hand. 'Can I see her handbag?'

He hesitated.

Jayne had to stop herself from saying, *Seriously?* 'I know it's evidence but you haven't sealed the bag yet. I'm gloved.'

He handed it over.

She reached inside and pulled the handbag so its open top was aligned with the top of the evidence bag. Looking inside, she could see the lipstick, the compact and the two wallets. Then she used her finger to expand the small compartment in the lining. She could see a maxi pad in there, still folded in its wrapper, but the glue at the edges wasn't holding fast. She handed the evidence bag back to Scott.

'You're going to want to look inside the pad.'

'What?'

'You should section it – carefully.'

After a pause, Scott gestured for them to follow him. He called out to the criminalist working at the far end of the garage. 'Tait, doc this inside and out.'

The criminalist labeled the handbag and photographed the exterior and interior. Once he was finished, Scott pulled the pad from the inner pocket and put it on the table.

'Okay, now open this up.'

Tait gave Scott a look like he thought this was a joke.

'*Now.*'

Tait instantly composed himself. 'Yes, sir.' He picked

up his camera and photographed the item with an evidence label before touching it. Then he used a pair of tweezers to peel off the soft plastic wrapping.

The pad was folded into thirds and he eased it flat before looking at Scott for direction.

Scott turned to Jayne. 'You said section it?'

She nodded.

He looked back to Tait, who used a scalpel to begin an incision on the side of the pad. Then he stopped and picked up a magnifying glass. 'There's already a cut here, sir.'

Scott leaned down and looked. 'Okay, peel it back from the existing cut.'

Tait carefully pulled back several layers to reveal an object that had nothing to do with moisture absorption. It was a small piece of paper, folded many times and pressed flat as though with an iron.

The criminalist photographed the item with a ruler and an evidence label before opening it with his tweezers. Then he stepped back to let the others see. Visible inside the folds of the paper was something written in faint pencil:

793 Cobb /Agapanthus

Jayne spoke. 'You said the shelters gave the women code names. That might be a code she was trying to keep hidden.'

Before she even finished speaking, Scott pulled his cell phone from its holster, his eyes fixed on the piece of paper. Jayne and Steelie started to leave and heard him say, 'Eric. Is 793 Cobb an address on your list? You're there right now? Okay, check this: Patterson may have been associated with the word Agapanthus.'

Just outside the garage, Scott caught up with Jayne. His

face was full of admiration. 'How in the hell did you know to look in the pad?'

'You said Patterson was at least fifty-one years old. She was likely menopausal. So the pad didn't fit. It was possible, but not probable.'

29

As he stood in the reception area of Sanctuary House listening to Scott through the phone, Eric looked at Aviva Goldsmith. She reminded him of a nun even in the way she waited for him to finish his call. She was calm, placid even, and gazed at his BlackBerry like it was an odd, worldly object she had no need of and felt sorry for him that he did. She switched her gaze to his when he ended the call.

'We have reason to believe that you would have known Eleanor Patterson as Agapanthus.'

Aviva Goldsmith didn't break eye contact but he saw her left eyelid twitch. She steadied it with a finger.

He said quietly, 'Please look at the photo again.'

'I don't need to. Agapanthus never arrived.'

He pounced on her use of the past tense. 'What do you mean, "never arrived"? So you expected her? How was she supposed to get here?'

He felt Angie's hand on his arm so stopped shooting questions at Aviva Goldsmith, who had been trying to get a word in.

'Let me explain,' she said. 'Our system here is that when we're contacted by women who need sanctuary, we don't ask any questions of them. We only give them our address and instructions on how to get here. We don't know their names, anything about them, or where they're

309

coming from, other than if they're out of state or will be arriving with children... oh, and which day. We need only enough information to determine if we have enough space to accommodate them. If they're coming from out of state, like Agapanthus...'

She paused and only then looked again at the portrait in Angie's hand. 'We instruct them that on arrival at the airport, they should take the bus to our nearest stop at the Naval College. We tell them which number bus to take and to walk here to the house. This makes it harder for their abusers to track them because it reduces the number of people they interact with, particularly by not using taxis, and it gives them a way to get here that makes them appear to be local. They're instructed to travel without baggage so they don't appear to be tourists. All of this is designed to reduce their vulnerability while in transit. The bus also provides some safety in numbers.'

Eric caught Angie's eye.

Aviva Goldsmith must have noticed the exchange because she asked, 'Is that important?'

Angie asked, 'You instruct them to use a bus from Atlanta Airport?'

'Ye-es.' She looked at them, her eyes questioning.

Angie said, 'I'm afraid that those instructions may have put Eleanor Patterson directly in the path of a predator.'

Eric thought Aviva Goldsmith looked upset and he wanted to get information from her before that rendered her useless. 'We need to know what day Eleanor Patterson was supposed to arrive at the airport. And we need to know if you've got any other women who didn't show.'

She looked into the middle distance.

310

He asked, 'Are you alright?'

'No, I'm not alright.' She blinked back the wateriness in her eyes and focused on him. 'I'm damn angry.' She turned on her heel, went to the inner door and punched buttons on the security panel.

Watching her, Eric wondered how he could ever have mistaken her for a nun.

The agents went to the window and watched her open a file drawer to pull out some manila folders. She put the items on the window ledge for them.

'There are only three women who haven't arrived at Sanctuary House after making first contact. That's three women since we opened in 1990. In these files are the records of our contact with them and you'll see what dates we expected them.'

Angie immediately began going through the files, her notebook and pen at the ready.

Eric looked at Aviva Goldsmith. 'Were you ever concerned about why these women never arrived?'

She smiled at him wearily. 'Human beings are complex creatures. Women being abused by the person they love or the father of their children have yet another layer of complexity. Even after they've decided to leave the abuser, they can change their minds and stay, or they leave but decide they don't need a place like Sanctuary House to assist them. To exercise choice is a woman's right and it's a crucial one. It has been our practice to assume that a woman who didn't arrive after first contact with us has exercised choice. We know there are alternatives...'

Her hand strayed to the roots of her streak of white hair and he noticed fine scar tissue on the backs of some of her fingers.

'For example,' she was saying, 'we know that it's possible that in the act of leaving, abuse victims face an even greater danger from their partners. But I must say that we had not thought that, having left the abuser, they would encounter someone yet more dangerous.'

She stopped touching her scalp and looked directly at him. 'May I ask how you knew this woman's code word? They're instructed to avoid writing it down or sharing it with anyone.'

Eric was limited in what he could say at this stage in the investigation but he wanted to give her something.

'We think she didn't trust herself to remember something so important. She wrote it down but hid it well. But the fact that she wrote it down may help us find her killer.'

'Her killer?' She echoed him. 'You only said she had been harmed by this person.'

'Yeah. He harmed her by killing her.'

This time, he recognized Aviva Goldsmith's expression; she was angry, damn angry.

Angie closed the last file and gathered up her notebook. 'Got it. Let's go.'

*

Tripper waited until the electronic display came up, acknowledging the cash he'd fed into the machine: *Go pump at #4*. He walked to the motorcycle and began to pump the gas. Through his helmet, he could hear a newscaster's voice coming from the small television screens mounted above the pumps. The man's tone was breathless.

'*Back to our breaking story. We're just now getting*

312

the vision we promised you from Northside where it's understood that police and FBI officials have made a break in the case of several unsolved Atlanta homicides. Teri is live at the scene. Teri?'

Tripper's grip relaxed on the pump and he turned to look at the screen. The camera was focused on the field reporter's heavily made-up face as she lowered her finger from where she'd been covering her ear.

'That's right, John. I should add that, so far, neither the police nor the FBI have made an official statement as to what is taking place in the house that is just about halfway down the block on this quiet street, but it's widely believed to be related to the discoveries of dismembered human remains around Atlanta, all still unidentified. As you can see behind me, law enforcement vehicles are continuing to arrive and they have put up crime scene tape to keep us some distance away.'

The camera shifted from her face to the street behind her and attempted to focus on a house partially obscured by one in the foreground. In the corner of the screen, a box materialized with a view of the same street with a subtitle: *Earlier Today.* Several people were visible emerging from an SUV and crossing the street. Tripper raised the visor on his helmet and stared hard. Jayne Hall and Steelie Lander were unmistakable as they walked behind Special Adversary Houston.

'… and although we have no official word on the case being investigated, the families of missing women in Atlanta are already beginning to congregate here, hoping for some word on their loved ones. Back to you in the studio, John.'

Tripper's anger was so great that it outweighed the zing

of fear that shot through him and made his toes tingle. His plan to go back to California and cause those bitches as much trouble as they'd caused him was no longer enough. They'd interfered one step too far now. He had to eliminate them *and* Houston. It would mean having to take a risk by going to the Mead Street house, which was in violation of The Transition Plan. But he would have to accept that risk.

Tripper lowered his visor with a snap and turned back to the motorcycle.

*

As Angie drove them back to her office, Eric made a series of calls. First, he confirmed that King was indeed working at Atlanta Airport on the day that Eleanor Patterson was due to arrive there. Then he contacted the relevant Transport Police units to track down any CCTV footage from in and around the airport. Without a time frame for Patterson's arrival, they would have to scan through all the footage from that day and hope to see some contact between Patterson and King. They needed a strong link to solidify the case against him because they didn't have proof that he was driving his van when her dismembered arms fell out of it on the freeway. Nor was her purse in his garage enough proof to convict him of killing her.

By the time Eric and Angie walked into the briefing room, the airport's CCTV footage was waiting for them.

The stationary camera had been trained on the information desk and picked up about fifteen feet of tiled floor in front of it. Numerous people passed back and forth in the room and the fast-forward made them appear to be involved in some complicated dance, sometimes appearing to twirl in the center of the floor when they were apparently consulting different monitors mounted around the room.

Angie stopped the first tape several times for false alarms: women who looked like Patterson on fast-forward but then were revealed to look completely different once the tape was put on play. There was no sign of a man cleaning the floors as King was alleged to have been doing that day.

Then Angie exclaimed, 'Whoa!' and rewound the tape. 'You said Houston described a big off-white handbag in the shed at King's house? I think I just saw one.' She pressed *Play*.

At first, the image was just the floor, the desk and the man working behind the desk. Then a woman came into the shot from the right, the airport terminal side, and stood in the center of the floor, turning slowly as if deciding which way to go. Angie paused the tape while the woman was turned toward the camera. The time marker read 16:22:12. Eric looked at the portrait on the projection screen and then back at the frozen CCTV footage.

'That's her,' he stated.

'Yeah. Definitely. Same square jaw, same features, same type of hair. Big, pale bag.'

'Play it, Angie.'

As they watched, Eleanor Patterson turned and walked to the information desk. She kept her handbag tucked under her arm as she stood talking to the attendant. It was while she was doing this that another man entered the shot from the left at time marker 16:26:34. His head was tilted down and he was walking backwards slowly, which was confusing until it became clear he was dry-mopping the floor, shuffling back so that he wouldn't walk on areas he'd just cleaned.

'Shiiit,' Angie hissed.

The man with the mop passed close behind Patterson while she was leaning into the counter to look at something. He paused as though to stretch his back and pulled a kerchief from a back pocket. As he wiped his forehead, he glanced at her. At the moment he put the kerchief back in his pocket, Eric pressed *Pause*.

'That's him. That's King, the sonofabitch.'

'She doesn't even know he's there.'

'He means nothing to her at this stage. If she even noticed him. He's just the guy cleaning the floor. We have to see how he gains her trust.' He restarted the tape.

King carried on mopping until he was out of the shot to the right. Patterson finished the conversation at the desk and walked out of frame to the left, toward the curb pick-up and bus stop area. The time marker read 16:31:02. Then King was back, now entering from the right and working backwards. He seemed to be mopping faster. At 16:40:36, he was no longer visible on the CCTV footage.

Angie exchanged the tape for one that showed the exterior of the transport lounge. They would examine the rest of the interior tape later. She fast-forwarded the tape to the right time and they saw Eleanor Patterson walk out of the building, cross a few lanes for other busses, then stand at the third island across. They had a clear view of her. Over a period of twenty-four minutes, four buses came and went and Patterson didn't get on any of them. Once, she waved at someone on a bus who may have spoken to her and she held up three fingers as if to suggest she was waiting for the number 3 bus.

At time marker 17:03:00, she appeared tired of standing

316

and sat on the bench, keeping her handbag close to her body. And at time marker 17:07:20, a van pulled up to the bus stop. It was a good match for the van Eric had spent two days watching in Mesa, Arizona. In the passenger window was a neat, hand-lettered sign: *Athens*. The town where Sanctuary House was located.

The agents watched Patterson go from waving the van off to shrugging to scanning for the bus again. Then someone opened the passenger door from the inside. Eric lunged forward to hit *Pause*. In the freeze-frame, the driver's wrist was visible. They would get the tape enhanced. He let the recording begin again.

Eleanor Patterson got into the van and closed the door behind her. After exactly three seconds, at time marker 17:08:10, the brake lights on the back of the van went off and it pulled forward, its Georgia license plate clear. It accelerated at a sedate pace until it was out of the frame.

Eric fast-forwarded the tape until they saw the number 3 bus arrive at the stop four minutes later, belching exhaust and canting slightly to one side. He didn't know how late the bus was but it was too late for Mrs. Patterson.

30

When Greg Parker, the archaeology professor, hailed Jayne and Steelie, they came over from where they had been showing his graduate students how to discriminate between human and non-human juvenile bone. Greg was using a trowel to expose a partial, skeletonized hand. The arm it was attached to had some tissue still adhering to the bones. The rest of the arm disappeared into the wall of the depression Greg had created in accordance with the grid pattern laid over the yard. When he had the hand sitting on a pedestal of soil, he leaned back on his heels, holstering the trowel on his tool belt. 'Take a look.'

Jayne got on her knees and peered at the bones. 'Can I borrow a brush?' He handed her a small paintbrush. She gently brushed the cut edge of the bones and confirmed what she thought she had seen: a bright, dry cross-section and a general absence of fractures radiating from the cut edges. Then she let Steelie take a look.

In short order, Steelie said, 'Postmortem cuts.'

Jayne nodded. They all sat back on undisturbed soil and pulled down their masks.

Greg launched in. 'As you can see, I came at that hand from this side of the grid, so I know the fingers aren't here. They're gone. And this isn't the first area of the yard where I've come across this.'

Jayne asked, 'You're thinking someone dug through this

318

body when digging another hole?'

'Maybe he wasn't paying attention to where he buried previous bodies and he hit things with his shovel as he buried someone else?' Greg offered.

Steelie weighed in. 'This actually reminds me of some of the graves around Zvornik.'

Jayne knew what she meant. They hadn't worked directly on the Drina River flanking Serbia but it was common knowledge that mass graves there had been 'robbed' of the bodies of people killed near Srebrenica during the war in Bosnia. Someone had attempted to remove the bodies and hide them in a second location but, because the exhumations were done hastily, perhaps at night and with the clumsy broad strokes of a backhoe bucket, body parts or fragments of clothing were left behind.

Jayne looked back at the hand in question. She could see that there was nothing beyond their cut edges, just soil all the way to the fence-line. Greg Parker had done a nice job of isolating the feature.

Steelie said, 'I'm not sure that this is someone accidentally cutting through previous interments. I mean, *some* of it may turn out to be just Ge— the perpetrator double-digging in one spot, but not this. This is someone taking out parts.' She looked across the yard. 'And they may not all be here.'

Dr. Penman had joined them. 'Are you saying we might dig up this whole yard and not find all the parts of a single body?'

'I'm saying it's a possibility,' she replied. 'I'm not up on serial killer behavior but I'm not sure that the person who wants to kill and dismember is the same person who wants to go back and move already-buried decomposing parts around his backyard just for fun.'

'Yeah,' said Greg. 'The latter sounds more like what you guys are known for.'

Jayne glanced at Steelie and they stood up. An uncomfortable silence followed that Greg tried to fill.

'Like the Body Farm,' he said uncertainly. 'At UTK... Tennessee...?'

Dr. Penman stayed on topic. 'What do you recommend?'

Jayne looked around the site. 'Look, you were always going to have to grid off the whole yard. I'd suggest that you carry on with that process but be alert to any remains that show disturbance or fragmentation from postmortem damage. Then carefully go from the known to the unknown wherever you see it. Since you're likely dealing with dismembered bodies, it's going to take just that much more attention to whether the cuts are peri or post.'

'So, I'm looking for the usual perimortem signs? Radiating fractures, lifting and bending?'

'Yes.' She looked at Greg, who was getting to his feet. 'And Greg can cover what's familiar to him with postmortem breaks from the archaeological setting.'

Steelie patted Dr. Penman on the back. 'You guys are a dream team.'

He huffed. 'I've just realized it takes two of us to do what just one of you can do.'

'Perhaps, but neither of us can tell a stone tool from a chipped rock, nor could we analyze stomach contents.'

'Nor would you want to,' Greg laughed lightly.

Scott came over. 'What's going on?'

Dr. Penman explained the apparent disturbance of the burials.

Scott looked serious. 'Do you know how many people you've got so far?'

'A minimum number of three, based on the fifteen body parts we've exhumed so far. We've had two right clavicles with the sternal end fused and one left clavicle with a fully unfused sternal end.'

'In English?' Scott said.

Steelie answered him. 'Collarbones. Two right collarbones, so that's two people, and they're both fused at the business end, so both people are probably over twenty-five years. Then one left collarbone from someone under twenty-five, which makes three. Minimum. Though only one cranium so far.'

'Okay,' Scott replied. 'From the garage, we've got ID cards or driver's licenses from eight different people so far. All female. We'll be cross-checking to see if any of them have missing person reports, besides Eleanor Patterson and the two names I recognize of local missing sex workers. Not all the trophies may be from women the suspect killed; there could be some assault victims we don't know about yet. But if you've only found three people so far, keep looking.'

'Say no more,' Greg said, walking away.

'And I'm afraid, Dr. Penman, that I've got to take away these two ladies. They've got a plane to catch.'

The ME shook hands with Jayne and Steelie as though they'd known each other for years and then the women joined Scott. He spoke under his breath. 'I wanted you two to see this.' He was holding a set of transparent evidence bags, which he fanned out in his hands. 'King made copies of those photos from Kigali.'

Steelie flicked on her flashlight and concentrated it on the corner of the top photograph. 'Look at the photo board, though, Scott. The others had a UN Civilian Police case number. These are different.'

Scott turned the photos toward him. The board read *EK-001*. He whistled softly before translating. 'Eugene King: first victim.'

'A perfect trophy,' Jayne said.

'Yeah,' agreed Steelie. 'Anyone seeing them thinks they're legit crime scene or case photos. He can explain them away too; after all, he was an FBI employee at the time and who knows what you weird Bureau people carry around.'

Scott dropped the photos to his side. 'Alright, I've got your ride out front. He'll drive you back to your motel, drop you with some dinner and then we'll be sending an Agent Carter to take you to the airport. He'll have your boarding passes.'

Steelie detoured to say goodbye to Greg's students while Jayne preceded Scott into the house. As she mounted the back stairs, she noticed it was getting dark. She turned on her flashlight and felt the chill of that house go into her bones again. She could barely believe she actually knew the person who lived here and was responsible for what was in that yard. That partial hand bothered her. Where was the rest of that person?

She came out from the house and was halted by the scene in the street: a knot of people holding lit candles and something else... Jayne gradually perceived that they were photographs, but only photos of women. Some portraits were big, while others were snapshots; women holding children, women laughing, women looking dubiously at the camera, women in graduation clothing. Women who were alive. Alive but missing.

Then Scott was in the doorway next to her. 'They already know, Jayne. Or they suspect.'

Scott's tone was so flat that she looked at his face and found that he was trying to compose himself before speaking again.

He cleared his throat. 'I recognize some of the relatives of women who went missing on my watch,' he said before he set off for the FBI tent.

Jayne looked at the relatives one last time. She felt they were identical to the group of relatives who'd waited outside their UN exhumation in Kigali in '96. The team had driven slowly out of the site with the body bags strapped down in the back of their pick-up and the relatives had pushed forward to touch their hands to the truck. *Everyone is the same, everywhere.*

Jayne followed in Scott's footsteps, feeling like she could be in Kigali, walking into the UN's morgue tent, then stripping off mask, booties, gloves – just like this. Putting everything into red biohazard bags – just like this. Movements so familiar, she could have done them in her sleep back then. Now, inside this tent, she couldn't tell where she was, what year it was. She could go out and find that it was 1996 again and Gene would be there; everything was the same and the families were waiting.

When she was ready, she hesitated to leave the tent.

But Scott was back in action mode. He gave her hand

a quick, encouraging squeeze. 'Follow me. When I stop to talk to the relatives, keep going to my right. The black Suburban has an agent in it, waiting for you. Just get in. I'll send Steelie over when she's done.'

Jayne followed him out into the deepening darkness. She noticed a television camera when a bright lamp suddenly came on. She heard Scott announce his name and title and tell the press that there was no official information yet. She kept walking, focused on the dark bulk of the Suburban beyond the crowd.

Then a hand pulled her to the side.

31

Half-empty pizza boxes sat in the middle of the conference table in the FBI briefing room. Agent Mark Wilson chewed anti-gas pills as he watched the CCTV footage of King's van pulling away from the airport with Eleanor Patterson in the passenger seat at 5:08PM. He had lost track of how many times he'd examined the footage but he kept doing it in the hopes that he would glean some clue as to where King was now.

*

Agent Angela Nicks watched Mark from her seat at the head of the table as she tapped a pencil against the papers in front of her. She had drawn circles around King's name and the names of the missing women and what they knew about each. She was looking for ways the circles might overlap and give them a lead on where King could be hiding now. So far, it wasn't working too well. The modus operandi that King had displayed at the airport with Eleanor Patterson appeared to be the only time he had used it. They didn't know how he might have adjusted the MO when he wasn't at the airport but he had got the women back to his house somehow. Angie switched to tapping the eraser end of the pencil against the tip of her nose. She knew that sometimes worked.

*

Agent Scott Houston was temporarily *not* thinking about King as he used the computer to connect to the internet and check on the status of the return flight Jayne was due to board that evening with Steelie. The Bureau's state-of-the-art, encrypted broadband connection was slower than he wanted it to be and he waited, emptying his brain as he stared at the screen. Then he realized something.

'Did anyone check the Agency 32/1 email account for the messages from King?'

He was met with silence, which was enough to get him to bail out from the airline website and switch to the web-based Thirty-Two One account. Mark came over with the password that Jayne had left with them and Scott typed it in. After what felt like a delay, the inbox appeared.

'Jesus.' Scott sat up straighter.

'What time zone is that stamp?' Mark pulled up a chair.

Angie and Eric immediately came over.

Mark explained, 'King sent them a message today. Depending on what time zone the account's set to, he might have sent it just a few hours ago.'

Scott had clicked on the message, whose subject line was 'Hi from San Fran'.

They read the message on screen.

Jayne: bk yr way nxt wk. Dinner? GK

Angie leaned in closer to the screen. 'That's not an email; it's a text message.'

Scott gestured at the screen. 'It's an email. It came on email.'

'But it was sent from a cell phone,' she persisted. 'Look, hit *Reply*. See what happens.'

Scott followed her instructions and the 'To' field was

326

filled with an email address made up of letters and enough numbers to resemble a telephone number.

'Angie, can you—' Scott turned but she was already on her phone.

'Tech unit? I need a check on a cell number. This is priority one.'

*

Standing at the dressing table in the motel room, Jayne placed the candle in her bag and thought about the woman who'd stopped her in the street by Gene's house. She hadn't looked very old but her skin had made Jayne think of parchment. She'd been holding a photograph, its subject obscured by her fingertips. She'd smiled at Jayne but had kept a hold on her arm until another woman had joined them.

The second woman had been a bit younger but still mature, with brown skin. She'd arrived to offer an unlit candle ringed by a paper collar to catch dripping wax. Jayne had accepted it with a nod. Then the two had smiled and turned away as though their work was done and, in that moment, Jayne had no longer felt confused about what year it was or where she was. It was where she always was and where she always would be: halfway between the living and the dead, helping to work a link that transcended time and space because the need for it was timeless and crossed all borders. It existed wherever the living searched for the missing and wherever people died deprived of their names. Jayne had held the candle on the ride to the motel and now she would carry it home to Los Angeles.

She heard the knock at the door that she and Steelie had

been expecting: Agent Carter, arriving to drive them to the airport. She glanced at Steelie to see if she was ready. Steelie was zipping up her bag so Jayne went to open the door.

The man standing there was dressed in motorcycle leathers and helmet, which was unexpected. He raised the visor and said, 'Hello, again.'

Even before Jayne heard the voice, she'd recognized Gene's eyes.

Abruptly and belatedly, she shoved the door closed but it bounced back at her fast and she was pushed off balance. As she stumbled backwards, she was aware of Steelie charging Gene with a cry that sounded far away and of him coming across the threshold, and then her vision went gray at the edges, closing down further and further, until there was nothing.

*

Scott had ceded his seat in front of the computer to Mark, who had navigated into the settings page of the Agency 32/1 email account.

'There.' Mark pointed to the screen. 'The account is on Pacific Time. But incoming messages could still be stamped with the time at the sender's location.' He looked up at Scott. 'Do we believe this? That King's in San Francisco?'

Scott was standing with his arms crossed, watching Angie on the phone with the technical support unit. 'No. No way. I don't know what game he's playing but he's here in Atlanta. We tracked him here in Wayne Spicer's car.'

Eric said quietly, 'We don't have a firm ID from the paramedics or anyone else who got eyes on the driver of the Spicer car.'

Scott gave his partner a withering look and Eric put his hands up in surrender. Just then, Angie turned toward them, a hand raised as she listened to her phone. They turned toward her expectantly.

'Okay, okay,' she said and then covered the mouthpiece of the phone as she addressed the three men. 'The text message was sent from a cell phone today at 1:07PM Eastern.'

Scott walked up to her. 'Is it turned on right now? Can they track it?' He all but took the phone from her hand.

She said, 'It doesn't need to be turned on – hang on.' She listened, thanked the person on the other end and then cut the call. 'So the cell doesn't need to be turned on for the phone company to ping it and get a location within one hundred feet. But first we gotta get a warrant out to the phone company.'

'This is bullshit!' Scott fumed. 'This is high priority, did you tell them that?'

'We might have another way.' She exchanged a glance with Mark. 'The detectives in Missings at Atlanta PD have the technology to ping cells.'

Scott looked at each of the agents in turn. 'APD Missing Persons? You know any of those detectives?'

Angie's mouth was set in a line. 'I've got a couple of favors I can call in. It might not be enough.'

'If they're like other detectives I know, they'll scratch you this time if you're ready to scratch them next time. What's it gonna take, Ange?' Scott implored.

'Let me make some calls.' She turned to leave the room.

Eric was hard on her heels. 'I'll start the warrant process in case we need it.' The door slammed behind them.

32

Jayne blinked her eyes to full openness and felt total confusion about where she was. Her head hurt and her mouth was dry. She tried to swallow and felt cloth – *a gag?* – holding her mouth open, wicking her saliva away. She instinctively raised her hands to remove it but discovered she was lying on her arms and they were bound behind her. She looked up and saw a doorway she didn't recognize. And then it all came back. *The motel, Atlanta, Gene. Oh, God.* She shivered convulsively and raised her head to look down the length of her body. She saw duct tape binding her ankles and then noticed movement across the room.

Gene was dressed entirely in white Tyvek with the hood pulled over his hair and surgical gloves on his hands, eyes staring wide as he bent over Steelie – *Steelie!* – who was stomach-down on the bed, arms tied behind her back, her face turned away from Jayne. And then she registered the sounds. Gene grunting with exertion, the noises coming from lips thinned with effort, interspersed with higher-pitched sounds that had to be coming from Steelie as he tied a gag at the back of her head.

Suddenly, Steelie kicked out at Gene with her bound legs and managed to connect with his lower back. He muttered something and stepped away from the bed to yank at her legs, pulling her backwards. As she fell to the floor, she twisted to avoid landing on her face and the movement

330

allowed her to see Jayne. They locked eyes and when Jayne saw tears in Steelie's, her own tears welled up instantly, but the connection was quickly lost as Gene yanked Steelie up to her knees. She bucked and twisted, so he clamped her against him as he groped her body roughly, his fingers spread wide.

Jayne screamed but the sound went nowhere, hampered by her dry throat and truncated by the gag. She frantically rolled to the left but couldn't get past her own shoulder to get up. She cried out once more in desperation, heart pounding, and craned her neck again. Steelie was trying to slam her head backwards into Gene's face as he bent over her. Jayne felt a rush of hope. *That's it. Get him. Get him!*

But Gene just strode forward, pulling Steelie on her knees until she was against the edge of the bed. He pushed her over easily, using one hand to keep her head buried in the covers as he used the other to pull open all the snaps on Steelie's cargo pants. Jayne's eyes widened. *Christ!* She had to get him away from Steelie. She looked around wildly and saw the bathroom window was open. Hoping he would be afraid she could raise the alarm from the bathroom, she started pushing backwards over the threshold, making as much noise as she could.

She looked back to see if Gene had noticed her and almost stopped breathing when she saw that he was smiling to himself. But then she saw why: he'd located Steelie's cell phone in one of her pockets. He'd been frisking her – violently – but he'd found what he wanted and had stopped. Dragging Steelie by the neck to the head of the bed, he began tying her to the frame, keeping her face to the wall.

Jayne felt her lungs start to function again and she threw her energy into rolling to the right this time, hoping to get all the way over onto her stomach, but her knees smacked into the side of a bathtub with a loud thud before she completed the revolution. Almost immediately, she felt a foot on her ribcage, rolling her on to her back again.

She tried to yell, 'Get off me,' but it just came out as noise so she was left to simply glare at Gene. There was a large bruise between his eyes that had leaked blood into the whites, making his pale irises yet more preternatural.

He smiled down at her, a bag in one hand. 'Thanks for getting yourself in here. This is exactly where I want you.'

He closed the window and opened the bath taps to full blast. When the water hit the empty tub, the initial noise was deafening and Jayne had a frightening image of Gene drowning first her and then Steelie. But he sat on the tub's edge, keeping a foot on her while retrieving an object from his bag. Jayne couldn't see what it was because his hand was clasped around it but the glimpse between his fingers suggested a grenade. It had to be something else.

He leaned toward her and held the object to her ear, pressing it to her skin. 'I will remove your gag, but if you start yelling, I pull the pin on this baby, which gives me time to leave and you time to die. Got it?'

'Pin' only meant grenade to Jayne. She tried to look at what he was holding to her head but he wouldn't let her. It was cold enough to be metallic but it could have been hard plastic. Now she understood that he had the faucets blasting so that anyone passing the room couldn't overhear while he got some piece of information from her before killing them like he must have killed all the others. She wanted to cry, to give up. She closed her eyes.

'I said, got it?' He jammed the object even harder against her ear.

She forced her eyes open and nodded.

He pulled her gag down and in so doing leaned his foot hard on to her diaphragm, making her convulse as her stomach muscles tensed. He looked at her like she was a specimen in a dish and then tut-tutted her. 'Jayne. I'm surprised you didn't recognize my MO the second you came to the freeway in LA.'

She actually felt her eyes darting around in their sockets as she took in the implications of his words. She tried to make some saliva. 'How did you know I was there?'

'I was watching you. And I must say, for an "expert", you didn't put two and two together at all because I haven't changed my cuts since Kigali.'

Jesus. He really did kill that woman in Rwanda. 'I didn't know about Kigali.'

Gene cocked his head. 'You surprise me. I was sure Gerrit would have sent you the crime scene photos. It was such an unusual crime for Rwanda at the time. Quite evolved compared to all the other killing.'

Jayne couldn't hide her disgust.

He rolled his eyes. 'You've always been too soft, Jayne. I've heard you talking to your so-called clients—'

She felt her cheeks flush. 'What are you talking about?'

'Why don't you just tell them that if their daughter's missing, she's already dead?'

'So you *are* the one who bugged my phone!'

'You shouldn't give them false hope like you do.'

'Why did you come and see me? I don't understand.'

Jayne knew she sounded needy and plaintive but couldn't help her tone. Details from the past two weeks were jostling for position in her mind.

'I wanted to know what you knew.' He gestured with the object clasped in his hand and Jayne was finally sure: it was a grenade. Small, dusty, lethal. 'I had to know how much time I had before I needed to go to ground. And everything I heard put me at ease. You suck at your job as bad as Houston does. And I would've left you alone, given how incompetent you are, but then you told Houston about me. Now you have to pay for that.'

Scott? 'I – I didn't tell him anything.'

'You never were a good liar, Jayne. I saw you at my mother's house. You were there today, leading Houston right in.'

'But I wasn't! He found you and your house himself!' She was almost shouting over the noise of the open faucet.

'Spare me. He's an *agent*. He can't find his own backside without help.'

He sounded petulant and Jayne suddenly saw a way in. She tried to push down her fear and changed her tack, wanting to keep Gene talking long enough for the FBI driver to arrive and end this nightmare. She didn't know what time it was but the airport pick-up had to be any minute now.

'You've got some issue, don't you?' She was trying to sound conversational, as though she wasn't lying on the floor trussed up in twine and duct tape, but her underlying fear was making her shiver and her voice was uneven and trembly. 'Some kind of grudge against agents? What, did you apply and they wouldn't take you? Too old, were you?'

She wasn't ready when he lunged at her and slapped her face, his hand open, the rubber of the surgical glove burning her skin. Tears stung her eyes but she knew she'd hit a nerve. 'That's it, isn't it?'

'Shut up!' He was clenching and unclenching the hand he'd used to slap her.

'So you applied,' Jayne pressed on. 'And you didn't make it – for whatever reason. Though I'm surprised they didn't take you, what with your postgraduate degree, obvious intelligence, previous Bureau history, plus you're active and athletic.' She was almost gagging on her words but her voice was getting stronger. 'I would have thought you were perfect agent material. You know you're good, right? No matter what they say.'

She watched the compliment take its effect. Gene's back straightened perceptibly, his mouth relaxed.

She went further. 'You were already a Bureau employee in the lab. Why was it so important to become an agent?'

He didn't respond initially, but when he did, his eyes were fixed on the grenade. 'I wanted to stay in Rwanda another year but the Bureau said extensions were only open to agents.'

Jayne hadn't expected this and couldn't immediately think of a follow-up question. 'So?'

His eyes bored into her. 'If you hadn't noticed, not a single one of those "special" agents can investigate their way out of a paper bag. Not only did the Bureau prevent me from carrying on my work in Rwanda, but two years later, they decided to send a team to Kosovo for the UN and what happens? They send that stupid piece of shit *rookie* in my place. *My* place.'

335

Jayne frowned. 'What rookie?'

Gene rolled his eyes at her like she wasn't keeping up. 'Houston,' he sneered. 'There I was, with all my forensic experience as well as a previous UN mission – I even advised them on who to get for the team – and who gets passed over? Me. And who goes? Scott Houston. I don't think so. No, uh-uh, the Bureau was only going to fuck me over like that one time. I resigned immediately and deprived them of my talents. I've been making sure they know what a mistake they made on Houston ever since. I've taken my time but I'm about to see that dirtbag stripped of every accolade he's received. I've shown he can't even solve a couple of homicides, that he's a fantasist who sees serial killers around every corner. He can't even close a couple of local missing person cases, for Chrissakes!'

While Gene had been ranting, Jayne had been hearing that familiar, superior tone applied to Scott like he was a target. To her knowledge, Scott had actually joined the FBI in 1994 and didn't even know Gene. She was struggling to understand how she had missed the signs that Gene was a sociopathic killer in the time she'd been side by side with him in the graves. She was suddenly assaulted with the images from the FBI briefing room. The technicolor of Rwanda bleached out by midday sun, the rich soil wetted anew with fresh blood, and then she remembered what she'd seen as it happened: Gene at The Cadillac one night. He'd shocked everyone by skirting UN guidelines to approach a table of known escorts and select a young woman. He'd only danced with her, hadn't taken her home – hadn't even bought her the customary cold drink despite the crush of heat and noise and twirling disco ball light. But the young woman had been dancing with death and hadn't even known it. Not only that, Gene's colleagues hadn't seen him fully and hadn't protected her.

Jayne was mortified to feel tears springing to her eyes. 'So you... murdered that woman in Kigali. You killed someone in a place that had just survived a *genocide*?' Her voice trembled audibly.

He fed off her display of emotion. 'But even you understand why it was the ideal place to do it, don't you? What was one more dead body in Rwanda? People were too busy with eight hundred thousand other corpses to pay attention.'

'But... but you were there as a forensic scientist! You were supposed to be helping people, not victimizing them. How could you do that?'

He shook his head. 'Still such an idealist, aren't you, Jayne? Let me tell you the truth about these victims you put on such a high pedestal. The cases we got at the Bureau were *all* about stupidity. The vics were stupid to get themselves into a situation where they were killed and the killers were stupid enough to leave behind trace. After a few months of scraping dried shit out of people's underwear after they'd voided their bowels, I knew the world was a better place without people like them, but I had no intention of being caught getting rid of 'em.'

Jayne gazed up at him in wonder, forcing herself to skip over his obviously willful ignorance of the way bowels can sometimes relax upon death, leaving feces free to flow into anyone's underwear, regardless of their IQ. 'You're saying that you think some people deserve to die? You think that young woman in Kigali *deserved* to die?'

337

'I'm saying I don't want stupid people in the gene pool.'

Jayne almost spluttered. 'Who the hell are you to say who's stupid?'

Gene exchanged the grenade for a ball of twine he pulled from his bag. 'Hey, I give people the opportunity to make a choice: go with an instinct for survival or go with the social fiction of Trust in Others. If they can't make the choice to survive, they shouldn't be allowed to live, let alone reproduce. It's the same choice our ancestors had when they came face-to-face with a lion in the savannah. I give them that choice, they usually make the wrong one and I get to clean up while I simultaneously drag Houston down.'

He flashed a grin at her. 'Who said men can't multitask?'

Jayne pictured Eleanor Patterson meeting a man like this when she was at her most vulnerable. Gene was justifying his murders with some kind of perversion of evolutionary biology when, really, he had victimized women, first out of career frustration and then out of misplaced revenge. But his reasons didn't change anything. She couldn't fake a plaintive tone any longer; Gene was deeply wrong and he needed to know it.

'You haven't been giving people choices; you've been giving them bait-and-switch. All you've done, Gene, is *betray* people's trust.'

He stood up, towering over her as he placed a foot on either side of her waist. 'You and Steelie have always had a way of sounding holier-than-thou.'

Holding one end of the twine, he tossed the ball of ragged, twisted thread into the other room. The ball unwound readily until it hit the motel room door. Then

338

Gene dropped down onto her, trapping her with his knees. 'We've talked enough. You're going to lie here in this bathroom, Jayne Hall, the lure on a hook for Houston, and when he comes through that door looking for you – and I know he will because he likes the chase and you've been giving him one hell of a chase for quite a while now – uh-uh, don't try to deny it – he's going to walk in and trip the line to this grenade I got specially for you.'

He leaned down toward her face. 'I lied when I said I hadn't kept up with where you went after Kigali. I heard about Kosovo and the mine your team blew, so you should enjoy this. You'll get to watch Houston and Steelie bite it. You'll probably survive it with a few limbs intact. Now, you start the show by calling Lover Boy to reel him in and I'll rig the room. If you tip him off to my plan, I pull the pin the second the words come out of your mouth. You don't mind if I frisk you, do you?' He began going through her pockets.

Jayne panicked. She didn't want to die and she knew Scott wouldn't be the one to come through that door. It would be the FBI driver. Another innocent, just like Benni in Kosovo – only there because she was there. She had to stop this before Gene could attach the twine to the pin, before he could even reach back into his bag for the grenade. He had located her phone and rocked back as he held it aloft, compressing her tailbone against the tile floor. And suddenly all the fear and pain mixed in with his weight on her hips to trigger an old, old memory – she'd been young, on a mat, in a class, being taught: *Defend yourself.*

She screamed with all her might and Gene reacted just as she'd hoped, lunging to push the gag back into her mouth, his weight now forward and, crucially, off her hips. Using strength she didn't know she had left, she thrust her hips up as hard and high as she could, sending him head-first toward the cold, hard toilet bowl, shutting her eyes just before his knees smashed into her face.

*

Scott attempted to be patient as he watched Angie from the doorway of her office.

When she finally slammed down her phone, she shouted, 'We got it! Guys, we got it.'

Scott felt warmth spread across his chest and went to her, his hand up for a high-five. She hit it and they merged it into a down-low, followed by one of their old handgrips.

Eric came in from the hallway. 'You got the location?'

'Not yet,' she replied, grabbing an FBI-marked windbreaker from the back of her chair. 'It's in Northeast. We can go mobile and I'll keep in cell phone contact for them to give us the hundred-foot radius.'

'Okay, I got the warrant underway, so I'm coming with you.'

Mark was out of his seat. 'I'll drive.'

The four agents ran down the stairs and out the back of the building to the motor pool.

Mark shouted, '4-8-6! Flak jackets and shotguns.' The others diverted course to the black Suburban with the corresponding license plate. Within seconds, Mark had them underway, activating the red and blue flashing lightbars in the front and rear windows. They left the Bureau parking lot at speed.

Angie's cell phone rang. She listened and then said to

Mark, 'Get to the expressway and take the first exit. We're keeping the line open.'

Mark swerved around a double-parked delivery truck and then braked hard as a taxi veered into their lane. 'Come *on*!'

Angie's voice came loud. 'We got him! Last ping is from near Eden and 45th. We're almost there.'

Mark slowed when they approached the intersection and turned off the emergency lights.

Scott looked out the front window, saw the motel across the street, dismissed it and then did a double take. 'Back it up, Mark. Now!'

Mark threw the vehicle into reverse and pulled to the curb with a screech of rubber. Scott held a hand to his ear as he made a call on his phone.

Eric said quietly to the others, 'That's the motel where Travel put Jayne and Steelie when we all flew in this morning.'

Angie and Mark both uttered expletives.

Scott holstered his phone and then spoke, his voice taut. 'Carter's here, in the parking lot. He arrived early to pick them up, heard bath water running, assumed someone was bathing, so was waiting until the appointed time to go back and knock.'

Eric cut in, 'King's got to be in there with them; no way one of 'em's having a freaking bath right now.'

'No shit. Let's get our gear on. We're going in on the presumption that King is armed. We are *not* waiting for further back-up. Got it?'

The others assented. When they ran to the building, they split into two pairs to cover both of the exterior staircases

341

up to the second floor. They positioned themselves on either side of Jayne and Steelie's door, guns drawn, while Mark held a small battering ram. Scott nodded at him and he rammed the door. It slammed open with a crack as they all shouted, 'Federal agents! Drop your weapon!!'

They were met with silence and they charged the room.

Scott saw Eric rush to the bed, where Steelie was on the floor against the wall, but his eyes were taking in the emptiness of the rest of the room. He felt rising panic as he imagined King taking Jayne away with him. Then he heard a shout from his left.

'Call a medic!'

He spun around and Angie's concerned expression gave him a stab of worry. He pushed past Mark to get to Angie in the bathroom doorway, heard a squelching noise and looked down. The threshold was soaking. His eyes followed a film of bloody water across the floor. There were two bodies by the toilet: a man collapsed around the bowl, his knees obscuring the head of someone contorted underneath. *Jayne.*

33

Scott stood next to Jayne's hospital bed, looking at the clipboard he'd removed from the door of her room. She murmured and he looked at her, but her eyes hadn't opened. She was semi-reclined under a blanket and her forehead looked discolored. He could see abrasions on her arms where the short sleeves of the hospital gown ended. When he heard footsteps in the hallway, he darted out in time to stop a nurse, who gave him a polite, interrogative smile.

He held up his Bureau badge and the clipboard. 'What does all of this stuff mean? Why is she out cold?'

'She's not out cold. She's sleeping.' The nurse took possession of the clipboard and slotted it back into the holder on the door. 'There's nothing to be concerned about, sir. She took a knock on the head that had a mild concussive effect and the doctor wanted to keep her in for observation. Please don't disturb her.'

Scott sighed and ran his hands through his hair. 'What about Lander? Steelie Lander? They would have come in together.'

'Around the corner in 808. I believe one of your colleagues is already there.' The nurse continued down the hallway.

Scott turned to look at Jayne again. Her mouth was hanging open slightly and the fluorescent light above the bed was shining bright on her forehead. He went back over to switch off the light, half-hoping the noise would wake her. He wanted to ascertain that she was really alright, to apologize for putting her in danger.

He reached down to her cheek but remembered what had happened when he'd picked her up off that bathroom floor and pulled the gag from her mouth. She had opened her eyes but hadn't been able to focus on him. Even when he'd repeated her name, she hadn't recognized him, and then the paramedics had arrived, pushing Scott aside while castigating him for moving someone without first establishing the nature of their injuries.

He had been forced to stand on the sidelines, watching them tend to both Jayne and an unconscious Eugene King. Scott realized that he hadn't even thought about the effect the same sight would be having on Steelie, who'd been standing just behind him, supported by Mark and Eric. He should talk to her.

He stepped away from Jayne's bed and saw that Angie was watching him from the doorway.

She looked him up and down as he approached. 'You got a chance to change clothes?' She kept her voice low.

'When I logged the evidence.'

'Any sign of SSA Franks?'

Scott shook his head.

'What about the grenade?'

'Contained. Bomb techs have it.'

Angie's eyes went to Jayne. 'How's she doing?'

'Nurse says she's fine. Just sleeping. What's the word on King?'

'The doc won't let us have him yet. Seems he's

experienced two separate traumatic "events" involving his head in the last twenty-four hours. He won't be out of the woods for a day or two.' She paused as she looked over at Jayne. 'She's tough. Wouldn't think it to look at her.' Angie made to leave, then turned back. 'Don't let that one get away.'

Scott tried to acknowledge this suddenly personal directive with a casual response but only succeeded in producing a strangled noise.

Angie regarded him with a smile for a moment and then set off down the hallway.

Scott took a final look at Jayne before going in search of Steelie's room.

When he looked in her door, he saw Eric sitting on the side of Steelie's bed, his hand closed over her fist. He was saying, 'Keep the thumb on top. That's key.'

Scott took in the bruise coming up on Steelie's chin. Her hair was sticking out in every direction at once, making her head look huge over a thin body lost in a voluminous hospital gown.

'Welcome to fight club,' she said when she noticed Scott. 'The first rule of fight club is... know how to fight.' She pointed at Eric. '*That's* key.' She rested against the pillows.

Scott sat down in the chair just inside the door. 'Eric giving you lessons?'

'Yeah, which beats him giving me medical tests. A minute ago, he asked me how many fingers he was holding up. It was just the one. The middle one.'

Eric smiled as he stood up. 'I don't get to run that joke too often.' He crossed to the door. 'I'll be back in five.'

Steelie asked, 'Is Gene here as well?'

Scott nodded.

'You've got him under guard, right?'

'He's not going anywhere.' He cast around for something to say. 'I just came from Jayne's room. She was sleeping. She's going to be fine.'

'The doctor told me.'

They fell silent. Scott leaned his elbows on his knees and looked at the floor. He was uncomfortable but spoke anyway. 'Steelie, I owe you both an apology. I should have known—' He broke off to see why she was groaning.

Steelie was trying to sit up. 'Should have known what?' she challenged. 'That Gene was lying in wait for us? That he's got a mean right hook? What are you, a mind reader?' She sank back onto the pillows.

He had never seen her look so angry. 'Point taken.' Waiting for her to compose herself, he averted his eyes and took in the IV stand next to her bed. The tag on the bag of fluids appeared to read: *Lander, Sandra*. He frowned and tried to focus on the first name and then quickly looked over at Steelie, hoping she hadn't clocked him reading it. He was almost sure it had her name as Sandra. He went over to the side of her bed.

'Look, Steelie, when I was driving back from Phoenix with Jayne, I had a… situation.'

'Yeah, I heard.'

'Right. Well, then you'll know she bailed me out. Which made me wonder who bails her out, when she needs it. Is it you or is there someone else?'

She raised her eyebrows at him but didn't speak.

He continued. 'Because I think Jayne needs it. At least to deal with the seriously bad dreams I think she's having.' He waited. 'I'm only asking because I care about her. A lot. No one should be alone on this... or groping in the dark. In the Bureau, we don't even get a choice about getting debriefed. Can you guys access follow-up debriefs from the UN?'

'In our day, we never got debriefings, only check-ins.' She seemed to assess him. 'But, in my humble opinion, Jayne wouldn't have these repercussions if it weren't for one particular incident, which jumbled up some of her reactions to other, normal things. In lo these many years that you two have been talking on the phone I would have thought you'd have covered this.'

Scott frowned. 'Covered what?'

'She still hasn't told you about Benni?'

'Who's he? Or she...?'

'He.' Steelie inhaled. 'Benni was one of our NATO escort soldiers in Kosovo. French, all of twenty years old. One of our teams was scouting for a clandestine gravesite so they were off the tarmac, like always, but using a path that had been de-mined.'

Scott felt a sense of dread.

Steelie said, 'Somehow Benni, who was up front, tripped a mine – antipersonnel, so he didn't die right away. He bled out a few feet from Jayne. She told me she couldn't even go to him because the de-miners were screaming for everyone to stop moving.'

'Jesus.'

'Yeah. Her recurring nightmare since then involves her stepping on a mine but, like, a Bouncing Betty?'

'Pressure-release.'

'That's the one. In her dreams, she steps on it, hears the click but can't move. She has to tell everyone around her to stay away. Even the de-miners are looking at her with pity because it's only a matter of time before she loses her balance or falls asleep. That's when she wakes up.'

Steelie paused. 'I've heard you've got a good six hours to intervene before a traumatic memory fixes itself like fucking concrete in your brain. No one talked to Jayne, or anyone else on that team, for three days, and even then it wasn't a private debrief. So...' She reached for her bedside control and began reclining the bed. 'You know anything that can break up concrete?'

After a moment, Scott met her gaze. 'Freeze-thaw usually works.'

She gave him a slight nod. 'Then get to it, Houston, because – to answer your question from earlier – there ain't no one else.' Closing her eyes, she settled back on the pillows. 'Now, I'm an invalid and I know my rights, so stop hassling me. Sheesh.'

He took a chance and looked at the nametag on the IV bag again from much closer. *Lander, Sandra*. Then he pulled the covers above her shoulders, looking at her bruised chin one more time. 'It's good to have you back, Steelie.'

'Yeah, I'm great,' she mumbled.

Scott closed the door softly behind him but stood with his back to it, trying to absorb what he'd just learned about Benni's death. Trauma like that would have a different character than the trauma he'd expect either Jayne or Steelie to have from their work as forensic anthropologists. Scott didn't know the ins and outs of survivor guilt but he could guess that Jayne felt half-dead inside. And yet... when he'd been imploding by the side of the road, she'd been the one to give him a lifeline. She was vibrant, electric, alive.

Scott pushed off the door and started toward her room. He wanted to take her away, out of this hospital – out of this *world*. He wanted to be the one next to her when she had a nightmare. He wanted to wake her from it, take her from it. He wanted to give her something else to dream about.

Feeling a tug on his arm, he found Eric alongside, animated and urgent. Sound came in next. Scott hadn't even heard his partner calling his name.

'What's happening?' From Eric's expression, Scott assumed the worst: King had managed to die in the last half-hour.

'You won't believe this.' Eric was drawing him back toward the elevators. 'You know the cell phone sim cards the criminalists found at King's house?'

Scott nodded.

'Tech support pulled the numbers off them to cross-check against those suspect numbers on our missing sex workers' call records.'

'King called the victims,' Scott deduced.

'Nope. He called our old boss Franks.'

'*What?*' Scott halted.

Eric pulled on his arm again to get him into the elevator and pressed the button for the ground floor. 'One of the sims shows a call to our anonymous tip line and two show a call each to SSA Franks.'

'*Direct* to Franks?'

Eric nodded. 'They date to after you started the media campaign for information on the van. Each call is about six months apart. We don't know the content yet but SSA Franks is going to have to give up his own phone log. My

349

bet is that King was the anonymous tipster SSA Turner referred to when he quizzed me in LA – the guy whose tips Franks was relying on to crucify you and get us transferred out of here.'

Scott felt anger and vindication in equal measure.

Eric looked at him. 'King was playing him like a violin, man.'

They left the elevator and walked out to the Crown Victoria Scott had left parked in an area for emergency vehicles. 'You think Franks will go down for this?'

'If he doesn't go down, he'll at least go sideways. It'll be up to OPR. They'll decide how much more he should have done to verify the information in the tips before he used it to make operational decisions. You want me to drive?'

Scott hesitated at the car door and looked back at the hospital, where only every third light or so was still on at this late hour. He tried to work out which one was Jayne's room and then realized he didn't even know which side of the building she was on. But he did know she was sleeping and that was the best thing, for now.

Scott turned back to his partner. 'Who's on King's door?'

'We've got two guys on loan from Atlanta PD.'

'Do they know he's dangerous?'

'Houston, he's concussed. *And* handcuffed.'

'Do they know he's dange—'

'They came personally recommended by Angie.'

'Okay then.' Scott threw his partner the keys over the roof of the car. 'You shoulda said that first.'

*

350

When Scott woke in the hotel room to the sound of his cell phone ringing next to him, he felt like he'd only just got to sleep. He saw it was Eric calling and answered in the dark.

Eric didn't bother with preliminaries. 'King's conscious and talking.'

Scott was immediately alert. 'Who to?'

'Whoever'll listen. But he's made it clear that he refuses to talk to someone he calls "Special Adversary Houston". That would be you.'

Scott sat up. 'Oh, I'll get him to talk to me.'

'No, Scott, I think we need to use this. Keep you out of there.'

'I don't think I can do that, Eric. I need to get this guy's confession.'

'He's more likely to confess if he thinks he's getting us to jump through hoops at the start. We can show him our good faith.'

'This is bullshit.'

'This is tactics,' countered Eric.

Scott lay back down and thought for a moment, running a hand through his hair. 'Okay, but you've gotta start with Patterson because we've got an evidentiary link with her personal effects at his house, and then you want to get corroboration with Spicer's evidence, so we can nail King with the biological traces from the van—' He sighed. 'Sorry. You know what to do. Who are you going in with?'

'We'll start with Angie, see if he wants to boast in front of a woman. If that throws things, we'll switch in Mark.'

'Good. They both know the case.' Scott paused. 'I want ears in the room.'

351

'You'll get 'em. You can be next door, down the way, whatever you want.'

'Fine.' Scott tried to switch into support mode. 'What else are you going to need?'

'Well, if he doesn't confess straight off, I need whatever we can get from his property that rules out someone else using his backyard as an abattoir. But I think we'll get a confession. If he'll spill it to Jayne—'

'Jayne?'

'Angie interviewed her.'

'*When?*' Scott strained his neck to see the clock on the bedside table. 'It's the middle of the night, for Christ's sake! Are you at the hospital? Have you talked to her?'

'Scott? I'm right here at the hotel, okay? I can practically hear you shouting from down the hall, in fact. No, Angie talked to her while you were at headquarters.'

'Why didn't anyone tell me?'

'We were just doing the routine. Jayne was lucid, so gave her evidence.'

Scott recollected Angie's comment that Jayne was tougher than she looked. So Angie would have already heard Jayne's account of whatever King did to her in that bathroom. Scott felt he was being left out of his own investigation even though he knew that wasn't what had happened.

Eric began again. 'So... if you can liaise with the ME's office on the IDs for body parts coming out of King's yard and also take over my link to the criminalists?'

Scott exhaled. 'You got it.'

'I'll drop you at HQ. See you at 0800 out front?'

'Ten-four.'

352

Scott hung up and let the phone rest on his chest as he lay in the dark, listening to the climate-controlled air conditioner kicking on. He hated sleeping in air conditioning and had never become used to it even when he had lived in Atlanta. Now here he was, sleeping in it again, dealing with the same case, and he wasn't even going to get to interrogate their suspect. He felt immensely irritated. He put the phone on the bedside table and lay on his back, drawing in deep breaths and letting them out slowly, willing a few more hours of sleep.

DAY ELEVEN

Friday

34

Scott pulled into the hospital parking lot at 11:30AM. He'd finished his morning punch list and was supposed to be on his way to the room neighboring King's, where Eric had set up a station for Scott to hear the interview. But he was taking a detour to see Jayne. He turned into her room at speed and almost collided with a cart of cleaning supplies. The bed was empty; it didn't even have bedding. He went back to the desk he'd sailed past a moment ago when ignoring staff who'd tried to ask if he'd needed assistance. He got the attention of one of the nurses and flagged his badge.

'I'm looking for Jayne Hall. 813? Admitted yesterday.'

The nurse consulted a sheet of paper taped to the wall. '813 was discharged.'

'When?'

The nurse looked at the sheet again. 'Nine-thirty this morning.'

'But I – who authorized that?'

The nurse answered like his tone was raising a flag. 'Dr. Reid, the attending. Is there a problem?'

Scott told himself not to shoot the messenger, so shook his head and set off toward Steelie's room. It was also empty. He backtracked to the elevator and ascended to the police-protected area where King was being held. He showed his badge to the Atlanta police officer in the hallway,

357

who directed him to the room with the listening station.

Scott found Mark already inside, sitting at a table and wearing a headset that was plugged into an audio playback device. Mark held aloft a second headset. Scott shook his head and indicated that he wanted to talk.

Mark removed one earpiece. 'You haven't missed much.'

'Where are Jayne and Steelie?'

Mark glanced at his watch. 'Probably in the security line at the airport.'

Scott impatiently rolled his index finger over backwards, as if rewinding a tape.

Mark got the message. 'They were cleared by the doctor and had no reason to – or interest in – staying around, especially with King upstairs here. Carter org'd their flights and took them to the airport. He's escorting them right up to boarding.'

Scott swallowed an expletive.

Mark put a hand on his earpiece and then pointed at Scott. 'Here we go.'

Scott got his headset on and sat down. He didn't recognize the voice he heard so it had to be King.

King:	*I didn't need a uniform back then. And I was using the van.*
Eric:	*How'd you get them to go with you, then?*
King:	*It's the red light district. How do you think I did it?*
Eric:	*You were a John?*
King:	*I wasn't a John. I posed as a John. Two different things.*

Eric:	So you asked the women to get in your van. Then what?
King:	You don't have to ask them to get in! They ask you. Or haven't you cruised the district, SA Ramos? Houston'll tell you; they're desperate to get in. Isn't that right, lady?
Angie:	It's Special Agent Nicks, Mr. King. Answer the question.

Scott pulled off the headset. He couldn't focus on this but he knew what to do to get back on track. He indicated to Mark that he'd return and went in search of the hospital's post office.

When Scott resumed listening a few minutes later, he could tell the interview had moved on.

Eric:	The garden and the garage. Why did you use them?
King:	First rule they teach us Bureau criminalists, something a lowly agent never learns: every contact leaves a trace. So I had to hang on to the bitches. Took 'em up the garden path. Literally. Ha!
Eric:	Why the dismemberment?
King:	Running out of space. Easier to transport from the back of the van. You ever move a dead body? It's heavy. Because of the water or the bones, or both.
Eric:	But you didn't just dismember. It looked

359

like careful cutting.

King: I'm flattered that you noticed. Yes, for show pieces, I took great care.

Eric: Show pieces?

King: The ones I've been scattering across the country in one long love letter to Special Adversary Houston.

Eric: You mean the ones you left in Los Angeles?

King: [Laugh] Uh, no, SA Ramos. He's a bit slow, isn't he, lady? Let's ignore him. You, lucky lady, will find body parts everywhere between here and California.

Angie: These are people you killed in other states?

King: No, they were not people I did in other states. The body parts are from the same pros I picked up on Atlanta's fine boulevards. I've dumped them along the interstate.

Angie: Why did you do that?

King: Well, I'll tell you. The glorious day finally arrived when Special Adversary Houston went public with his warning that a serial killer was loose in Atlanta and he gave a decent description of my van. I seem to recall you were next to him, Ramos, but you stayed silent like the good little partner that you are. And that was the signal for me

360

to start making it look like those bitches were killed elsewhere. I had some body parts frozen solely so I could dump them in places where they'd defrost in time to look fresh to the cops who'd find them. I left clues that different truckers came through Atlanta with regularity, picked up pros, took them interstate, and killed them while on the road. Houston would have been following that trail, with me leading him by the nose. And that would have been the end of the serial killer theory, the end of the interest in my van, and the end of Houston.

Angie: We're not aware of body parts being found outside Atlanta, besides the ones you lost in Los Angeles.

King: Yeah, well, the cops are stupid. First they have to find the stuff, then they have to scratch their asses. It would have worked, in time.

Angie: Mr. King, if you're going to do a deal with the prosecutors, you're going to have to give up the locations of these women's bodies.

King: I am, am I? Listen, you don't tell me how it's done. I tell you how it's done. [Mutters] Bitch.

Eric: Watch your mouth, King. Agent Nicks is right. They will not deal with you unless you give us locations.

Scott pulled off the headset to answer his cell phone, which had begun vibrating and displaying the Los Angeles number of his boss, Craig Turner. He walked into the hallway as he answered.

'Morning, sir.'

'Houston. I've got your fax from this morning. The suspect's declined legal representation?'

'That's correct, sir.'

'Is the interview underway?'

'Yes, I'm at the hospital now and Ramos and Nicks are in with him.'

'And?'

'It's going well. They're stringing him out, taking him round corners.' Scott didn't mention that his own name was coming up in the interview because he didn't understand it yet.

'Good. What have you got for material to ID the bodies coming from the suspect's backyard?'

'I spoke to Atlanta Missings this morning. They're going back over the misper reports for cases that fit the suspect's activity period. They'll transmit any biological information direct to the medical examiner's office. But we've got another issue. The suspect has just alleged that he dropped body parts along the interstate between Atlanta and LA. We need to find out if any of the material's been recovered and why it hasn't been ID'd yet. If we can get proof on those ones, we can charge him on each count.'

'I'll call Cates at CJIS; he'll get you an NCIC liaison.'

'Sir.' Scott could hear his boss switch the call to speakerphone and he waited for him to continue. He thought about how the head of the whole Criminal Justice

362

Information Services Division might not be too pleased to get a direct call about an NCIC issue, but he couldn't help it if SSA Turner wanted to show off.

'Office of Professional Responsibility interviewed me last night.' Turner sounded more casual now, as though he was leaning back in his chair. 'Never liked internal affairs myself but I try not to hold it against the rank-and-file.'

Scott smiled as he imagined the cross-grilling tactics Turner probably used on the agents trying to question him.

Turner stated, 'I made it clear that my assessment of the situation is that, during the course of this investigation, you have not displayed activity that warrants disciplinary action.'

'Thank you...' But his boss was still talking.

'Now, Houston, the only way I could do that was to *actually* assess the situation. I see now why you chose this Agency 32/1. Why's it called that? Do you know?'

'Uh, it's named for the Geneva Conventions, article thirty-two, protocol one.'

'Geneva? As in the laws of war?'

'Yes, sir. I understand that the part the agency's named for deals with the right of families to know what happened to their relatives – where their bodies are buried, and so forth.'

'Huh. Well, your fax this morning shows that Thirty-Two One led you to the firm ID that's become crucial for building the case against the suspect. Is that correct?'

'Patterson. Yes, sir.'

'And now you tell me we've got body parts strung across the Bible Belt, the Corn Belt *and* the Rockies?'

'Yes, sir.'

SSA Turner went from the speakerphone back to the handset and Scott quickly ran down a mental list for what his boss could hit him with next.

THREE DAYS LATER

Monday

35

San Fernando Road, Los Angeles: 2PM. Carol was having a vacation day, so when the mail carrier came in the front door, Jayne went to meet him. She gave him the outgoing mail and he handed over the incoming pile. Jayne heard Steelie call out to her, so she diverted to the laboratory, mail still in hand.

Steelie was sitting at the light box, looking at a rectangular X-ray that measured about an inch and a half on each side. She turned when Jayne walked in and said, 'Can you look at this?'

Jayne put the mail down, checked out the bruise on Steelie's chin for new color changes then focused on the X-ray. It showed several upper teeth in a human jaw.

'Got anything besides a bitewing?' she asked.

'This isn't a buffet,' Steelie parried. 'Would you say that's a root canal plus a post or just a root canal?'

'Got any dentist's notes?'

'No. When they archived these they lost all the paper notes. The only things left were these bitewings, probably because they were stapled onto the folder itself.'

'Hmm, I'm leaning toward root canal but I'd put a note about the possibility of a post. We don't have enough information to do more than that.'

Steelie pulled a magnifying glass from a jar on the counter. She used it to look at the X-ray again. Jayne

367

walked to the end of the room and started rummaging through a drawer.

After a while, Steelie swiveled her stool. 'What on earth are you looking for?'

'Didn't we have some candlestick holders in here? From when the power was always going out?'

'Oh, you mean in the days *before* a generator?' Steelie was expansive. 'Who even remembers those days?'

'Seriously. And where did you move that candle those women in Atlanta gave me?'

'Both items are in the top drawer of the other cabinet.' She swiveled back to the light box.

Jayne pulled open the drawer and brought out a holder. She put the candle in but it was too narrow to stand up on its own. Lighting a match to melt the wax on the bottom so that the candle would stick, Jayne saw the wick within. Then she remembered Scott saying that thing about the wick going all the way through.

They had been in the Sunkist parking lot – the reunion. He had been right, both about the wick and about how the two of them were at opposite ends of the same effort. They were all identifying people, whether starting with a body or a missing person. Watching the wax melt, Jayne decided that Scott was right about a lot of things and the memory of their embrace on the side of the road surged forward in a rush – his hands in her hair, her mouth on his, the desire.

And the desire was now only part of it. When she'd become aware of Scott lifting her up from that disgusting, bloody motel floor, she'd felt truly alive. But she hadn't been able to make any words come out. Later, when she'd asked Angie where Scott was, she'd explained that he was logging evidence and had offered to take him a message. But by then, Jayne just wanted to show him how she felt. They'd talked enough. She hadn't called him; she'd just been waiting – in excruciating, deeply pleasurable anticipation – for him to return to LA.

The telephone rang. Steelie called out, 'My turn,' as she rolled over on her stool to answer it.

When Steelie called out, 'Scott!' Jayne turned around, half-expecting to see him in the doorway.

But Steelie was listening intently to the phone and made a thumbs-up sign. 'Hang on, Houston, let me put you on speaker.'

Jayne came to stand by Steelie, who pressed a button and turned up the volume while telling Jayne, 'They're still in Atlanta. You gotta hear this.'

'Scott?' Steelie called out. 'Tell Jayne what you just told me.'

After a pause, Scott said, 'Jayne.'

It gave her a jolt to hear his voice. 'Scott. Hi.'

'Hi. So, what I said was, we've got a full confession from King on the Georgia cases, plus the body parts on the 101 Freeway.'

She and Steelie called out questions simultaneously. Scott described how King had preyed on the women who worked in Atlanta's red light district and later posed as a shuttle driver to pick up Eleanor Patterson. 'He had also stopped a woman while dressed as a cop. But not you, Steelie. At least, he denies it so far.'

Steelie exclaimed, 'It never occurred to me that it was Gene!'

Jayne said, 'And if it wasn't, that means someone else

out there is still posing as a cop and assaulting people.'

Scott replied, 'We've checked in with LAPD and the Sheriff's Department on this and it turns out that people posing as cops happens in LA County more than you might think. Most of the time, the ruse is part of a shakedown for cash. Sometimes sexual assault. But it doesn't generally result in murder and the local guys have caught a fair few of the perps. Then there are a few cops who've abused their badges. But Steelie? Don't worry. They'll catch up with him eventually. As for King, the prosecutors are dealing with him by rolling some charges together in exchange for getting locations on body parts he's dropped across the country.'

Jayne immediately thought of how she and Steelie were bruised but alive while the families waiting outside Gene's house might soon have answers of a different sort.

She asked, 'What has he said about Kigali?'

'Nothing yet. He won't be drawn on the details. I'm sure he doesn't want to see the inside of a prison overseas. So we're talking to Gerrit Leuven, seeing if he can get the UN involved.' He paused. 'Leuven's got a lot of good things to say about both of you. Of course, I cautioned him that his information was ten years out of date.'

She laughed and was rewarded by hearing a laugh come back through the speaker. She pictured his lips curving into his usual half-grin and said, 'Thanks for giving us the low-down, Scott.'

'Well, we owe you... for a number of things on this case.' He cleared his throat. 'Bringing me to the next point. Let me get Eric over here.'

Eric's enthusiasm was in his voice when he came on the

370

line. He intoned, 'Ladies...' like a DJ in a hazy nightclub.

'You sound good, Agent Ramos,' Steelie remarked, starting to go through the mail that Jayne had dropped onto the counter.

'Just a little demob happy.'

'When are you guys actually demobilizing?' Jayne asked, hoping it wasn't obvious that she just wanted to know when Scott would be back in Los Angeles.

'Good question,' Eric replied. 'The Bureau won't pay for us to stay out here for more than a week—'

'You gotta be kidding me,' exclaimed Steelie as she slid a square envelope addressed to Jayne in her direction.

'Actually, they would, but Houston and I would have to double up and, trust me, no one wants that.'

Scott cut in. 'Can we get back on point? Jayne, Steelie: our supervisor, Craig Turner, has asked us to draft an MOU with your agency, for this and future cases.'

Jayne paused in the act of opening the envelope and saw that Steelie's eyebrows were raised about as high as her own. She clarified, 'You're saying the FBI wants a memorandum of understanding with our nonprofit organization so we can help you again?'

'Yes, as you just did on this case, minus the personal endangerment. This is on the up-and-up. It would be an official agreement for implementation on an ad hoc basis. And SSA Turner's already got a request for you in the hopper. We need better antemortem info on our missing Atlanta women since King's ensured that their remains are going to come in as separate bones from different places. A couple of the family members out here are already asking after you. They were pretty surprised to see two women and such, quote-unquote, young women, walking out from the crime scene at King's house.'

The sound of the bells jangling on the agency's front door traveled back to the lab. Jayne addressed the phone. 'Look, someone's at the door and Carol's off, so we gotta go. We'll... get back to you on that offer.'

'Alright, Thirty-Two One.' Scott sounded amused. 'Sounds to me like you're playing hard to get, but you should know: two can play that game.'

Jayne had to bite her lip to stop from smiling as she hung up.

Steelie made for the hallway but she was looking at the envelope in Jayne's hand. 'Who's that from?'

Jayne finally looked at it. No return address, an Atlanta postmark and something with a shiny border inside. Her heart started to pound. *Scott?* She slid out the card. It was a gilt-edged invitation to dinner with him at In-N-Out Burger that Friday.

This time, her grin was so broad and came on so quick that she couldn't hide it from Steelie, who rolled her eyes and set off down the hallway. Jayne enjoyed the bursting-with-happiness sensation for a full thirty seconds. Then she went to join Steelie and meet the next client of Agency 32/1.

Acknowledgments

Thank you to my publisher Helen Huthwaite and my tremendous editor Amy Baxter. Our collaboration is the stuff dreams are made of and I am thrilled to be one of your authors.

I am indebted to my brilliant literary and film agents, Anna Soler-Pont and Carla Briner. Thank you to the Pontas team for the shared commitment to an ideal and the dedicated work on my behalf. Anna: from the connection all those years ago in Barcelona, we go on!

I am grateful, as ever, to Suttirat Anne Larlarb. I warmly thank the Larlarb family – Vachree especially – for decades of support and love, and Kris Rucker, who has been there from the beginning.

Profound thanks to Dawn Hague. You have kept me under your wing and taught me to fly.

Marsha Koff, Peter Brown and the ladies of GG: your enthusiasm for my books carries me forward more than you know.

I have unending gratitude for my family, who are my first readers, my last readers and everything in between. Most of all, I thank my parents, Msindo and David (rest in peace, Pop). I couldn't do it without you.

Jayne and Steelie
will return